A DEADLY HOMECOMING

Also by Jane Bennett Munro

Murder under the Microscope
Too Much Blood
Grievous Bodily Harm
Death by Autopsy
The Body on the Lido Deck

A DEADLY HOMECOMING

A TONI DAY MYSTERY

JANE BENNETT MUNRO

A DEADLY HOMECOMING
A TONI DAY MYSTERY

iUniverse books may be ordered through booksellers or by contacting:

iUniverse
1663 Liberty Drive
Bloomington, IN 47403
www.iuniverse.com
1-800-Authors (1-800-288-4677)

ISBN: 978-1-5320-5490-7 (sc)
ISBN: 978-1-5320-5492-1 (hc)
ISBN: 978-1-5320-5491-4 (e)

Library of Congress Control Number: 2018910949

Print information available on the last page.

iUniverse rev. date: 10/25/2018

Praise for *Murder under the Microscope*

Murder under the Microscope is an exemplary first novel.
  —*The US Review of Books*

As a winner of an IP Book Award for Excellence, I wasn't the least surprised that this book was selected.
  —*GABixler Reviews*

Praise for *Too Much Blood*

Munro's writing is entertaining, believable, and fast-paced. She takes you into the autopsy room, shows the fragility of the characters, and makes the readers feel they are inside the story. Readers will definitely be looking forward to solving more cases with this character.
  —*The US Review of Books*

Exceptional realism that only comes from personal, hands-on experience. Munro writes with captivating flair, and her story line is believable and realistic.
  —Charline Ratcliff for *Rebecca's Reads*

Praise for *Grievous Bodily Harm*

Sassy pathologist Toni Day shines in this modern-day mystery of corporate shenanigans and hospital politics … A smart, enjoyable summer read.
  —*Kirkus Reviews*

Munro's story is a roller coaster ride of suspense and intrigue, with twists and turns that will entertain a lover of mysteries and forensic crime novels for hours.
  —*The US Review of Books*

The author brilliantly shares her expertise in forensic pathology, allowing readers inside the room during the autopsy, and sharing her expertise and knowledge.
  —Fran Lewis, *BookPleasures.com*

Praise for *Death by Autopsy*

A solid mystery far from DOA.
  —*Kirkus Reviews*

If this is your first Toni Day novel, you'll want to go back and start the series from the beginning.
—*BlueInk Reviews*

Fans of medical drama and mysteries will be sure to love this fast-paced and fact-laced romp through the world of pathology.
—*The US Review of Books*

This book is a fantastic crime thriller. You won't be able to put it down until you finish reading it. I loved it. I gave it 5 stars, but it deserved many, many more. I highly recommend this book to everyone especially if you enjoy crime and thriller books. You will love this one. I look for more from Jane Bennett Munro.
—Marjorie Boyd-Springer for *Goodreads*

Praise for *The Body on the Lido Deck*

An entertaining murder mystery to cruise through.
—*Kirkus Reviews*

The Body on the Lido Deck will keep readers guessing until the action-packed end. And when it's all over, the story's satisfying solution will leave them eager to explore Toni Day's other adventures.
—*BlueInk Reviews*

This book offers believable dialogue, a breakneck pace, and a unique story that breathes new life into the literary murder-comedy genre. It's Jessica Fletcher meets *CSI*, with the usual crime-scene gore and droning medical jargon now wrapped up in a charming, entertaining package.
—*Clarion Reviews*

The mystery's nomadic setting—on a cruise ship still on course for its vacation destinations—and the protagonist's go-getter attitude make for an enthralling beach read.
—*The US Review of Books*

In memory of my own British mum, Ida Mudd
Keywood Tripp Bennett Hines (1907–1987)

I lifted a corner of a quilt and peered underneath. As I did so, the all-too-familiar odor of decomposing flesh assailed my nostrils.

There was, indeed, someone else in the house with me.

And he was dead as the proverbial doornail.

CHAPTER 1

Remember, it's as easy to marry a rich woman as a poor woman.

—William Makepeace Thackeray

My husband, Hal, and I were sitting out on our back deck, enjoying the warm June weather and drinks after work and watching the dogs run around in the backyard, when my cell phone rang.

"Kitten, I have a huge favor to ask."

My heart sank. The last time my mother had asked for a favor, it was because Nigel had prostate cancer.

Nigel Gray was my stepfather, a homicide detective chief superintendent retired from Scotland Yard. He and Mum had met six years ago, in 2008, on the *Queen Mary* in Long Beach, California, and it was love at first sight for both. They were married four years ago, right here in our backyard in Twin Falls, Idaho.

They lived in the house that I grew up in from the age of three with Mum and my father's parents, my grandma and grandpa Day, who had both passed away when I was in high school.

Mum and I had emigrated from England to Long Beach at their invitation when I was three years old. My own father, an American serviceman, had been killed in a hit-and-run accident on a busy London street when Mum was only seventeen and pregnant with me. Mum had never shown the slightest interest in remarrying until she met Nigel.

Not that she hadn't had plenty of opportunities over the years.

That was more than forty years ago, but it hadn't had the slightest effect upon her accent, which was as crisply British as it had been then. Mine, on the other hand, had all but disappeared.

"Is it Nigel?" I asked.

"Oh, no, kitten. It's my friend Doris Maxwell, from work. You remember her, of course?"

Of course I remembered Doris. She and Mum had worked together for forty years at the corporate headquarters of a large drugstore chain. Mum had been executive secretary to the CEO, and Doris supervised the employee benefits department, specifically their health insurance. They frequently went shopping together, and that's what they'd been doing when Mum met Nigel; they had been taking a break from Christmas shopping, having lunch on the *Queen Mary*.

"What's wrong with Doris?"

"I don't know if I told you, kitten, but she remarried a few months ago."

Doris's husband, Bob, had died just before Christmas. "She didn't wait long, did she?"

"No, dear. Dick simply swept her off her feet. And then they moved into this truly fantastic old house that Dick inherited from his great-uncle. They no sooner moved in than weird things started happening. Voices coming out of nowhere. Furniture moving around by itself. Things falling off shelves and breaking. Things disappearing and reappearing. Doris felt as if she were losing her mind, because Dick never noticed anything, never heard the voices, and told her she was just imagining things. And now *Dick's* disappeared."

"Disappeared? When?"

"About a week ago now."

"Did she report it to the police?"

"Of course she did," my mother said tartly. "She's not a complete idiot. But they haven't found him, and she said she couldn't stand to be in that house all alone with the spooks, so we invited her to come stay with us."

"That sounds serious."

"It is," Mum said, "and besides that, she's not well."

I got up and moved over to the railing where a collection of redwood tubs that I'd planted the previous weekend bloomed merrily, the plants having recovered from their initial transplant shock. "Not well how?"

"It didn't seem like much at first, dear," Mum said. "She was having a lot of headaches, and sometimes she seemed confused and had no appetite, and then she started having diarrhea, and then she began vomiting and having leg cramps."

"When did that start?"

"It's been happening for several months now. It sort of comes and goes, she says. But she's losing weight, and she just doesn't look good."

"Has she been to a doctor?"

"Certainly. I insisted. They even put a scope down her but didn't find anything. They've given her some medicine to take, and it seems to help, but she still doesn't feel good."

I plucked off a dead leaf and tossed it into the yard. "I'm so sorry, Mum. Is that what the favor's about?"

"Yes, dear. I wonder if you and Hal could see your way clear to come visit for a couple of weeks."

Hal picked up his empty beer bottle and my depleted glass and went into the house.

"Now?" I asked.

"Yes, kitten, now. Doris needs help. Nigel and I thought if you could come for a while, you could investigate the haunted house and maybe figure out where Dick could have gotten to. I know how you love a good mystery."

My propensity for getting involved in matters best left to law enforcement had become a point of contention with both my mother and my husband over the last few years. The fact that Mum was actually *asking* me to investigate Dick's disappearance was alarming.

My name is Toni Day, and I'm one of three pathologists at our local hospital, Cascade Perrine Regional Medical Center. The three of us are partners in an independent pathology group that contracts with the hospital, unlike many of the other doctors whose practices are managed by the hospital, making them essentially hospital employees.

Hal came back out, having fetched himself another beer and refreshed my drink. He handed me my drink and leaned on the railing next to me, bending over to give me a kiss.

My husband, Hal Shapiro, towered over my petite five foot three by a foot and outweighed me by at least a hundred pounds. With his thick blond hair and moustache (now mostly white), bright blue eyes, and ruddy complexion, he looked more like a Viking than the mild-mannered college professor he actually was.

"I'd love to, Mum, but I have to check with my partners and see if they can do without me for a couple of weeks. And Hal ..."

"Don't worry about me, sweetie," Hal said. "School's out, and I'm free as a bird."

Usually he taught summer school too, but now that he was sixty, he'd decided not to.

"I'll let you know tomorrow, Mum," I told her.

"We'll pay for your plane fare, of course."

"Oh, no, you don't have to do that," I protested, but I knew it was useless to argue with my mother.

"Nonsense, kitten. I insist. Besides, your fiftieth birthday's coming right up, and we must celebrate."

I groaned. "Don't remind me."

I ended the call and went back over to the table. Hal followed and sat down across from me. "I take it we're making a trip to sunny Southern California."

I told him what Mum had said.

"Is she serious? She actually *wants* you to get involved in this? It sounds positively gothic."

"I know, right? Usually she hates it when I investigate things. She's afraid I'll get hurt."

"I can see her point," Hal said, "because you usually do. How many times have you been knocked unconscious now? Five?"

"Something like that. Anyway, they want us to come and see what we can do."

Hal snorted. "Sounds to me like they need an exorcist, not a pathologist."

"Antoinette!"

Only one person in the world was allowed to call me that, and that was only because I couldn't stop her.

Hal and I had just emerged from the Delta SkyWest terminal at Long Beach Airport after retrieving our luggage. My mother's green Chevy Malibu was parked at the curb waiting for us. Nigel was driving, and Mum had her arm out the passenger window, waving wildly. Our 6:30 flight from Twin Falls had arrived in Long Beach at 9:20, after a layover in Salt Lake City.

Nigel popped the trunk and came around to help Hal get the luggage into it. He slung an arm around me and gave me a kiss. "I say, Toni, old thing—what a sight for sore eyes," he said. "Your mother has been frantic."

My stepfather resembled the actor Bernard Fox, who played Dr. Bombay on the sixties' sitcom *Bewitched*, which I'd watched as a child; he had wavy

salt-and-pepper hair and a moustache, was a little on the stocky side, and favored vests with watch pockets.

Nigel grunted as he tried to lift my suitcase into the trunk. "What have you got in here? Bricks?"

I climbed into the back seat and leaned over it to kiss my mother's cheek. "Nigel says you're frantic."

"And that's throwing roses at it," she replied with a sigh. "I do so hope you and Hal can help Doris. I'm at my wit's end."

As a young woman, Mum had been a dead ringer for Susan Hayward, a gorgeous actress from the fifties with a mop of curly red hair and green eyes, and had frequently been mistaken for her by those old enough to remember. She continued to wear her hair in the same style, even though now it was mostly gray. She and I had the same green eyes, but my short, curly hair was black and my complexion olive, like my father's. She was shorter than me and heavier, but even so, she still had a shapely figure that I'd caught Nigel admiring more than once.

Mum and I were both lucky to have found men who preferred their women with a little meat on their bones.

Long Beach was overcast and foggy. I remembered that June was frequently like that here and how frustrated I'd been as a teenager because I'd wanted to lie out on the patio and work on my tan. Not now, of course, since everybody knows about the dangers of sun exposure. As a pathologist, I saw evidence of it under my microscope every day at work. I never went out without sunscreen on.

Hal came around and opened the car door next to me, motioning for me to shove over behind Nigel so that he'd have more leg room if he sat behind Mum.

The trip home from the airport was short and quick because the morning rush hour was over, and the streets were relatively empty. As we turned into the driveway of my childhood home, I felt a sense of loss.

The place had changed a lot since I'd lived there as a child. From the street, it looked like the same red-tile-roofed, white stucco, Spanish-style house, but back then there was a lawn, which it had been my job to mow and edge as soon as I was big enough and Grandpa Day's health had begun to decline. On the parkway, there had been two date palms that produced inedible dates that I had to rake up before I could mow, as the pits would jam the mower blades. Not to mention cleaning up contributions from George, the dog next door. Large oleander bushes had shaded the front stoop from the afternoon sun.

All that was gone.

Because of the severe drought conditions in Southern California over the past years, many residents gave up on trying to water their yards, or were forced to stop doing so by city ordinance. Like its neighbors, the yard had been xeriscaped. The lawn had been replaced by gravel and paving stones. Where there had been palm trees, there were now cacti. Yuccas grew along the front stoop but were not tall enough to shade anything.

It was depressing.

The main house had two bedrooms and a bath. When I lived there as a child, Grandma and Grandpa slept in the master bedroom at the front of the house off the living room. Mum and I lived in the apartment off the back of the garage. Back in the day, it had probably been a maid's quarters. It consisted of one large room, with a bath and a kitchen. Mum and I had screened off two sleeping areas by the artful use of bookcases and folding screens and left ourselves a more than adequate space where she could watch TV while I did my homework on the dinette table in the kitchen.

Between the main house and the apartment were a one-car garage, a carport, a screened-in patio, and an open patio partially shaded by an extension of the garage roof. This extension was bordered on both sides by latticework upon which Mum had grown roses.

The roses were also gone now.

The spare bedroom in the main house was too small for both Hal and me, so we always stayed in the apartment when we visited. After Grandma and Grandpa were both gone, Mum and I moved into the main house, where she slept in the master bedroom, and I slept in the spare room.

Right now, the spare bedroom was occupied by Doris.

When Nigel pulled into the carport adjacent to the garage, Doris came out the kitchen door to greet us. She was several inches taller than Mum and much thinner than I remembered her. Her iron-gray hair was clipped short, as it had always been, but her naturally ruddy face was now gray and drawn, as if she'd been getting chemotherapy. She wore sneakers and jeans and a blue plaid shirt with the sleeves rolled up above her elbows.

I got out of the car and waved at her over the top of it. "Hi, Doris!"

She came hurrying around the car, arms outstretched. "Hey, you kids! How was your flight?"

We hugged. "Just fine. How are you?" I asked, as if I expected her to be just fine too, even though I knew she wasn't.

She held me away from her and peered into my face. "Well, now, I expect your mother has filled you in on how I am, hasn't she?"

"She has," I said, "and I'm so sorry about Bob."

"Thank you, sweetheart. It was a massive heart attack. One minute he was there, and the next minute he was gone. Quite a shock. Have you kids had anything to eat? I made a coffee cake. I thought you might be hungry."

Doris's coffee cake was to die for. "Well, even if I wasn't, I am now," I told her.

"Oh, now, Doris, you didn't need to do that," my mother said. "You should be resting."

"Resting!" Doris said. "I've had quite enough rest. I actually feel pretty good today. Coffee should be ready by now."

We trooped into the kitchen, which smelled divine, and through the dining room into the living room, where I sank into Mum's capacious couch with a sigh. Mum and Doris busied themselves in the kitchen while Hal and Nigel took our suitcases out to the apartment. Soon we were all settled with plates of coffee cake and cups of coffee or tea.

"I suppose," Nigel said, "the first thing we ought to do is go look at the house."

"Oh, no," Doris objected. "Don't you want to get settled before you do that?"

Apparently, Doris didn't share my mother's sense of urgency.

"We've got all day," I said. "Don't you want us to get started?"

"Oh, there's no rush," Doris said. "You should take the time to get unpacked first, don't you think?"

I noticed that Doris's hands were shaking as she lifted her coffee up to her lips. Was it fear, or was it because of her illness? Despite her upbeat greeting, she really didn't look well.

"Doris darling," Mum said, "you may as well do it and get it over with, you know."

"If you haven't figured it out by now," Nigel said, "Doris has been dreading this. She's scared to go back into that house."

"We'll all go," Mum reassured her. "There's strength in numbers."

Doris sighed. "I suppose you're right, Fiona."

"Where is this house?" I asked.

"It's the MacTavish house," Doris said. "Surely you've heard of it. It's on Country Club Drive."

"I think I have," I said. "Is it that house off Country Club Drive that's kind of up on a hill, with trees all around it so you can hardly see it?"

"That's the one," Doris said.

"The kids in school used to say it was haunted," I said.

"I think it is," Doris said with a shudder. "It was built back in 1920 by Dougal Alexander MacTavish, who intended it to look like a Scottish castle. I believe he actually had some of the stones shipped here from Scotland. It's supposed to be really authentic."

"That sounds like William Randolph Hearst," I said. "He had entire ceilings shipped over from France and Italy to put in Hearst Castle."

"Well, this is on a much smaller scale," Doris said. "Dougal had some marble imported and bought antique furniture from several Scottish castles that were on the auction block because the families that owned them couldn't pay the death duties."

"And Dick inherited all that?" Hal inquired.

"Yes. From his great-uncle."

"Is Dick a MacTavish too?" I asked.

"No, he's a Campbell. MacTavish was his mother's maiden name."

"But surely a house like that must be a historical site," I said. "I'm surprised it hasn't been acquired by the city."

"I don't think so," Doris said. "Dick never said anything about that. I should think that if the city owned it, we wouldn't have been allowed to live there."

"I can't wait to see it," I said. "Let's get the dishes cleaned up and get going!"

CHAPTER 2

There's a fascination frantic
In a ruin that's romantic;
Do you think that you are sufficiently decayed?

—Sir William Gilbert

I was excited to finally see the MacTavish house up close and personal, because I'd never actually seen it before.

As a curious child, I'd ridden my bike along Country Club Drive, admiring all the rich people's houses, until I came to the winding road that led up the hill. But when I got to end of the road, I'd find the lane leading to the house blocked off by a wooden gate with signs that said No Trespassing and Keep Out. Even from that vantage point, the trees and bushes blocked my view of the house. Back then I'd been too scared to go any closer.

Now I was going to not only see it but actually go inside.

By the time we finished our coffee and coffee cake, the sun had come out, and it had become quite warm. Hal and I left our jackets behind when we all piled into Mum's Chevy and headed for Country Club Drive with Hal driving.

We drove north on Lemon Avenue to Bixby Road, past Charles Evans Hughes Junior High, where I'd gone to school, and continued west, past Atlantic Avenue and Long Beach Boulevard, until we reached Country Club Drive as it passed by Del Mar Park. Just south of the park, a lane branched off Country Club Drive and wound up the hill through a thick tangle of trees and shrubs. The No Trespassing and Keep Out signs were gone. In their place was a metal gate, which was closed.

"Now what?" Hal asked.

Doris rummaged in her purse. "Sorry, I should have ... just a minute ... oh, here it is." She held up a small black handheld device and pushed a button. The gate slowly creaked open.

Hmmm, I thought. *That's not like Doris.* The Doris I knew would have had her remote out, all ready to go.

Hal drove in slowly. We still couldn't see the house, not until we'd gone around several more curves. Finally, we pulled up in front of the house and got out of the car.

The canopy of eucalyptus trees over the house all but blocked out the sky. The sun managed to penetrate in a few places, but even as we stood there, clouds moved over the sun, and the wind came up, swishing through the trees with an eerie howling sound.

The house, which had looked merely picturesque while the sun was out, now seemed to loom over us threateningly. It was built of dark gray stone and was at least three stories tall. I wasn't sure if there was a fourth story hidden somewhere up there in the treetops. I didn't know how anybody else felt about it, but I had no trouble believing this house was haunted.

Doris fished a key ring out of her purse and said, "Shall we?"

I looked up at the turrets on either side of the roof and shivered. I wished Hal and I had kept our jackets with us. I hoped the house was warmer inside than it was out here but didn't hold out any hope. It was June. The heat, if there was any, would be off.

"Let's go," I said—and did not add, "and get this over with," although that's how I felt.

A wide staircase with flaring stone balustrades on either side ending in posts with bronze lions' heads on them led up to massive double doors carved of dark, almost black, wood, with knockers, also shaped like lions' heads, and ornate brass handles. Doris inserted a key into a keyhole and pushed the double doors open. We stepped inside.

Inside, it was just as cold as I'd feared—and dark. Doris flipped a switch, and a huge crystal chandelier blazed to life overhead, revealing a vast foyer. An ancient Turkish rug covered the stone floor, or maybe it was Persian. When I looked up, I couldn't see a ceiling. Doris saw me looking. "This foyer reaches all the way to the tower on the fourth floor," she said. "The drawing room is straight ahead." She flipped another light switch, and another crystal chandelier illuminated an even larger room that contained a massive fireplace. It was surrounded by a marble mantelpiece supported by columns that rose from a marble hearth. Neatly stacked wood appeared ready to light, but I didn't see any matches. This oversight was explained when Doris walked over to it, her sneakers squeaking on the hardwood floor. "Let's take the chill off, shall we?" she said and flipped another switch. The wood burst into flame.

"Huh," Hal said. "Gas log?"

Doris nodded. "This fireplace goes through into the library behind it," she explained. "That's where we spend most of our time. The TV is in there, and Dick's recliner and my couch, and we both have our computers in there."

I looked around, noting the dusty antique furniture. I know absolutely nothing about antiques, but none of it looked comfortable enough to actually sit on for any length of time. Two love seats faced each other in front of the fireplace, with a coffee table between them. Delicate little end tables stood at each end of the love seats, with lamps on them. Tall brass candelabra with white candles stood on the mantelpiece. A portrait in a heavily gilded frame hung over the mantelpiece and depicted a severe-looking man of indeterminate age in nineteenth-century clothing and a powdered wig. Huge tapestries depicting hunting scenes covered the stone walls. Without them, I thought, the room would be even colder than it was.

I walked over to one of the arched windows and looked out. The stone walls were at least a foot thick. Around the room, I saw other groups of chairs, tables, and lamps. Some of the lamps looked like they could have been Tiffany, and I asked Doris if they were.

"They're all Tiffany," Doris said. "And those tapestries all came from Scotland."

"Was all this here when you moved in?" Hal asked.

"Most of it," Doris said. "Everything in here belonged to Dick's uncle. Back here, in the library, is less formal. As I said, that's where we spend most of our time." She led us through a passageway that opened out into another vast room. On this side, the fireplace and hearth were brick, and the mantelpiece was made of the same black wood as the front door.

The furniture clustered around the fireplace was dwarfed by the size of the room and the height of the ceilings. It formed a cozy nook in which to read and watch TV. I recognized Bob's leather recliner, Doris's couch, an assortment of end tables and lamps, and a coffee table that had come from their house. A flat-screen TV had been mounted into the space above the mantelpiece. Modern-looking sound equipment occupied glass-fronted cabinets on either side.

The rest of the walls were covered by bookcases that reached the ceiling. A library ladder stood in a corner, ready for anyone who needed to retrieve a dusty tome from the top shelves, although the layers of dust covering the ancient books had clearly not been disturbed in decades. More modern books occupied space on the lower shelves, even some paperbacks.

An elegantly carved conference table stood at the other end of the room, in front of another fireplace, surrounded by matching chairs with high backs and leather seats, all large and ponderous enough to have been original furnishings. Incongruously, Dick's computer and a printer occupied one end of the table.

The walls separating the library from the hallway and the hallway from the kitchen, at least those that were not weight-bearing, had been removed. From where we stood, we had a clear view of a huge medieval-looking kitchen, its main feature being a fireplace large enough to roast an entire ox. Its walls were blackened with soot. Massive black iron tools hung on the whitewashed stone wall above it. At five three, I was able to walk into it and stand up straight, and so could Mum, although she demurred. "It's so sooty," she objected, wrinkling her nose. "Kitten, please watch your head!"

Involuntarily, I ducked. Soot-covered chains and pulleys hung over my head, no doubt having been used to hoist the ox up over the fire. I hadn't seen them in the darkness. But there had clearly not been a fire in there in years. The floor, although soot stained, had been swept and decorated with an assortment of candles of varying sizes and colors, some in glass jars and some on stands of varying heights. It was a pleasing arrangement.

"How long does it take to get all those lit?" I asked.

"Twenty minutes," Doris said, "and even longer to blow them all out. We only light them when we entertain."

I wondered when, or if, they'd ever had occasion to do that.

An antique black rolltop desk stood in the alcove to the right of the fireplace. "Dick sits here when he pays bills," Doris said.

"He doesn't use the computer?" I asked in surprise. I'd used Quicken for years to keep track of our finances, and most of our bills got paid online.

Doris shuddered. "Heavens no. He's terrified of being hacked."

I shrugged. She had a point. I wondered what he *did* use his computer for. Porn?

I changed the subject. "Could you have a fire in here if you wanted to?" I asked.

"No, the chimney's completely blocked. Dick says there hasn't been a fire in here for at least fifty years."

Although the kitchen may have been nearly a hundred years old, the appliances were modern. The stove, the two refrigerators, and the upright freezer were shiny black. The washer and dryer at the end of the kitchen were new. They were tall and a gorgeous shade of candy-apple red. I'd seen recent advertisements for ones like them on TV. Next to the washer and dryer was a deep utility sink with a spray hose, and an ironing board that folded up into the wall, like the one in Mum's kitchen, which had been used more for parking purses and grocery bags than for actually ironing anything.

Hal and I had an extra refrigerator and freezer too, but they were out in the garage. Did Dick and Doris have a garage? I wondered.

"What's this?" Mum inquired from the alcove on the other side of the fireplace. "Doris, is this a dumbwaiter?"

She was standing in front of a square stainless-steel door in the wall at chest level, with two switches in the wall next to it. I went over to get a closer look. I'd heard of dumbwaiters but had never seen one.

"We had one in our house when I was a child in England," my mother said.

"How does it work?" I asked.

"I don't know," Doris said. "We've never used it."

"It's used to transport things up and down between floors," Mum said. "One opens the door, like this …" She pushed upward on the door handle, and the door slid up and locked into place with a click. "Oh."

"Oh, what?" I asked, peering into the opening. I saw nothing except some rails and cables running up and down the walls on either side of the shaft. Brownish smears on the back wall suggested either rust, not likely on stainless steel, or that something had spilled in transit. "I don't see anything."

"There should be a car," Mum said. "It must be on another floor."

"Got a flashlight?" Nigel asked.

Doris opened a drawer and took one out. "Here you go."

Nigel took it and aimed it into the space. "Here, take a look. The car is on the second floor."

I stuck my head into the opening and saw the rails and cables on either side running up into the blackness above. "I can't see anything," I complained. "Why don't we just bring the car down?"

"Go ahead," Nigel said. "Carry on."

"Okay." I pushed the red switch on the wall from Off to On and the black switch from Up to Down. Nothing happened. "Now what?"

"The car shouldn't move unless the door is closed," Mum said.

"So we'll close it," I said and pulled down on the handle. The door didn't move. I let go of the handle and sighed. "Now what do we do?"

"Maybe you have to release it," Hal said. "It clicked when you pushed it up."

"I don't see a release mechanism," Nigel said. "Maybe it's inside." He stuck his head back into the shaft and aimed the flashlight at the top of the door frame.

"Ah, here it is," he said. And then—"Watch out!"

He backed up so suddenly that he nearly knocked me off my feet as the car plummeted down precisely where his head had been.

A loud crash announced its arrival on the basement level.

"Are you all right, lovey?" my mother inquired solicitously.

Nigel nodded as he brushed dust off his shirt. "Bloody hell, that's a bit unsafe," he said with typical British understatement.

"A bit unsafe, my ass," Hal said. "It's a fucking deathtrap. There's got to be a safety mechanism."

"If there is," Nigel said, "it's not bloody working."

"Has this ever been serviced?" Mum asked.

Doris shrugged. "Not since I've been here. Like I said, we've never used it."

"But you've had any number of repairmen and carpenters and electricians and plumbers in here since you moved in," Mum persisted. "That's what you told me."

"Apparently we had to," Doris said. "Dick said his uncle really let the old place go, living here all by himself the last ninety years or so, so we've had workmen in here removing dry rot, mold, and mildew, replacing baseboards, repairing electricity and plumbing, you name it."

"But have any of them worked on the dumbwaiter?" I asked.

"I can't imagine why. We had no intention of using it."

"Did you keep an eye on them, to see what they were doing?"

Doris shuddered. "Oh heavens, no. I stayed out of their way and let Dick handle everything. It's his uncle's house, and after all, isn't that what husbands are for?"

Maybe they are, I thought, *and maybe they aren't*, but the bottom line was that Doris wouldn't know if they had worked on the dumbwaiter or not. And that wasn't like the Doris I knew either.

"We can't leave it like that," Hal said. "It's a liability. If we can't fix it, we should at least disconnect the car and leave it in the basement. Where would the motor be? Any idea?"

Doris merely shook her head.

"It's got to be in the basement," Nigel said. "Let's go take a look at it. Doris? How do we get to the basement?"

"There's a door out here in the hallway," Doris said. "Let me show you."

We followed her out into the long hallway that led past the parlor and the library and ended just past the kitchen in a rather dark alcove. Doris reached up and pulled a cord that we hadn't even seen in the gloom. A ceiling light revealed two doors at the end of the hallway. Doris opened the one on the right.

"Here it is," she said. "Be careful on the stairs; they're steep."

I peered past Nigel and saw the stairs leading into impenetrable darkness. "Isn't there a light down there?"

"I don't know," Doris said. She shivered, hugging herself as if trying to get warm. "I never go down there. It's creepy, and there are spiders. Black widows. Hobos. Brown recluse."

At that, I shivered too. As a teenager I'd been bitten on the toe by a black widow spider. My whole leg had swollen up to the point where the skin began to split, and the doctor had told me to keep my weight off it. Consequently, I'd had to ride the bus to high school on crutches for the first three weeks of my sophomore year. Needless to say, I was not overly fond of spiders.

"What about Dick?" I asked.

Doris waved a hand. "Oh, he went down there all the time. He has a workshop down there. I have no idea what he worked on though."

"Maybe he was digging the Panama Canal," I suggested, thinking of *Arsenic and Old Lace*.

"Then p'r'aps we'd better watch our step," Nigel said dryly. "How about that flashlight?"

"Oh, sorry. I should have thought of that," Doris said. The old Doris wouldn't have needed reminding. She gave it to Nigel, who handed it to Hal.

"You go first," he said. "If the stairs will bear your weight, Toni and I should be safe."

"Thanks a lot," Hal said, but he took the flashlight and aimed it down the stairs, which looked just about as decrepit as I expected them to, given their age. At least two of them were broken, and one was missing altogether. I wondered why in tarnation the workmen hadn't repaired them. Perhaps Dick didn't want them to, for God only knew what reason.

The flashlight also illuminated a cord hanging from the ceiling just like the one in the hall. "Here's our light," Hal said, pulling it.

Nothing happened.

Hal said, "That figures," and aimed the flashlight up at the light fixture. There was no bulb in it. "What the hell?"

"I'll get one," I said and went back into the kitchen. "Doris? Have you got any light bulbs?"

"I'm sure I do," she replied. "Why, is that light out again? Dick just replaced it."

"There's no bulb in it," I told her.

She rummaged in a drawer just below the junk drawer. "Well, I can't imagine why that would be," she said. "Here's a hundred-watt. Will that do?"

"It should," I said, taking it from her. "How about a stepladder?"

"There's one here next to the refrigerator," my mother said, holding up a kitchen stool. "Will this do?"

"That looks like just the thing." I took it and the bulb back to Hal.

With a bulb in place, the light illuminated the stairs quite well. Besides being in bad repair, they were very steep, and there was no railing. But the darkness beyond the stairs remained impenetrable.

"This looks like a broken hip just waiting to happen," Hal commented.

"I suggest you go down backward," Nigel said. "That way, you can at least use your hands."

"Good idea," Hal said and started down. The staircase swayed alarmingly under his weight. "You two had better wait till I get down," he said.

I thought perhaps I should have taken a seasick pill, but all of us managed to reach the bottom without incident. I hoped we'd be as lucky getting back up that rickety staircase as we'd been coming down and resolved to look for an alternate exit from the cellar.

"Why the hell didn't those workmen fix these?" Hal asked irritably as he aimed the flashlight around. "The dumbwaiter should be right over there," he said, pointing to the left. Then he handed the flashlight to Nigel, at which point I objected.

"Hadn't we better find out if there are more lights before you go off with that flashlight and leave the rest of us in darkness?" I inquired.

"Toni, old thing, do give over," my stepfather admonished me. "There's another cord hanging just there." He pointed straight ahead.

Hal said, "Let's hope this one has a bulb," and pulled the cord. A bank of overhead fluorescent lights blazed into life with a rather alarming buzzing noise. They continued to flicker and buzz while I wondered what they'd do first—quit buzzing or quit working. But in the meantime, we could now see what was down there.

16

Nobody had dug the Panama Canal. It was a perfectly solid stone floor with no holes that I could see.

To the left was still darkness, into which Nigel departed with the flashlight. To the right, a veritable wall of boxes, festooned with cobwebs, all but blocked access to whatever lay beyond them.

"Looks like Doris hasn't even unpacked," Hal observed.

"We need to see what's behind those boxes," I said. "Maybe Dick is back there on the floor, dead from a heart attack."

"We'd be able to smell him by now if he was," Hal said. "I sure hope there's another light over here," he grumbled as he plunged into the darkness. A metallic clatter ensued. "Shit!"

"Are you okay?" I asked.

"I will be as soon as I quit hurting," he said. "Try to find a light switch, will you? I can't see a thing back here."

"You should have kept the flashlight," I said, knowing it would piss him off but unable to help myself. It's a wife thing.

"Well, that's no help now, is it?" he replied, annoyance clear in his voice.

I was singularly unwilling to blindly brave the dark cavern that was apparently strewn with metallic objects that could cause me injury as they had Hal—not to mention walking into spiderwebs, no doubt with resident spiders, possibly black widows. I shuddered and wondered if Doris had more than one flashlight. But before I could say anything, Hal said, "Never mind, I found it," and a second bank of fluorescents lit up the space beyond the boxes.

It seemed that Dick was either obsessively organized or a total slob, or maybe both. A workbench ran the length of the far wall with shelves upon which stood a succession of clear plastic containers with neatly labeled drawers containing perhaps every size and type of nail, screw, nut, bolt, washer, and hook known to man. A pegboard upon which the outlines of tools had been drawn filled the rest of the wall, but most of the tools were piled on the workbench or on the floor.

There was no body.

Perhaps it was Dick's great-uncle who had been obsessively organized, and Dick who was the slob.

While Hal poked around on the workbench and the shelves, I checked out the ancient glass-fronted apothecary cabinet that stood against the wall opposite the workbench. One of the doors was closed, but the other dangled crookedly from the top hinge. The other hinges were missing altogether. The items in the cabinet and the glass shelves upon which they stood were coated with decades of dust, rust, and encrusted spills.

But one item stood out from its neighbors by virtue of its total absence of dust. It was at the back of its shelf, behind other bottles, as if someone had tried to hide it. I began to move bottles around to get at it, and Hal turned around and asked me what the hell I was doing.

"You'd better be careful," he told me. "You don't know what you're getting into. You should wear gloves to handle that stuff."

"Does Dick have any gloves in that mess?"

"There's a pair of work gloves, but they're way too big for you."

"Better than nothing," I retorted, and held out my hand.

"Wait a minute," Hal said. "Here are some painting gloves down here among the paint cans." He handed me a box.

I took it, extracted a pair of gloves, and pulled them on.

Nigel reappeared. "Might there be a pair of pliers and a screwdriver in all that mess?"

"Phillips or flathead?"

"Phillips."

Hal fished the items out of the pile on the workbench and handed them to Nigel, who then turned to me and inquired, "What have you gotten into, old dear?"

"Take a look at this," I said. "See that bottle way in back?"

"Why isn't it dusty like all the rest?" he asked.

"Exactly my thought."

"Let's have a look then."

I reached into the cabinet and removed the bottle. It was clear glass and was half-full of a white powder. The label was printed in red and badly faded, but under the glare of the fluorescent lights, I could make out the words. "Cowley's Rat and Mouse Exterminator," I read, "active ingredient, arsenic trioxide. Wow. That hasn't been used to kill mice in decades. I wonder how long this has been here."

"Close to a hundred years, I should think," Nigel said.

"Well, then, I should think it'd be a lot dustier than this," I said. "It looks like it's been wiped off. Why wipe this one off and not the others?" Experimentally, I tried to unscrew the cap, expecting it to be welded in place by decades of corrosion, but to my surprise, it turned easily. "Hey. This has been used recently."

"To kill mice, I expect."

"There's a box of D-Con right over there on the workbench," I pointed out. "Why wouldn't he use that?"

"Well, then, what would he use this for?"

"Use what for?" Hal inquired. "What *is* that?"

Nigel took the bottle from me and handed it to Hal. "That, old boy, is pure white arsenic, famed in song and story as number one on the poisoner's hit list."

"That's what I was thinking," I said. "Hal's going to think I'm reaching."

"Try me," Hal said.

"Doris has been sick since she married Dick. I'm just saying."

Hal put the bottle back in the cabinet. "You're right. I do think you're reaching."

"There's a surprise," I remarked. "I think I'll have a heart attack and die from that surprise."

"You think Dick was systematically poisoning Doris with arsenic?" Hal asked, ignoring my sarcasm. "What for?"

"The usual reason. Money."

"Doris has money?"

"She could. Maybe she has a lot of insurance. Bob was an insurance agent, remember? He could have left her very well off; plus, he could have insured *her* for a lot of money too. She could have already made Dick the beneficiary."

"Spot on, old girl," Nigel said.

Hal frowned. "You mean she's right?"

"Don't act so surprised," I snapped.

"Fact of the matter is," Nigel went on, "that Bob did very well in the insurance business and insured both himself and Doris for half a million dollars. Each."

"And is Dick the beneficiary?" Hal asked.

"Not sure," Nigel said. "You'd best ask her. Are you done poking around there?"

"I guess so," Hal said. "Oh, wait. This might come in handy." He held up a small can with a spout. "Machine oil. You might need it."

"Thanks," Nigel said. "Let's get on with it."

We picked our way over to the other side of the cellar, where Nigel had found another bank of fluorescent lights and turned them on. The door to the dumbwaiter gaped open, exposing the stainless-steel interior of the car.

"Was it like that when you got here?" I asked Nigel.

"Yes, why?"

"Well, Mum said the car wouldn't move unless the door was closed. So how come we were able to send the car down here from the kitchen if the door was open down here?"

"Obviously, the safety mechanism isn't working," Nigel said.

I stood and watched as Hal and Nigel removed the wall panel below the dumbwaiter door to expose the motor and stood it against the adjacent wall. They struggled to get the cables back on the wheels from which they had come loose when the car plunged from the second floor to the basement, nearly taking Nigel's head off in the process. I wondered why we were spending so much time and effort fixing the dumbwaiter when we could be exploring the basement. Doris never used the dumbwaiter, and in any case, she wasn't living there anymore.

When they began to take the motor apart, I voiced my objections. "Maybe it would be better if you just disconnected the wiring," I suggested. "That motor could have a short in it and cause a fire."

"That's true," Hal said and proceeded to do just that.

Nigel got to his feet with a groan and dusted his hands off on his pant legs.

"Okay," Hal said. "Can we put this wall panel back now?"

"I don't see why not," Nigel said.

As Hal began fitting the wall panel back into place, I noticed something. The panel looked rough and unfinished. "Haven't you got that on backward?" I asked, pointing to the panel.

"That's the way it was when we got here," Hal objected.

"Let's see what the other side looks like," Nigel suggested.

Hal sighed. "Whatever." He turned the panel around.

We all gasped. A dark stain spread all the way across the top of the panel, and red-brown rivulets ran from there almost to the bottom edge.

"What the hell is that?" Nigel asked.

"Probably paint," Hal said.

"Could it be blood?" I asked.

"Here we go again," Hal commented.

"Somebody put that panel on backward to hide it," I argued. "Why bother if it's only paint?" I bent down and sniffed. "It sure doesn't smell like paint."

"It's dry," Hal said. "You wouldn't expect it to smell like paint."

I wet a finger, rubbed it in the stuff, smelled it, and grimaced. "It's not paint," I said and held it out to Nigel. "Smell that."

"She's right," Nigel said. "It's blood. What the bloody hell happened here?"

I didn't like what I was thinking. "Do you suppose what nearly happened to you happened to somebody else?" I asked.

"We can't tell unless we raise the car and look at the bottom of the shaft," Hal said.

"In that case," Nigel said, "I reckon we'd better fix that motor after all."

Hal groaned.

I picked up the flashlight. "While you two are doing that, I'm going to look around some more."

"Be careful," Hal cautioned.

"I'm always careful," I said. "Holler if you find anything."

While Hal and Nigel worked on the motor, I went back to the other side of the basement, past the boxes, into the darkness beyond. To my chagrin, I found my progress blocked by a solid brick wall. Surely the basement didn't end here, unless the rest of it hadn't been dug out, which seemed odd for a house this old and this large.

If Dick's ancestor had intended for it to be authentic, surely there would be a stone basement underneath the entire house. There wouldn't be a brick wall in the middle of it. A stone wall, perhaps, but bricks suggested that the wall had been built after the fact. I wondered why.

I turned to the left and started walking in that direction when I heard groaning and clanking followed by a loud bang.

"Toni!" It was Hal's voice. "We need the flashlight!"

I started back the way I had come. "Is it fixed?" I asked.

"Possibly," Nigel said. "In any event, the car is now on the first floor."

I glanced at the dumbwaiter. The door was closed.

"Is it possible to open the door when the car is on another floor?" I asked. "Because if it isn't ..."

"Only one way to find out," Nigel said and pushed upward on the door handle. He got it about halfway up before it stuck in place. "Here, hand me that oilcan, would you?" he asked Hal, and Hal handed it to him. I held the flashlight while Nigel generously anointed the track and pushed the door back down. "That's better," he grunted, and pushed it back up. This time, it went all the way up and stayed in place while Nigel put more oil into the track.

A red-brown splotch nearly covered the floor of the shaft, with splatter on the sides. I aimed the flashlight up inside the shaft to illuminate the bottom of the car, but even so, it was too dark to tell if the same stain was on it.

"Maybe some paint got spilled in here," Hal persisted. "It doesn't necessarily have to be blood."

I took a closer look at the bottom of the shaft. "Would paint have hairs in it?"

"That does it," Nigel said. "It's blood until proven otherwise. We have to report this to the police. You may as well leave that panel off, old boy. They'll want it for evidence."

CHAPTER 3

Yet who would have thought the old man to have so
much blood in him?

—Shakespeare, *Macbeth*

When we got back upstairs, Doris and Mum were relaxing on the couch, watching TV. "Did you find anything?" Mum asked.

"We certainly did," I said.

"It appears as though someone was killed in the dumbwaiter," Nigel said. "Nobody could survive an accident like that. If it was an accident."

Doris sat up straight on the couch, suddenly showing interest. "What do you mean, *if* it was an accident? Do you think it was murder? Who … wait, do you think it was *Dick* who was killed?"

I opened my mouth to speak, but Nigel beat me to it. "There's really no way to know at this point."

"There was blood and hair on the bottom of the hoistway and the bottom of the car," I explained. "Like there would be if someone's head was crushed by the car coming down to the cellar level. Like what almost happened to Nigel."

Doris put her hand to her mouth and looked sick.

"That's enough now, Antoinette," Mum said.

"But that's not all we found," I protested. "There's a half-empty bottle of Cowley's rat poison in the apothecary cabinet down there that looks like it's been used recently."

"One would expect mice in an old house like this, surely," Mum said. "What would it matter if it's been used recently?"

"That's not the point," I said. "Cowley's is pure arsenic trioxide. That hasn't been used to kill rats for at least fifty years. But the bottle's not dusty like all the other things in that cabinet, and the lid should have been stuck, but it came right off."

"Toni seems to think that Dick's been poisoning Doris with it," Hal said.

Doris gasped, turned white, and broke out in a sweat. She fanned herself vigorously. "Oh, God, oh, God, I can't breathe," she moaned. "My chest hurts. I think I'm going to pass out. I think I'm having a heart attack."

"Now look what you've done!" Mum exclaimed. "Did you have to mention arsenic right in front of her like that?"

"I'm sorry," Hal said. "Actually, it was Toni who mentioned arsenic."

Mum shook her head with annoyance. "Hal dear, really, what does that matter?"

"She's not having a heart attack," I said. "She's having a panic attack. And she's hyperventilating. Doris, where do you keep grocery bags?"

"I'll show you," Mum said. We went back to the kitchen, where I fetched a brown paper bag. I took it back to Doris and instructed her to breathe into it.

To my relief, she recovered quickly. "I never used to get panic attacks," she murmured. "Now I get them all the time. It's so stupid. Oh, I feel sick."

Her pale face was again beaded with sweat. "We've got to get her out of here straightaway," Mum said. "I'm afraid she's going to be sick."

She'd barely gotten the words out of her mouth when Doris bolted from the couch and scurried down the long hallway to the bathroom at the end of it.

Mum sighed. "I had hoped she wouldn't be doing that anymore. She said she felt better this morning, but now …"

"I'm going to call the police," Nigel said.

"Shouldn't we look around first to see if we can find Dick before you do that?" I asked.

Nigel shook his head. "It won't make any difference. Someone was killed by that dumbwaiter. Even if it wasn't Dick, it should be reported."

I shrugged. "Okay, but I still think we should look around. Even if it wasn't Dick who was killed, there's got to be a body somewhere."

Hal was still skeptical. "Surely the police looked all around when they were here before."

Doris came out of the bathroom in time to hear Hal's remark.

"They didn't," she said. "I called them to report Dick missing, and they came to the house and interviewed me, you know, about where he liked to go, and who his associates were, all that sort of thing. They didn't look around at all."

"Do you know what their names were?" I asked. "So if you needed to call them, you'd know who to ask for?"

"They each gave me a card," Doris said. "I think I left them on the desk in the kitchen. Let me look." We followed her into the kitchen where she riffled through the piles of papers on the rolltop desk and eventually located them and held them out to me. The cards were identical, bearing the logo of the Long Beach Police Department and the words Violent Crimes Division. I stowed the cards away in my pants pocket.

"Well, if the police didn't look around," I said, "maybe we should. We'd look pretty stupid if Dick's body is lying somewhere around the grounds in plain sight."

"You mean they'd look stupid," Hal pointed out. "They didn't do their job. Besides, if there's a body lying around out there, wouldn't we be able to smell it by now? Did you smell anything when we got here? Because I didn't."

Mum, Doris, and I just shook our heads. Doris's face twisted into an expression of severe distaste at the suggestion.

"What's out back?" Hal asked. "Any other buildings?"

"There's a barn out back," Doris said. "You can go out that way." She indicated the door at the end of the kitchen by the laundry area.

Outside the back door, a grove of eucalyptus trees amid a tangle of bushes shaded the side of the house and prevented us from going anywhere except along the side of the house to the back, where a huge barn stood. It looked large enough to house farm equipment. The door was secured by a padlock.

I went back into the kitchen to ask Doris for the key. She looked confused. "We need to look in the barn," I explained.

The old Doris would have given us the key right off the bat. We wouldn't have had to ask.

Her face cleared. "Oh, sorry. I should have thought of that. Just a minute." She fished around in the junk drawer and produced a huge key ring. She detached one and handed it to me. "There you go."

The padlock yielded to the key without too much resistance, but it took both of us to shove the huge sliding door open to reveal the dark, cavernous interior, which was empty except for a beige Mercedes sedan and a stack of boxes that stood behind it.

"Whose car is that?" Hal asked, as if he expected me to know.

"I'm guessing it's Dick's," I said. "I'm sure Doris's is at Mum and Nigel's, because she rode over here with us. That's interesting, don't you think?"

"Why?"

"Because wherever Dick went, he didn't go there in his own car. Did he just walk off? Did somebody come and pick him up? Where was Doris while all this was going on?"

"I'm sure the police asked all those questions," Hal said.

Maybe. I wasn't so sure. "You don't suppose he just walked out here somewhere and had a heart attack or something and is just lying somewhere in all these trees?"

"Like I said before, don't you think we'd smell it by now?"

A horrible thought occurred to me. "What if he's inside the car? With the doors closed, we wouldn't be able to smell him."

Hal made a face. "Then I suggest you take a look inside before opening the door."

"Good idea." I peered in the window. Nobody was sitting in the front seat. I moved to the back windows. Nobody was lying in the back seat either.

Hal opened the driver's side door, reached in, and popped the trunk.

Dick wasn't there either. Just a spare tire and a golf bag.

"What do you suppose all these boxes are doing here?" Hal asked. "If the boxes in the basement are Doris's stuff, what are these?"

"Or," I said, "maybe these are Doris's, and the ones in the basement are something else."

"Well, whatever they are, they're all too small to put a body in," Hal said with an air of finality.

We did a quick search of the barn, shining the flashlight into the corners and other dark spaces. No Dick. Although Hal kept pointing out that if Dick's body was there, we'd smell him.

"We should probably look upstairs," I said. "There must be tons of rooms that have been closed up for decades. He could be in any one of them."

"They're probably locked," Hal pointed out. "We'll have to get the keys from Doris."

We went back inside. Mum was back on the couch. "Doris and Nigel are upstairs," she told us. "Nigel wanted to look in all the closed-up rooms, even though Doris told him she'd already looked in them when Dick first went missing."

"In that case," I said, "I want to look around outside some more."

"Why?" Hal asked.

"I'm curious about the basement," I said. "I want to know if it goes all the way under the house."

"What do you mean?" Mum asked.

"I tried to go back beyond the boxes and the tool bench," I told her, "but there's a brick wall there, and I couldn't go any farther."

Hal shrugged. "Maybe that's all there is to it," he said. "Maybe that's all they dug out. Maybe there was rock, and they didn't want to blast, or whatever they did back then."

"Well then, why didn't they build it of the same stone they used for the rest of the house?" I asked. "Why use brick?"

Hal shrugged again and followed me back outside.

We made our way around to the west side of the house, hugging the walls because the underbrush was too thick to allow passage any other way.

We stopped when we encountered a cluster of huge blue spruces up along the side of the house. Their branches actually touched the house. We couldn't go any farther.

"What's that?" I pointed to something that appeared to push some of the lower branches upward.

"What's what?" Hal asked. "I don't see anything."

I got down on my hands and knees and crawled under the branches, ignoring the twigs and needles tearing at my hair and clothes, until I could see what it was.

"Aha!" I said. "Cellar doors! This basement *does* go all the way under the house!"

"There's no way to get those open," Hal said, "unless we cut those trees back. You didn't happen to find Dick in there, did you?"

I giggled. "Not hardly."

"Let's go see if Nigel found anything," Hal suggested.

We retraced our steps and brushed each other off outside the front door. "Shit," Hal said as he attempted to pick needles out of my hair. "You've got pitch in your hair. Don't try to comb it or you'll tear it right out of your head."

I promised I wouldn't, and we went back inside. Doris was back on the couch, and Nigel was in the recliner. "No joy," he reported. "All we found was dust."

"I told you," Doris said.

"Well, we didn't find him either," Hal said.

The doorbell rang. "That's probably the police," Nigel said.

"I'll get it," I said.

When I opened the front door, two detectives in plainclothes stood there next to each other. One was compactly built and not much taller than I was, with salt-and-pepper hair and dark eyes; the other was huge and black. The disparity in their sizes reminded me of my son-in-law Pete, who was a homicide detective for the Twin Falls Police Department, and his partner, Bernie Kincaid. Come to think of it, the short detective even kind of looked like Bernie, except that his hair was grayer.

When he saw me, an expression of shock crossed his face. I stared back at him. "What?" I asked.

The detective finally found his voice; and it sounded angry.

"Sonia? What the hell are you doing here?"

It was my turn to stand there with my mouth open. Who the devil was Sonia?

Hal, Mum, and Nigel joined me at the door. "Is there a problem?" Nigel asked.

"We heard shouting," Mum said reproachfully.

The big detective rescued me. "That's not Sonia," he said to his partner. "I know her. She graduated from Poly with me. Didn't you? Weren't you a Polyette? Toni, right?"

Recognition dawned. "Tyrone? You're a *cop* now?"

Tyrone Jeffers had played football for Long Beach Polytechnic High School, and the only reason we knew each other was that I had been a member of Polyettes, the high school drill team that did the halftime performances on the field, and pep rallies at school on game days. Mum hadn't been particularly supportive of my participation in something that she called "all that jumping up and down" and threatened that she'd make me quit if I got a single B.

Long Beach Polytechnic High School was one of five high schools in Long Beach, located smack-dab in the middle of that part of the city occupied mostly by black families. The student body, when I was there, had been 50 percent black and 25 percent Japanese. I'd been in a minority there.

Tyrone laughed. "Detective Sergeant, Homicide. And you were gonna be a doctor. Did you make it?"

"I certainly did. I'm a pathologist now."

Tyrone looked surprised. "You mean like a medical examiner?"

"Not quite," I said. "I'm hospital based, although I've gotten involved in the odd homicide from time to time."

"Far too many," my mother interjected. "If you ask me."

"Mum, this was your idea—remember?"

"Now I know who you are," the smaller detective said suddenly. "My brother talks about you all the time." He stuck out his hand, and I shook it. "Detective Lieutenant Mark Kincaid, Homicide."

"Toni Day," I replied, "MD."

No wonder he looked like Bernie. Suddenly everything fell into place. I remembered that Bernie had once mentioned that I was the spittin' image of his ex-wife. That must be who Sonia was, and clearly, she hadn't made any points with her former brother-in-law.

"So did you two know each other in high school?" Hal asked Kincaid.

Kincaid shook his head. "Nope. Bernie and I went to Wilson."

Back in the day, Long Beach Poly and Woodrow Wilson High School had been archrivals on the football field.

Nigel had clearly had enough of Old Home Week. "I say, gentlemen, shall we get on with it?"

Suddenly both detectives were all business. Tyrone and Mark followed Hal and Nigel down the hallway, with me bringing up the rear. "Careful on the stairs," I called after them. Tyrone was even bigger than Hal, and I wasn't sure those rickety stairs would survive his weight.

They did, though. We all reached the bottom safely, one at a time, and Nigel led them over to the dumbwaiter where the panel leaned against the wall, bloodstained side out.

"What is this contraption?" Mark asked. "I've never seen anything like it."

Nigel explained what a dumbwaiter was. "This thing nearly took my bloody head off earlier," he told them. "So we came down here to see if we could fix it, and Toni noticed that the panel was on backward, and then when we turned it over, there was this great bloody mess on the underside."

"Then there's this on the bottom of the shaft," I pointed out. "And some splatter on the walls and door frame."

"Actually, that's called a hoistway," Nigel said. "Not a shaft."

"So," Mark said, "what exactly do you folks think happened here?"

"The same thing that nearly happened to me," Nigel said. "Only that time it succeeded."

"Someone's head was crushed between the bottom of the hoistway and the bottom of the car," I said.

"So where's the car?" Tyrone asked.

"On the main floor," Nigel said. "We had to do that in order to look at the bottom of the hoistway."

"Is there blood on the bottom of the car?" Mark asked.

"I couldn't tell," I said. "It's too dark."

"Okay," he said. "Someone may have been killed here, but who? Where's the body? Is anyone missing?"

"Yes," I said. "Don't you guys talk to each other? Doris reported her husband missing last week."

Mark gave me that sharp look again. "Who's handling the case? Do you know?"

I pulled the cards out of my pocket and handed them to him. "These guys."

Mark glanced at them and said, "Hmph."

Tyrone looked over Mark's shoulder, shook his head, and said, "Oh boy."

"Are you trying to tell us," Hal interjected, "that those guys didn't exactly graduate at the top of their class at the police academy?"

"I wouldn't know about that," Mark said. "But they are a pair of lazy bastards."

"Amen," Tyrone agreed.

"We kind of got that impression from what Doris told us," I said. "She said they asked a lot of questions, but they didn't look around."

"Sounds about right," Mark said. "Maybe we'd better have a look-see."

"Do you want to look around the house?" I asked. "Doris could show you around."

"We've already looked in all the upstairs rooms," Nigel said. "The dust hasn't been disturbed in years."

"We're going to assume that Doris has already looked around the house for her husband," Mark said. "But we'd like to take a look outside. Are there any other buildings? Is her husband's car still here?"

"Yes, to both," Hal said.

"Then let's go," Tyrone said.

"Wait," I said. "There's something else I need to show you."

Hal did an eye-roll and said, "Oy vey."

I ignored him. "It's over here," I went on, and led them over to the other side of the cellar and the apothecary cabinet.

"Toni, for God's sake," Hal objected, "they can't do anything about that without something to link it to."

"About what?" Tyrone asked.

I pointed. "See that bottle way in the back that isn't dusty like the others?"

They looked. "What about it?" Mark asked, a little impatiently.

"It's arsenic," I said, "and Doris has been sick almost since she married Dick."

"Oh, now let me guess," Mark said with thinly disguised sarcasm. "You think Doris is suffering from arsenic poisoning. You think someone's been poisoning her. You've been reading too many detective stories."

He sounded just like his brother.

"Okay," I said. "You may laugh now, but if this turns out to be attempted murder, don't come blaming me for hiding evidence."

"Give it a rest, sweetie," Hal advised me. "You're wasting their time with this wild theory of yours."

Both Mark and Tyrone looked as though they agreed, so I gave up and led them back up the stairs and out the back door. I pointed out the barn and the car, told them Hal and I hadn't found anything, left them to it, and went back to the house to join Mum and Doris, who were back on the library couch, feet up on the coffee table.

"Doris is feeling much better," Mum said, "but I think she needs to go home and lie down."

"I'd better let the cops know we're leaving," Nigel said. "They'll want to know how to reach us." Suiting the action to the words, he went into the kitchen and out the back door to do just that.

"While he's doing that," I said, "I'd like to take just a quick look upstairs."

"Go right ahead, sweetie," Doris said. "I'll just rest here."

The staircase to the second floor was very narrow and curved. Doris and Dick's bedroom was the first room on the left. The door was unlocked. The room was large and contained a king-size bed covered with a floral duvet and cluttered with a profusion of throw pillows. Matching shams covered the king-size pillows. Matching draperies covered the window, shutting out the light. I went over to the window and drew them back to reveal a spectacular view of Del Mar Park.

The dresser, the highboy, and the wardrobe were all antique white with gilt trim. A set of silver brushes adorned the dresser and were engraved with the initials RAC. They were Dick's, I assumed, although the portrait of Doris and Dick that sat on the dresser showed that Dick was nearly bald. Only a rim of gray hair could be seen just above his ears.

The adjoining bathroom contained a claw-footed bathtub and the pedestal sink, clearly from the nineteenth century; only the toilet was modern. A tall cabinet alongside the sink, also painted antique white and gilt, contained towels, toilet paper, and a plethora of personal care items. One shelf, entirely given over to Dick, contained his razor, shaving brush, and shaving cream, a tooth glass in which Dick's toothbrush stood, along with deodorant, aftershave, and the like. Doris's makeup and creams and lotions occupied another shelf.

"Toni? Where are you?"

Hal had come looking for me. "In here," I called.

"We're leaving."

When we went downstairs, Doris was still on the couch but didn't look happy. "I've got to get out of this house," she said shakily. "Can we go now?"

So as soon as the detectives left, having given their cards to Doris—and also to Nigel at his request—and received permission to take the photo, we took her back to Mum and Nigel's house, where she apologized for being such a nuisance and went straight to bed.

CHAPTER 4

The female of the species is more deadly than the
male.

—Rudyard Kipling

Back at the house, Nigel immediately put the kettle on for tea.
"Any coffee left?" Hal inquired.

"Yes, but surely it's cold by now," Mum said.

"That's what microwaves are for," Hal said.

Mum and I went into the living room, where Mum sat down on the pink
brocade armchair, kicked off her shoes, and put her feet up on the ottoman.

I brought Mark Kincaid's and Tyrone's cards into the living room with the
intention of programming their numbers into my cell phone.

"So, kitten," Mum said, "I take it you don't think that arsenic was used
for mice."

Hal came in with a steaming cup of coffee and joined me on the couch,
leaving the recliner for Nigel. "That's what I would have thought," he said,
"but you know Toni. She just made a quantum leap on the basis that Doris had
been sick lately and immediately assumed that Dick had been poisoning her."

I looked up from my programming. "It's not that much of a leap," I objected.
"Can you say 'Lyda Southard'?"

In the kitchen, the kettle began to whistle.

"Anyone fancy a cuppa?" Nigel asked.

Mum and I assented, and Nigel went out to prepare it.

"Who's Lyda Southard?" Mum asked.

"Lady Bluebeard," Hal answered. "Idaho's most famous serial killer."

Nigel came back with three mugs in his hands just in time to hear that last remark. He handed Mum her tea and then gave me mine. "Do tell," he said with interest as he settled into the recliner. "I didn't know Idaho even *had* serial killers. Was this something recent?"

"Oh, no," I said. "She was born in 1892. She married a total of seven husbands, and the first four died of gastroenteritis or typhoid, or influenza, or ptomaine poisoning, according to their death certificates, but it turned out she was poisoning them with arsenic, which she got by boiling flypapers." I took a sip of my tea, but it was still too hot, so I put it back on the coffee table.

"Not only that," Hal said, "but she also poisoned her first husband's brother, and her two daughters also died under mysterious circumstances."

"And I suppose she killed her husbands for money," Mum suggested.

"Specifically for their insurance," I said. "That's why it occurred to me that Dick might have been trying to kill Doris for her insurance."

"She has quite a bit," my mother said. "Bob was an insurance man, you know, and he left her very well off. He'd insured himself very generously, and he'd insured her too, for the same amount; so Dick would have had a motive, if he knew about it." She picked up a magazine and fanned herself with it.

"Maybe he took out a policy on her as well," Hal suggested.

I took another sip of my tea; just right. "Too bad we can't ask him," I said.

Nigel got up and opened the front door, leaving the screen door closed, letting in the ocean breeze.

"Thank you, lovey; that feels much better. How much money did Lyda Thingummy get from all that?" Mum asked.

"Not much by today's standards," I replied. "Just a little over $28,000. One of her husbands had let his policy lapse by not paying the premiums, so she didn't get anything from him. She was said to have been a trifle testy about that."

Nigel took a large swig of tea and wiped his moustache with the back of his hand. "How do you two know so much about this?" he asked.

"Elliott's grandfather was the county prosecutor on the case," I said. "Elliott told us all about it."

Elliott was our next-door neighbor and also a lawyer.

"How'd she get caught?" Nigel asked.

"When her fourth husband died, a relative of her first husband, who just happened to be a chemist, got suspicious and went out to their ranch and took some samples. They had arsenic in them," I said. "Then Elliott's grandfather got involved and found the motive in the records of the Idaho State Insurance Company of Boise, which had insured all of them. They dug up all her husbands and her first husband's brother and one of her daughters, and they all had arsenic in them."

"Of course, by that time, she was already married to her fifth husband, who was in the navy and was transferred to Hawaii, and the law caught up with her there and brought her back for trial in Idaho," Hal said.

"That was in 1921," I said. "She got ten to life in the Idaho State Pen."

"But she escaped," Hal said, "and ended up in Kansas married to her sixth husband. They caught her and brought her back to Idaho."

"How long was she in prison?" Mum asked.

"She was paroled in 1941," Hal said, "and a few years after that, she married her seventh husband, and he disappeared two years later. Nobody ever saw him again."

"Maybe she poisoned him too," Nigel said and drained his teacup.

"Maybe," I said and drank the rest of my tea before it got cold. "Nobody knows. She died in 1958, and she's buried in Twin Falls."

Nigel got up and collected our teacups. "More?" he inquired.

Mum and I both assented. Hal got up and accompanied Nigel into the kitchen. I finished my programming and slid my cell phone into my purse.

"What a story!" Mum said. "Quite the thriller. What made you think of her, kitten?"

"Well, Bob was an insurance man," I said, "and Doris remarried only a few months after he died. You said Dick 'swept her off her feet.' So maybe Dick knew Bob, or maybe he knew how much insurance she had somehow. Plus, she started getting sick, when? Right after the wedding?"

Nigel and Hal returned with refills.

"Not quite," Mum said, "but maybe a couple of weeks after that. What do you think, lovey? Does that sound about right?"

"I'd say so," Nigel said, handing Mum her tea. "It's been going on for quite a while. But if Dick was poisoning her, wouldn't you think she'd start getting better now that he's gone?"

"I thought she was," Mum protested, "until today."

Nigel handed me my tea. "Can't she be tested for arsenic poisoning?" he asked.

"Certainly," I said. "Since she presumably hasn't ingested any for a week or more, it had better be urine rather than blood, although after that much time, they might have to test hair or fingernails."

"Can they test for it at the police lab?" Mum asked.

"Oh, heavens no," I said. "It would have to go to a reference lab. They have to use high-pressure liquid chromatography, and most hospital labs don't have that capability."

"But isn't there a quickie test they can do?" Mum persisted. "Not too long ago, I read a book by Dorothy Sayers in which they did something called a Marsh test to detect arsenic."

"I think I know that one," I said. "Was it *Strong Poison*? The Marsh test is really old. It was developed in 1836 and involves heating the test substance in acid, and it causes a silvery deposit on the glass tube. But antimony does the same thing, so it's not specific for arsenic. Besides, in that book, they used it to test some white powder that Miss Murgatroyd found in Norman Urquhart's office safe, which was pure white arsenic. The amounts likely to be present in urine are way smaller. It's measured in micrograms per liter."

"Micrograms?" Nigel inquired. "That's what—a thousandth of a gram?"

"A millionth of a gram," I said, "in a liter of urine."

"That's like a quart," Hal added helpfully.

"Yes, I know," Nigel said dryly. "Everything's metric in England. You Yanks need to get with the program, don't you know."

"So what do we do next?" Mum asked. "Take a urine specimen down to the police station and ask them to get it tested?"

"I think Doris needs to go to her doctor and ask to be tested," I said. "If she turns out to have arsenic in her urine or nails or hair, then her doctor can report it to the police and give them the medical records. Also, the doctor has to make sure that if there's enough arsenic there, the lab will fractionate it."

"Fractionate?" Hal asked.

"They have to separate organic arsenic from inorganic arsenic," I explained, "because it's inorganic arsenic that's toxic. We all have some organic arsenic in our bodies because it's in water and food. It's even in some California wines."

"Oh dear," Mum said.

"Relax. It's not enough to hurt us."

"That's all very well," Nigel said, "but if Doris does have arsenic poisoning, is there any way to treat it?"

"There are chelating agents that can be used," I said. "They bind heavy metals so that they can just be peed out."

The discussion sort of petered out after that, and Mum and Nigel decided to take naps, so Hal and I went out to the apartment to unpack and get settled. We'd only been at it for a few minutes when Mum came looking for us in a panic.

"It's Doris," she gasped. "I can't wake her up!"

Hal and I immediately dropped what we were doing to follow Mum back to the house at a dead run.

"Is she breathing?" I asked en route.

"I'm not sure," Mum said. "I think so."

We burst into the spare room where Doris lay on the bed, ominously still. Nigel had pulled a chair up to the bedside and was holding her wrist.

"Is she breathing?" I asked again.

"Just barely," he replied. "I'm having trouble finding a pulse, however."

"I'll call 911," Hal said and started to leave the room.

"Already did," Nigel said. "They're on their way."

I held a Kleenex in front of Doris's face. It fluttered with each breath. Doris's breaths were irregular. The pulse I felt in her carotid artery was irregular too. I pried up an eyelid. The bedside lamp was shining right into her face, and to my relief, the pupil contracted.

But then so did everything else. Before we could react, Doris was in the midst of a grand mal seizure. Nigel and Hal tried to hold her down.

"Turn her on her side," I said. "She may vomit."

"Shouldn't you put something in her mouth so she doesn't bite her tongue?" Mum asked anxiously.

"That's the least of our worries," I replied. "I just don't want her to choke."

It took all four of us to get Doris on her side. She was a tall woman and surprisingly strong.

"Is she epileptic?" Hal asked.

"Not that I know of," Mum said.

The doorbell rang.

"That must be the paramedics," Nigel said.

"I'll go," Mum said. She left and returned almost immediately with two paramedics wearing the uniforms of the Long Beach Fire Department. With lightning speed, they got an IV started and shot something into it; I suspected it was Valium, to stop the seizure. Gradually, it did so, and Doris lay limply on her side, still once more.

"She's not breathing," one of the paramedics said ominously, and within seconds, they had Doris intubated and were breathing for her with an Ambu bag.

"Is she epileptic?" asked one of the paramedics. "Is she on antiseizure medication?"

"Not that we know of," Mum said again.

"Does she have any heart issues?"

"No," Mum said. "But she does have high blood pressure."

"Does she take anything for it?"

"She does, but I don't know what," Mum said helplessly. "She's my best friend, and I should know these things."

While this conversation was going on, I'd been surreptitiously going through Doris's belongings. "Here we go," I said, holding up a Ziploc baggie of pill bottles. "She takes Lisinopril and hydrochlorothiazide."

The paramedic took the bag from me, opened it up, and looked at the prescription labels on all the pill bottles, writing them down on a form attached to his clipboard. "Any reason to think this was a suicide attempt?"

"No, but it could have been a poisoning attempt," I said.

The paramedic looked up from his clipboard, skepticism written all over his face. "With what?"

"Arsenic," I said. "She should be checked for it when you get her to the hospital."

"How long ago? Should we be pumping her stomach?"

"We think it's been going on for a while," I said, "although we didn't know about it until today."

"I see," said the paramedic, and he wrote "Suspicion of arsenic poisoning" on his clipboard.

"Where will you be taking her?" I asked.

"Memorial, unless she has another preference."

I looked at Mum, who shrugged. "We never talked about that. Up until now, she's never been sick. But I know her doctor is at St. Mary's, because he's my doctor too."

"St. Mary's it is," Nigel agreed. "Off you go, then."

Mum and Nigel decided to follow the ambulance in their car. Hal and I went back to the apartment to finish unpacking.

CHAPTER 5

Excuse my dust.

—Dorothy Parker, her own epitaph

"There's something I don't understand," Hal said. "If Dick's been missing for two weeks, why is Doris still getting sick?"

"I can think of two reasons," I said. "I think arsenic builds up in the body until there's enough of it to cause more severe symptoms and death. One has to give chelating agents to get it out of the body."

"So you think Doris has reached some kind of critical threshold of toxicity?"

"Maybe. Either that or she's still getting it somehow."

Hal frowned. "*Getting it somehow?* You make her sound like some kind of druggie."

"Well, Mum said she's been sick for months. But Mum never said anything about seizures and a coma. So if she hasn't been getting any arsenic for the last two weeks, why did she suddenly take a turn for the worse?"

"That's what I asked," Hal reminded me with monumental patience.

"Not exactly. You asked why she was still sick. I asked why she suddenly got sicker."

"Whatever. Let's not nitpick, okay?"

"Okay. So since Dick isn't here to give her arsenic, where's she getting it?"

"Maybe Dick put some in her food ahead of time, so she'd still be getting it after he left."

"Maybe," I said again. "But she wouldn't have brought any food here, would she?"

"I sure hope not," Hal said. "What if Fiona or Nigel ate some of it?"

"The only thing I can think of that she'd have to bring with her is her medicine."

"Which is all pills," Hal pointed out. "How would he get arsenic into her pills?"

"Maybe he put a little white arsenic into the prescription bottles, so it would cling to the pills."

"We can check when we go back to the house. Let's finish this up first."

But curiosity got the better of both of us.

The first thing I spied as we went in through the kitchen door was a tall orange can sitting on the counter next to the coffee maker. I picked it up and looked at the label. "Metamucil," I said. "I wonder who uses that."

"Never mind," Hal said. "Let's check her pills."

So we went back into the spare room, where Doris's pills still sat on top of her open overnight case. Hal opened the baggie and dumped the pill bottles out on the bed. We held each of them up to the light and couldn't see any white powder in the bottles or clinging to the pills.

"I think this is a nonstarter," I commented as I put the pill bottles back in the baggie. Then I took my cell phone out of my pocket.

"What are you going to do?" Hal asked.

I dialed Mum's cell phone. "Find out whose Metamucil that is," I told him. "I've never known either Mum or Nigel to use that before."

"Maybe one of them just started using it," Hal said.

Mum answered her phone. "Yes, kitten?"

I got straight to the point. "Who uses Metamucil?"

"It's Doris's. Why?"

"I'll tell you when we get there," I said. "Where are you now?"

"Doris is about to be admitted to the medical ICU," Mum said. "It's on Seven South."

"See you there," I told her, and rang off before she could ask any more questions. "Let's go," I said to Hal.

Hal turned up a palm. "Go where? And why?"

"That Metamucil is Doris's," I told him.

"You think that's where Dick …"

"Metamucil is an orange-flavored powder," I said. "It would be so simple to mix a bunch of white arsenic powder into it with no one being the wiser."

"Can the police lab test it?"

"They can if they have HPLC," I said. "I'll call Tyrone and ask. Let's get going. There's no time to waste!"

"But aren't you forgetting something?" Hal asked. "We don't have a car."

"We could use Doris's," I said. "Her purse is still here. Maybe her keys are in it."

They were. I handed them to Hal, and we went back outside. The carport was empty. "I don't suppose your mother has caved on the subject of garage door openers," Hal said.

"Doesn't look like it," I said.

Hal bent over, grasped the handle at the bottom of the door, and pulled. With a cacophony of squeaks and rattles, the door reluctantly rolled upward to reveal a dark blue Mercedes Benz SL550 roadster.

"Oh my God," I said reverently.

"Are you sure this is Doris's?" Hal asked. "She used to drive an ancient Subaru that didn't even have automatic transmission. What the hell happened?"

"She married Dick," I said. "He probably bought it for her. I agree, this is not her style, but it's definitely his."

"Boy, oh boy," Hal murmured. "Never thought I'd ever get to drive something like this. This thing has to go for over a hundred grand."

"I wouldn't be surprised," I said. "Let's get going."

The interior of the garage was so cramped that there wasn't room for me to get into the car on the passenger side until Hal backed the Mercedes out into the driveway. The interior was even plushier than the exterior, with rich burgundy leather upholstery and an instrument panel that would have looked more at home in a Boeing 747. Hal took a moment to figure out what did what before he continued backing out of the driveway.

On the way, I called Tyrone from my cell phone. He wasn't in. I left a message.

We reached St. Mary's Medical Center without incident. I stared in amazement at how much the place had changed since I'd done my internship there. The main entrance and the emergency room entrance were still off Linden Avenue, but the parking lot across the street had been replaced by a six-story parking structure. The old hospital building had been replaced by a seven-story tower, with a skywalk linking the two buildings at the fourth-story level. On the Atlantic Avenue side stood a gleaming, glass, three-story medical office building, where I knew that Doris and Mum's doctor had his office.

We parked, made our way inside, and took the elevator to the seventh floor. We found Mum and Nigel in the ICU waiting room. Mum jumped to her feet when she saw us. "Antoinette, really, what are you on about? You hung up on me!"

I ignored her question. "How's Doris?"

"Doctor's with her now," Mum said, "if you could call him that. He looks about sixteen."

"Probably an intern," I said. "If they even have internships anymore. He could be a first-year resident."

"Has the next class of interns arrived yet?" Hal asked. "Doris might have picked the worst possible time of the year to get sick."

"Not yet," I said. "Not until July 1. Doris has another week with the old crew."

"Well, I suppose that's a relief," Mum said. "Now, why are you here?"

"We think Doris is getting her arsenic in her Metamucil."

"Goodness gracious, I hope not," Mum said. "I've been using it too."

My stomach dropped. I sat down heavily. "Please tell me you're joking."

Mum sat down too. Her face had gone white. "So I've been getting arsenic too?" Her voice trembled. "What shall I do, kitten?"

"Fiona, do give over," Nigel said. "You don't actually *know* there's arsenic in that, do you now?"

"Of course not," Hal said. "We haven't even established that *Doris* has been taking arsenic. This is all just a figment of Toni's fertile and overheated imagination."

In my purse, my cell phone rang. I pulled it out and looked at the display. Tyrone.

"I need to take this," I said. "Excuse me just a minute."

Out in the hall, I asked Tyrone if the police lab could test for arsenic.

"Test what?" he asked. "Blood?"

"Metamucil."

"Meta-what?"

"Metamucil," I repeated and then explained what Metamucil is and what it's used for. "Doris takes it, and it occurred to me that it might be what Dick put the arsenic powder into. Dick disappeared about two weeks ago, but she's still getting sick, and now she's in the hospital."

"I'll check and call you back."

When I went back into the waiting room, Mum was sitting with her face in her hands. Nigel put an arm around her shoulders, and she turned her face into his shoulder. Nigel looked as if he wanted to say something, but at that moment, a nurse entered the room and came right over to us. "Excuse me. Whom are you here to see?"

"Doris Campbell," Mum answered. "How is she?"

The nurse frowned. "Are you related?"

"No, she's my best friend."

"I'm sorry," the nurse said, and she really did seem sincerely sorry. "I can't discuss her with anyone but a relative."

"Oh, dear," Mum murmured. "Can I at least see her?"

"In a few minutes. Her daughter is in with her now, and we can only allow one person at a time." She turned to go back into ICU.

"Don't worry," I said. "When Vicky comes out, we'll get her to sign a release."

In due course, a tall, slender woman with bangs and thick, straight brown hair to her shoulders came out into the waiting room. She had Doris's gray eyes and had changed very little from when we were in high school together. She spotted us immediately.

"Fiona! And Toni! Oh my God!" She held out her arms and hugged both of us. "I can't believe you're both here."

"Victoria darling, you haven't changed at all," my mother said.

"Hi, Vicky," I said. "Wow, it's so good to see you, although I wish it were under happier circumstances."

"Oh God, so do I," Vicky said. "I can't thank you two enough for being there for Mom. She's been having such an ordeal, and now Dick's disappeared. Doesn't anybody know where he is?"

"Not so far," I told her.

"Victoria, darling," my mother said, "the nurse said they can't tell us anything because we're not family."

"Oh, for God's sake," Vicky said. "I'll go right back in and tell them they can."

After a few minutes, the doctor came out. He looked very young and strangely familiar. "Mrs. Gray? I'm Dr. Parker, resident in the ICU today. We printed off a release form from the computer, and Mrs. Campbell's daughter has signed it." He turned to me. "That means I can discuss the case with you, Dr. Day, and you can in turn discuss it with your family. She put all of your names on the release."

It was weird to hear him refer to Doris as Mrs. Campbell, since she'd been Mrs. Maxwell to me my whole life.

"Wow, that was fast," I said.

"She gave me quite a piece of her mind," Dr. Parker said ruefully.

"So, Doctor," Mum said impatiently, "how is she?"

Dr. Parker glanced around the waiting room. A few other people had come in after us. "We probably shouldn't discuss it here. Let's use one of these family conference rooms."

I looked around. There were several doors labeled Family Conference. Dr. Parker opened the door to one of them, and we all filed in. There was a conference table with chairs around it, and we all took seats.

Dr. Parker stayed on his feet and began to pace the room. "Mrs. Campbell is about the same, I'm afraid. She still hasn't regained consciousness. We've got her on the respirator, and we're giving her some extra potassium and magnesium in her IV, because those were dangerously low, and she's also quite anemic, so we'll be giving her a couple of units of blood and possibly some iron …"

I interrupted. "Shouldn't you wait until you see if she has arsenic poisoning? You'll just be wasting the iron if you have to give her chelating agents. She'll pee it out right along with the arsenic."

The doctor frowned. "Dr. Day, what is your specialty?"

"Pathology," I said. "Anatomical and clinical."

"Really?" The frown disappeared. "Where did you train?"

"Right here in Long Beach. I did my internship and part of my residency here at St. Mary's, and the rest at the VA."

The frown was back. "But we don't have a pathology residency program here. Just internal medicine."

Taken aback, I said, "Seriously? Since when?"

He shrugged. "At least since I came here three years ago."

I was taken aback again. "You're a *third*-year resident?"

"Yes. Why? Do you think I look too young?"

"Well …"

He smiled. "It's okay. Everybody says that. When were you here?"

"Over twenty years ago," I told him. "And back then, everybody said I looked too young too."

"You did look too young," Hal said.

The young doctor laughed and stuck out a hand. "Please call me Jeff."

I shook it. "Please call me Toni. And this is my husband, Hal."

Jeff shook Hal's hand and then turned back to catch me staring at him. "Why are you looking at me like that?"

"I'm just wondering why you look so familiar."

"I don't know," he said. "I'm pretty sure we've never met before. But I look a lot like my dad. Maybe you know him."

"Parker," I mused. "There was a Tom Parker in my intern class here at St. Mary's. Last I heard, he was an anesthesiologist at John Wayne Memorial in Newport Beach."

"That's my dad!" he said excitedly. "Wow! Wait till I tell him I met you. He'll be jazzed. By the way, did you know my mother too?"

Uh-oh. Now we were treading on sensitive ground, because I knew Tom had gone through a nasty divorce a few years back, but I feigned ignorance so as not to say the wrong thing. I sensed both Hal and Mum holding their collective breaths, because they also knew the gory details.

But Jeff merely went on without visible emotion. "Because they're divorced now, and then Dad married the administrator there. She's really cool."

I let out a breath that I hadn't been aware I'd been holding. "I'm glad to hear it. So everybody's happy?"

"Yes, as far as I know."

"You are planning to test Mrs. Campbell for arsenic poisoning, aren't you?"

Dr. Parker stopped. "Why would I do that?"

"The paramedic wrote it down," I said. "Didn't you see it?"

Jeff frowned. "I guess I missed it. Why do you think she has arsenic poisoning?"

"It's a long story," I said.

"Okay." Jeff pulled up a chair and sat down. "Suppose you tell me what this is all about."

I told Jeff about Doris's sudden marriage, Dick's disappearance, Doris's symptoms, and finding the bottle of Cowley's Rat and Mouse Exterminator, which had made me suspect Dick of poisoning her.

"The thing is," I went on, "that Dick's been gone almost two weeks, and Doris has been out of that house since then, and she shouldn't be getting any more arsenic, but then she went into a coma and had a seizure. I can't think of any way she'd be getting more arsenic unless she brought something from her house that had arsenic in it, and the only thing she brought besides her pills was her Metamucil. So I just want to make sure you test her for arsenic."

Jeff leaned his elbow on the table and rested his chin in his hand. "That's quite a story. Sounds like something Agatha Christie might have written."

"And I've been using that Metamucil too," Mum said.

"So we might end up treating you too. Has the Metamucil been tested?"

"Not yet," I said. "I called the police about it, but they have to call me back." *Damn*, I thought, *what's taking so long?*

"By the way, who is Mrs. Campbell's regular doctor?" Jeff asked.

"Dr. Connors," I said. "He's Mum's doctor too."

"Well, that's handy," Jeff said. "He's right downstairs in the medical office building. I'll just give him a call from the nurses' station and let him know what's going on. Toni? Why don't you come with me?"

"Go ahead, kitten," Mum said.

I looked at my family and shrugged, then followed Jeff into ICU.

Wow, I thought, looking around. This wasn't the big open room with twenty-four beds all out in the open, separated only by flimsy curtains, that I remembered.

Now there were long rows of cubicles with doors one could actually close for privacy. The nurses' station was in the middle, surrounded by high counters one could lean on. A ward clerk barely looked up from her computer when we came in. I guessed if I was accompanied by a doctor, she knew I must be okay.

Vicky came out of a cubicle right opposite the nurses' station. "Toni? Did you want to go in and see Mom?"

"Thanks but not right now," I said. "Mum would, though. They're all in Family Conference Room 1."

"Okay," Vicky said. "I'll go tell her." She left.

"Let's go into this dictation room," Jeff said. He pulled out a chair. "Here, have a seat."

We both sat down.

Jeff dialed an extension from the phone on the wall. "Joe? Jeff Parker here. Yes, I'm the resident in the ICU. I just admitted your patient Doris Campbell." A detailed discussion of Doris's clinical condition and proposed treatment followed, after which Jeff said, "Oh, and by the way, it was your patient Fiona Gray that came in with her, along with her daughter, a Dr. Toni Day, who thinks she was poisoned with arsenic. Yes, that's what I said, arsenic." He turned and looked at me. "He wants to talk to you."

I'd known Dr. Connors for most of my life, so I wasn't really surprised. He'd followed my progress through high school, college, medical school, internship, and residency, and he knew all about my practice in Twin Falls and all the cases I'd been involved in, because Mum told him everything. I took the phone. "Hi, Dr. Connors."

His reassuring, booming voice came through the phone, instantly throwing me into a time warp. "So, Dr. Toni, what have you gotten yourself into now?"

I told him all about the Metamucil situation.

"Is she sick too?" he wanted to know.

"No, no symptoms, but she's a little panicked."

"Well, I can certainly understand that. It seems that I have a little time right now between patients, so tell her to come right down."

"Okay, I will," I told him. "Do you need to talk to Jeff some more?"

"Not right now. I'll come up and see Doris for myself shortly."

We disconnected. When I left the dictation room, I saw Vicky escorting my mother to Doris's cubicle. "I just talked to Dr. Connors," I told her, "and he can see you right now."

"Is he going to come up and see Doris?" Mum asked.

"That's what he said," I told her.

"Thank you, kitten," she said. "I'll see her when I get back." She left.

I went in and stood next to Doris's bed, marveling that this woman whom I'd known nearly all my life was now barely recognizable. I squeezed her hand. "Doris, I love you. Please get better."

I thought I felt her fingers move—or maybe it was just wishful thinking.

I looked back toward the nurses' station where Jeff was now sitting at a computer station inside the circular counter. Various nurses in dark blue scrubs came and went and pretty much ignored him. I pulled up a chair and joined him as he pulled up the hospital information system and logged into it. Then he accessed Doris's medical record.

"Now," he said, "with regard to arsenic, how should we go about this? Should I test both blood and urine? Obviously, this isn't something I have to deal with on a regular basis, so I'm a little rusty here."

"Well, if she's been getting arsenic in her Metamucil every morning, she may have some in her blood, but with chronic poisoning, it's more likely to show up in her urine. If that doesn't work, we could try hair and fingernails."

"How long will that take?" he asked.

"That depends," I said. "Does your lab have HPLC? Most hospital labs don't, so they send it out to a reference lab. Which one do you use?"

"Pacific Diagnostic Laboratories."

"Google them," I suggested.

Jeff did so on his cell phone and found out that Pacific sent all the tests for arsenic to Mayo Clinic. Googling Mayo Clinic Laboratory told us that blood and urine arsenic would take up to four days, and hair and nails would take up to seven days.

"Another thing," I advised him. "Be sure and ask for fractionation on the urine because it's the inorganic arsenic that's toxic."

"Good to know," he said. "I'll just add all this to the orders. How about we start with blood and random urine and go from there?"

"Sounds good to me," I said.

"Sounds like a bunch of crap to me," said a voice behind us.

Startled, I looked up to see a small, bespectacled man wearing a lab coat and a scowl. He wasn't much taller than me and didn't look much older than Jeff. His hair was short and black so that I nearly didn't see the yarmulke he wore.

His small dark eyes were fixed on Jeff. "Don't you think, Doctor, that you should discuss the case with your attending before going off half-cocked ordering a bunch of esoteric tests? Who is this patient anyway?"

Jeff was unfazed. "Toni, this is Dr. Seligman, the hospitalist on duty. The patient is Mrs. Doris Campbell, a sixty-six-year-old lady who was admitted after having become comatose and then having a grand mal seizure at home and is suspected of having chronic arsenic poisoning."

Jeff's equanimity seemed to infuriate Dr. Seligman further. "Suspected by whom? And who's this?"

Jeff introduced me.

"That still doesn't explain what you're doing back here," Dr. Seligman informed me.

"Mrs. Campbell is my mother's best friend," I told him. "She was at my mother's house when she had her seizure, and my husband and I witnessed it."

Dr. Seligman shrugged. "Then her coma is most likely postictal. Epileptics frequently have an altered neurological state after seizures."

"She was comatose before she had the seizure," I pointed out.

Dr. Seligman turned to Jeff. "Any significant medical history?"

"Hypertension," I said.

Dr. Seligman narrowed his eyes at me. "I was asking the resident. Please don't interfere."

"She's a doctor too," Jeff said.

"I'm a pathologist," I added.

Dr. Seligman seemed unimpressed. "Really. Where do you practice?"

"Twin Falls, Idaho."

Now Dr. Seligman seemed really unimpressed. "Whatever," he said, dismissing me. "Now, what's all this nonsense about arsenic?"

"Tell him, Toni," Jeff said.

"Her husband died in December," I said, "and she remarried in February."

Dr. Seligman interrupted. "What's that got to do with her condition?"

"Ever since she remarried, she's been unwell," I said.

"Unwell how? What were her symptoms?"

"Anorexia, diarrhea, vomiting, and confusion. Today she had a syncopal episode followed by nausea and vomiting, so she went back to bed, and when my mother tried to wake her, she couldn't. Then she had the seizure and hasn't regained consciousness."

Dr. Seligman interrupted me again. "Those symptoms are pretty nonspecific. What makes you think they're due to arsenic?"

"My husband and I found a bottle of Cowley's Rat and Mouse Exterminator in her cellar that looked as if it had been used recently."

"What makes you think it wasn't used to kill mice?"

"I'm sure it was, fifty years ago. Its active ingredient is arsenic trioxide."

Dr. Seligman turned his palms up. "So?"

"There was a box of D-Con in the cellar too. Why wouldn't they use that? Why mess with white arsenic powder?"

Dr. Seligman folded his arms. "You tell me."

This contentious little man was trying my patience. "I can only think of one reason. It's tasteless and odorless and easy to mix with food. I think it was mixed with her Metamucil."

"By who?"

"Whom," I said, taking a leaf out of Mum's book. "Her husband."

"You're seriously accusing this woman's husband of trying to poison her with arsenic? Where is her husband, anyway?"

"Good question," I said. "Nobody knows. He's disappeared, and the police haven't found him yet. It's been two weeks now. Doris has been staying with my mother since then, and she's still sick. Even sicker than she was before, so I think he put arsenic in her Metamucil, because it's the only thing she brought with her except her pills."

Jeff, who had said nothing during this whole exchange, possibly because he hoped that the hospitalist would forget he was there, held out Doris's baggie of pill bottles before he had a chance to ask about them. Maybe he thought that would catch Dr. Seligman off guard.

It worked. Dr. Seligman took the baggie and promptly dropped it. Jeff and I exchanged a smile, which, of course, was gone by the time the hospitalist straightened up with the baggie in his hand.

"Let's see what we have here," he grunted, and dumped the baggie out on the counter. "Lipitor, thyroxine, baby aspirin, multivitamin, fish oil. Aha!

Lisinopril and hydrochlorothiazide. Where's the potassium? She's on a thiazide diuretic; she should be taking potassium supplements."

"Not necessarily," Jeff said calmly. "Lisinopril is potassium-sparing."

Dr. Seligman fixed Jeff with a beady eye. "And what is her serum potassium, Doctor?"

"It's low," Jeff said, "and so are her calcium and magnesium, and they're being replaced as we speak."

"And why do you suppose that is, Doctor?"

"Because she's been vomiting and having diarrhea," Jeff said.

"Very good. Obviously, she's had a stroke. I'm cancelling these arsenic tests. Remember what you were taught, Doctor. When you hear hoofbeats, don't look for zebras. Arsenic is a zebra. Carry on."

With that, the hospitalist turned to go, but he was blocked by Dr. Connors, who stood behind him. Dr. Connors was nearly as tall as Hal, with a gray crew cut and blue eyes, and dwarfed Dr. Seligman, upon whom he bestowed an indulgent smile. "How's my patient, Sam?"

"Still comatose, as you will see. We are replacing her potassium, calcium, and magnesium, and we'll be transfusing her for her anemia, which is significant."

"What's the working diagnosis?"

"Stroke."

"What about the arsenic poisoning?"

Dr. Seligman sighed. "Do you really believe all this malarkey about arsenic, Joe? The whole thing sounds like an Agatha Christie mystery."

Dr. Connors was no longer smiling. "I've known both Mrs. Campbell and Mrs. Gray for decades. Both of them are intelligent, sensible women who are not in the habit of telling tall tales. If Mrs. Gray and her daughter—who's an excellent and highly respected pathologist, by the way—are worried about arsenic, the least you can do is test for it and rule it out. It wouldn't kill you."

"Now you sound like my mother," Dr. Seligman said, showing the first hint of a smile I'd seen since he arrived. "Okay, Doctor Day, if there's only one test you could do for arsenic in this patient, which would you pick?"

"Get a twenty-four-hour urine," I said, "and you don't want to lose any time."

"She's right," Dr. Connors said. "If she really has been poisoned, it's best to get her on chelating agents as soon as possible. She may even need dialysis."

"So, Joe, you don't agree that this is a stroke?"

"I don't know," Dr. Connors said. "She could have had a stroke too. But I'll tell you this, Sam. If she's comatose because of arsenic poisoning, she isn't going to wake up until we get her on chelating agents. I just hope it isn't already too late."

Dr. Seligman's face turned red. "You came all the way up here just to tell me that?"

"No, Sam," Dr. Connors said. "I came up here to check on my patient. It seems that Toni's mother has been using it too, so I'm getting both it and her tested. Have you got that Metamucil here, Toni?"

"No," I said. "I left it where it was. It'll be tested by the police lab."

"Let me know what you find out. Now I need to see my patient and get back to my office. Nice to see you again, Toni," and with that he disappeared into Doris's cubicle.

Dr. Seligman pulled a handkerchief out of his lab coat pocket and wiped his brow. "I'll be going too," he said. "I'll be back for evening rounds." And with that he was gone.

Jeff and I went back to the waiting room. Mum, Nigel and Hal were back out in the waiting room with Vicky. Mum was on her feet, hands on her hips, green eyes flashing. "Who was that thoroughly unpleasant little man who just came through here? He practically pushed us out of his way without so much as a how-do-you-do! Who does he think he is?"

"The hospitalist," I said.

"A bloody arsehole," Nigel commented. "I don't care what else he may be."

"Maybe it's just as well that Doris wasn't awake to hear him," I remarked. "Does he always treat you like that, Jeff?"

Jeff smiled. "He treats all of us like that. He's the type of guy that believes in treating house staff the same way he was treated. He hasn't caught on to the kinder, gentler type of residency program we have now."

"Oh, right," I said. "No more thirty-six-hour shifts."

"Did you have to do that, Toni?"

"As a medical student and intern, yes, I did," I told him, "but not in residency, thank God. We took night and weekend call, though. We still do."

"What the devil is a hospitalist?" Nigel asked.

"They're internists who take care of inpatients," Jeff said. "Dr. Seligman is on duty right now just for the ICU. He goes off duty at six, and another one comes on at six and stays until six in the morning. It's a good system, really. They stay in contact with the primary care physician, and the primary physician can see patients in his office without forever being called out for emergencies or having to make rounds, although they're welcome to do that if they want to."

"He's right, Mum," I told her. "We have hospitalists too, in Twin Falls. It works well, as far as I know."

"Antoinette darling," Mum said, "I'm fair knackered. Can we go home now?"

"Of course," I said. "Do you have to go to the lab and get your blood drawn, or give a urine sample?"

"I already did that," Mum said and pulled up her sleeve to show the purple Coban wrapped around the crook of her elbow.

Hal looked at his watch. "Jesus, look at the time. No wonder I'm starving."

I looked at mine too and was startled to see that it was after five o'clock. "I'm not surprised. Do you realize we haven't eaten since this morning?"

"Doris's coffee cake," Mum said sadly. "At the time, I had no idea …"

"None of us did, lovey," Nigel said. "I suggest we get something to eat. I'm sure you don't feel like cooking tonight. How's the cafeteria here?"

"It was okay back in the day," I said. "I don't know about now."

"No," Hal said firmly. "No cafeteria. I want to go to Hof's Hut. I'm craving a chili size."

Nigel looked bewildered. "What the devil is a chili size?"

"It's kind of like a chili dog," I said, "but it's a chili hamburger. They serve it open-faced with cheese and onions on top."

"I want extra onions," said Hal.

"And extra cheese," I said. Suddenly I was starving. I hadn't even thought of a chili size in years. Back when Hal and I lived in Long Beach, we'd gone to Hof's Hut frequently, usually after a movie or football game.

Or after visiting a friend in the hospital.

So we did that, and afterward, we went home and fell asleep watching TV. I woke up around two in the morning, saw where I was, looked around affectionately at my slumbering family, turned off the lights and TV, and tiptoed out to the apartment, where I fell into bed. I knew nothing until the next morning, when Hal woke me at nine thirty.

"The cops are back, and they want to talk to you."

CHAPTER 6

Better to hunt in fields for health unbought
Than fee the doctor for a nauseous draught.

—John Dryden

I reluctantly hauled myself out of bed, climbed into the same capris and T-shirt I'd worn the day before, performed my morning ablutions, and went back to the main house with Hal.

Mum was in the kitchen, pouring coffee, while the teakettle whistled on the stovetop. "Kitten, would you mind getting that?"

Hal went on into the living room, while I took the kettle off the stove and prepared tea for Mum, Nigel, and myself.

When I was finished, I went into the living room with three mugs of tea. I handed Nigel his and put Mum's on the end table next to the pink armchair. Both detectives sat on the couch. Mark Kincaid greeted me by saying, "Good morning, Doctor. Sorry to interrupt your beauty sleep."

I debated for a nanosecond whether to take umbrage at that sexist remark or blow it off. I decided not to make an issue. "Have you come to get that Metamucil?"

I looked straight at Tyrone as I said that, and he had the grace to look embarrassed. "Oh, jeez, sorry, Toni. I got sidetracked and never got around to calling you back."

Mark looked confused. "What Metamucil? What are you talking about?"

Tyrone explained. "Toni wanted to know if our lab could test the Metamucil for arsenic."

"It could," Mark said testily, "but why should it?"

"Because I think Dick put arsenic in Doris's Metamucil, and that's why she's still sick after almost two weeks," I told him. "I did touch it, I'm sorry to say, so my fingerprints are on it, but you can eliminate them. Want me to get you a grocery bag or something to put it in?"

"No," Mark said. "We don't handle evidence. We'll send a CSI over to do that."

Nigel cleared his throat. "I say, shall we get on with it? What was so important that you had to get us all out of bed?"

"We sent a couple of CSIs over to the MacTavish house yesterday," Tyrone said. "They took pictures, collected blood from the dumbwaiter, dusted for fingerprints, and collected material from Dick Campbell's personal items for DNA. They searched the house from top to bottom, including the cellar. One of the items they photographed was the portrait of the Campbells that was in the master bedroom."

"We looked for Dick Campbell in the system," Mark said. "He wasn't there. So, to make sure, we did facial recognition and got a match."

Mark picked up a manila envelope from the coffee table, removed a photograph from it, and handed it to Nigel. "Would you mind passing this around, please, and tell me if you know this person."

Nigel looked and handed it to Mum, who exclaimed, "Why, it's Dick, of course! Only ..."

"Exactly," Nigel said. "It's Dick, and yet, it isn't, not really."

Hal held out a hand. "Let me see."

Mum hesitated. "Neither you nor Antoinette have ever met Dick," she objected.

"But I saw the photograph of him and Doris that was in their bedroom," I pointed out. "Do you have that photograph with you, Lieutenant?"

"Right here," Mark said. He pulled it out of the manila envelope and handed it to me.

I held it up next to the photograph in Hal's hand. "It's a younger Dick," I said. "His hair is darker, and he has a lot more of it."

"He has a moustache too," Hal said. "I thought you said he wasn't in the system."

"He isn't," Tyrone said. "Not under the name Richard Campbell. This is Quentin St. George, and he was arrested five years ago on suspicion of having murdered his wife."

"With arsenic?" I asked.

Mark threw up his hands and flopped back on the couch. "What, you got some kind of fixation about arsenic or something?"

I folded my arms defiantly. "Okay, Detective Smarty-Pants, then *you* tell *me* how she died."

"Antoinette," my mother interjected, "don't be rude."

"Sorry," I said. "Please, tell me how she died."

"Nobody knows," Tyrone said. "She died at home, presumably of natural causes, but before she could be buried, her son accused Mr. St. George of murdering his mother for her money. He pressed charges, so we had to arrest him and send the body to the coroner."

"So what did the autopsy show?" I persisted.

Tyrone handed me the report. "I figure it'd be better for you to read that than for me to try to read it to you."

I thought so too, so I took the report and sat down on the arm of Mum's chair to skim through it. After a few minutes, I looked up. "Drug screen was negative."

"Right," Mark said. "That's why we couldn't hold him. We couldn't prove that she died of anything other than natural causes."

"But they didn't test for arsenic," I pursued. "They just tested for drugs of abuse. There's no testing for heavy metals of any flavor."

"Well, we certainly aren't going to exhume the body just because you've got a thing about arsenic," Mark said. "We need more proof than that."

"But that's a catch-22," I argued. "If you don't exhume the body, you can't get proof."

"Then I guess we're at an impasse," Mark said with an air of finality.

"You realize," Tyrone said gently, "that it hasn't been proved that Mrs. Campbell was poisoned with arsenic either."

"But it will be," I said stubbornly.

"That reminds me," Mum said. "We need to have our breakfasts and go see Doris. Perhaps there will be news."

"And that reminds *me*," I said. "Did the late Mrs. St. George have a lot of insurance?"

"That was the reason her son pressed charges," Tyrone said. "She was a widow, and her late husband had insured her for a million dollars."

"Aha!" I exclaimed. "Maybe he killed Dick for revenge. What was his name?"

"Derek Buchanan," replied Mark, "but look here, we don't even know yet that it was Dick who was killed."

"That could just be a coincidence," Hal cautioned me. "No point going off all half-cocked. Come on—let's go get dressed."

I assented, and we did that, but I couldn't help thinking of Commander Phil Harris, back in Twin Falls, who told me years ago that there are no coincidences when it comes to murder.

There had been no change when we all arrived at St. Mary's.

Doris was still comatose, still on the vent, and the twenty-four-hour urine for arsenic was still being collected and wouldn't be complete until afternoon, so it might not even get sent to the reference lab until the next day.

Jeff Parker went over her chart with me at the nurses' station while Mum sat with Doris in her cubicle. We kept our voices down so as not to be overheard by either Mum or Doris, should she actually be able to hear anything.

Doris had received two units of packed cells during the night, so her hemoglobin, while still low, was much better than before. Her renal function tests, however, were getting worse.

"Her kidney function's deteriorating," Jeff told me. "If we need to put her on chelating agents for arsenic, she'll need to be on hemodialysis."

"By the looks of this," I pointed out, "she may need hemodialysis anyway."

"True," Jeff conceded. "By the way, do you know if she's allergic to peanuts?"

"Peanuts?" I asked in amazement. "Why?"

"Because if we need to chelate her, we'll want to use dimercaprol, which is British antilewisite in peanut oil."

"I don't know," I said. "Let me ask Mum." I tiptoed over to the door to Doris's cubicle and did so.

"Not to my knowledge," Mum replied. "I've seen her eat them before without any ill effects."

I passed that on to Jeff. "That's good," he said, "because dimercaprol is injectable, but the other choice, succimer, is only available as pills. We'd have to crush them and give them via nasogastric tube."

"Are you planning to start her on dimercaprol before you know the results of the lab tests?" I asked.

"I'd rather not," Jeff said, "but as you can see, we're still collecting the twenty-four-hour urine, so it's still going to be two or three days after we get that sent off before we know anything, and if she keeps deteriorating like this ..."

"Will Dr. Seligman go along with that?"

"Not him," Jeff said. "No way. But Dr. Connors wrote the order and left it up to me when to start it."

"Dr. Connors sent Mum's blood off to be tested yesterday," I said. "Perhaps he'll get results before you do."

"Maybe," Jeff said. "So now it's just a waiting game."

I passed that along when I rejoined my family in the waiting room.

"Well, we don't need to wait here," Hal said. "I promised my folks that we'd stop by this afternoon."

"You did?" My heart sank. Visiting Hal's parents was the last thing I wanted to do; although I knew perfectly well that if we were in Long Beach, we'd have to do that sometime. Hal's father, Max, always treated me well, but his mother, Ida, didn't like me. The veneer of politeness that she affected whenever she had to interact with me was transparently thin and did nothing to hide her true feelings about her non-Jewish daughter-in-law.

"Yes, sweetie, I did," Hal said. "Already she's highly offended that we didn't visit yesterday."

"How the hell could we do that?" I asked. "Didn't you tell her what yesterday was *like*?"

"Mom doesn't care," Hal said. "It's all about her. You know that."

I did, to my sorrow. "I don't suppose you'd consider going without me, would you?"

"Seriously? Can you imagine how offended she'd be about that?"

"*She's* offended? How about me? She refers to me as 'that shiksa you married' whenever she thinks I can't hear her, and I shouldn't be offended?"

Hal raised his eyebrows. "Jesus, sweetie, you sound just like her. Are you sure you're not a closet Jew?"

I had to laugh. "Do you think that would help?"

Hal sighed. "Probably not. Okay, you don't have to go if you don't want to. What are you going to do instead?"

"Go shopping."

"Toni, you hate shopping. What are you really going to do?"

"No, really, Mum wants to take me shopping for my birthday," I said, glancing into the back seat where my mother sat directly behind Hal. "Right, Mum?"

She cooperated beautifully. "Yes, dear," she said with admirable restraint, considering I'd just made that up on the spur of the moment. "Anything you want, kitten."

Hal shot me a skeptical sideways glance. "Hmph. And this shopping expedition has to take place this afternoon why?"

"Because it's convenient, Hal dear," my mother said smoothly.

"Yes," I chimed in. "Besides, Bullock's is having a big sale, and it's just for today. Tomorrow would be too late."

Hal apparently knew when he was beaten, because he just sighed and lapsed into silence for the remainder of the drive home.

After he'd departed in the Mercedes for his parents' home, Mum fixed me with a stern eye. "Now, kitten, what is this all about? You do hate shopping. I know that, so what are you really going to do?"

"I want to go back to Doris's house and snoop," I said.

"But, my dear, you can't," Mum said. "Haven't the police declared it a crime scene? Someone was killed there. You'll get in trouble."

"I want to see what's in his desk," I said. "I want to see what's on his computer. We already know he isn't who he said he was. Don't worry. The police will never know I was there. I'll wear gloves, so I won't leave any fingerprints."

"Well, then, since you've made up your mind, do you need help? I could go with you, or Nigel could."

I shook my head. "No, I'll be fine. This won't take long."

I really believed that when I said it, but I had no idea what I was getting myself into.

I saw no evidence of police presence as I slowly drove Mum's Chevy up the winding drive and around the house to park behind it, out of sight of anyone who might come up the drive after me.

Actually, it might have been better to hide the car inside the barn, but I couldn't move that huge sliding door by myself. *Drat!* I thought. *I should have brought Mum with me after all. Or Nigel. Or even Hal.* There was no reason to be in such a rush to explore the MacTavish house. I just didn't want to go to Hal's parents' house.

Oh, well. I was there now, armed with a flashlight, a hammer and a screwdriver, cell phone, and keys to the house in my pocket. I'd seen yellow crime scene tape across the front door, but there wasn't any across the back door. I pulled on a pair of latex painting gloves I'd found in Mum's garage, let myself into the kitchen, and closed the door noiselessly behind me. I tiptoed across the vast kitchen to the rolltop desk, pulled out the chair, and sat down.

The rolltop was open, just as Doris had left it when she looked for the cards the first pair of detectives had left with her, so I didn't have to wrestle with that, but the first drawer I opened emitted a screech like a cat with its tail stepped on. Startled, I stopped and held my breath, listening for any sound from elsewhere in the house while my heart rate slowly returned to normal.

Idiot, I thought, *you're the only person in the house. There's no reason why anybody else would be here, so quit dithering and get on with it.*

Systematically, I went through all the drawers. I found Dick's checkbook, a box of cancelled checks, pens and pencils, envelopes and stamps, a stapler and a staple puller, Scotch tape, scissors, and all the usual paraphernalia and detritus one would normally find in someone's desk.

Then I noticed that one of the smaller drawers had a false bottom. When it was closed it looked like two drawers, but when pulled out, the other drawer came with it, and it was only as deep as a single drawer.

I turned it over and pushed and prodded at the bottom until it slid open. Inside were four passports, all under different names, only one of which was Richard Campbell. But the photo on each of them was of Dick, each at an earlier age than the one before it. The earliest one had expired in 1984. There were also three driver's licenses corresponding to the three other passports. I imagined that Dick's driver's license was probably in his wallet and that he hadn't left the country because he'd left his passport behind.

The next most recent was Quentin St. George.

Now what?

If I took them away with me, I'd be messing up the trail of evidence; but if I left them there, somebody might take them before the police had a chance to see them. So I laid the all the driver's licenses out on the desk and photographed each one with my cell phone. Then I opened up all the passports and did the same, after which I put them back in the secret compartment and slid the drawer back in where it belonged, then sat back and heaved a sigh of relief.

Then I remembered what had happened on the Caribbean cruise we took the year before to celebrate Mum's retirement, when both my cell phone and my laptop had been stolen, so I sent each of the pictures to my email address, which I could access on my laptop, which was safely stashed in the apartment at Mum and Nigel's.

Then I pulled out the file drawer, thinking I might find insurance policies that might prove Doris had made Dick her beneficiary, but no dice. The drawer was empty.

Jane Bennett Munro

Perhaps the CSIs had taken them; but why would they have left the passports and drivers' licenses? Because of the drawer with the false bottom? I didn't think so. If I could figure that out, so could they.

I was pretty sure Doris didn't know about them, because if she had, she wouldn't have kept them secret. She would have given them to her lawyer and divorced Dick.

But it was possible that she'd taken the contents of the file drawer. Maybe they were in her room at home. I made a mental note to look when I got home.

If they'd neglected to look in Dick's desk, they might have left his computer too. I headed for the library where Dick's computer and printer stood in lonely splendor on the exquisitely carved conference table. But as I circled the table, my foot caught in something, and I went sprawling.

What the hell, I thought as I picked myself up and retrieved my flashlight, hammer, and screwdriver, which had gone in three different directions. Luckily my cell phone was safely zipped into my jacket pocket. I turned on the flashlight and found that my foot had caught on a length of fishing line, which was invisible in the gloom of the library. One end of it was tied to the leg of the chair opposite Dick's computer. The other end was another matter. I traced it across the room to an armchair in the corner. The line passed under the armchair and ran along the far wall to the fireplace. From there, it ran up the wall and disappeared into the gloom at the top where I lost sight of it.

What was up there?

When I'd been upstairs the day before, we'd been in Dick and Doris's master bedroom, which faced Del Mar Park. The room directly above the library would have to be the room on the other side of the hall. I hadn't had a chance to check it the day before, but surely the CSIs had.

Now was my chance to check out the upper floors, especially the fourth floor. All I'd had time to see the day before was the master bedroom on the second floor. I wanted to see if all the floors were open to the foyer so that I could look down into the foyer from them. I went all the way up to the third floor where the stairs ended.

There had to be another staircase leading to the fourth floor. Doris had referred to a fourth-floor tower, so maybe the stairs to it would be at the other end of the hall. Sure enough, that's where I found it, an extremely claustrophobic, dark, and steep spiral staircase in a space no bigger than a closet. I could see light at the top because it was daylight, but at night, that staircase would be in total darkness. One would have to feel one's way, and coming back down would be even scarier than climbing up. The stairs were slippery too, almost as if someone had waxed them, and there was no rail to hold onto.

I came out in a space that was divided in half by a waist-high carved railing, over which I could lean and look down into the foyer fifty feet below, a dizzying height.

Pushing someone over that rail would surely result in death.

Now why in hell did I have to think of that just now? And why was the hair rising on the back of my neck and my arms suddenly covered in goose bumps?

Suddenly I was absolutely sure that someone was behind me. I turned, but nobody was there. Feeling stupid, I rubbed my arms to get rid of the goose bumps and stepped away from the railing. All I wanted to do now was go back down those stairs and get closer to the ground as quickly as possible.

What the hell, I thought. I'd never been scared of heights before. *What's going on here?* Was this a premonition or something?

I tried to dismiss the thought, but the feeling of unease remained in the back of my brain. It was with grave misgivings that I stopped on the second-floor landing instead of going all the way down to the ground level.

The master bedroom was the first room on the right, which would put it directly over the kitchen. That fireplace would be right above the one in the kitchen. There was a switch in the wall next to it. I flipped it on, and the gas log burst into flame just like the ones in the fireplaces on the ground level. I turned it off and went back out in the hall.

The door to the room opposite was locked.

Now what?

Well, I did have a hammer and a screwdriver. I could just pry the door open. It would do a lot of damage, though.

Then I remembered the key ring in the junk drawer in the kitchen. Maybe one of those keys would unlock this door.

So I ran back downstairs and retrieved the keys. There were an awful lot of them. It would take some time to try all of them. *Oh, well*, I thought, *nothing ventured, nothing gained.*

As it happened, the third key I tried unlocked the door. It opened with a dreadful creaking. I wished I'd thought to bring some WD-40 with me. Of course, everything in the house creaked; it was nearly a hundred years old.

This must have been Dick's great-uncle's bedroom. Heavy draperies closed out all the daylight. I felt around for a light switch and didn't find one. I switched on the flashlight and looked around. There were gas jets on the walls, but not a single electric light did I find. Even the bedside lamp was an oil lamp. There was no oil in it.

I crossed the room and opened the draperies to let in some light, and in so doing, I let loose a cloud of dust that set off a sneezing spell I thought would never end. I was making so much noise that if anyone had entered the house, I never would have heard it.

Eventually, the sneezing stopped, and I blew my nose and prepared to get on with it. Everything in this room was covered in decades of dust. I couldn't really tell what color anything was; it all looked brown. A tall portrait in a massive gilt frame of a dark-haired lady in nineteenth-century clothing looked down from above the fireplace on the wall opposite the bed. Dick's great-aunt? I hadn't heard anybody mention that Dick's great-uncle was married. Perhaps she died young. I wondered if there had been any children. Dying during childbirth was a likely cause of dying young in those days.

The corner by the fireplace was dark, but with the flashlight, I could see an area where there was no dust on the floor. That in itself was a clue. Hadn't the CSIs seen this? I got down on my knees and felt around the baseboard. To my surprise, it came loose to reveal a small space in the wall, which contained a reel of fishing line and a small battery-operated tape recorder.

Well, well. What have we here?

Experimentally, I pressed Play. Instead of music, I heard a cacophony of creaks, groans, footsteps, screams, and maniacal laughter.

Someone had a perverted sense of humor, and I was pretty sure it wasn't Doris. I picked up the fishing reel and discovered that the line ran down through a crack in the floor.

Hmm. How did Dick do that?

Experimentally, I tried to pull the rug back to see. To my surprise, it came up easily to reveal a ring embedded in the floor.

A trapdoor, by golly. I scrambled to my feet, stepped to the side, and pulled up on the ring. The trapdoor creaked open to reveal a shelf about four inches below it. I reached down to feel around the edges of the shelf in case there were any more hidden treasures and found an opening. I curled my fingers around the edge and found that the shelf slid back to reveal a pretty good view of the library below.

Wow, I thought, *wait till Nigel sees this*. This was the explanation for the weird noises and moving furniture that Doris attributed to the house being haunted.

I put the shelf back the way I found it, closed the trapdoor, replaced the baseboard and the carpet, and picked up my tools. As I straightened up, I noticed a switch in the wall next to the fireplace.

That's odd, I thought. Surely the logs in this fireplace were real. There was no such thing as gas logs in the 1920s. But my curiosity got the better of me, and I flipped the switch.

Nothing happened. So what was the switch for?

I turned it off again, and as I did so, the wall moved. Fireplace and all.

What the hell, I thought. How was that possible? Fireplaces were supposed to be attached to chimneys. Clearly this was a fake fireplace. I peered into the gap and saw only darkness. My flashlight showed only a bare floor. With footprints in the dust.

What was a secret room doing behind the fireplace? What would it be used for? Since it had been built at the beginning of Prohibition, it might have been used to hide hooch.

On the other hand, Dougal MacTavish had built it to be a replica of a Scottish castle. I didn't know Scottish history well enough to figure out what this room would be used for, or when.

Someone had been in there recently. Probably Dick, working out another trick to play on Doris.

The man really had been a right bugger, as my mother would have said.

But why have a secret door if there was nothing behind it? That made no sense. I had to see what was in that room. But I was reluctant to actually go inside. After all, in the mystery TV shows I'd seen and mystery novels I'd read in which there was a secret door, the heroine always got trapped inside.

But then I reasoned that since I was armed with tools, I'd be able to escape. I even thought of sticking the screwdriver in the opening, but the door instantly shut behind me, before I could even move, plunging me into total darkness.

CHAPTER 7

And so from hour to hour we ripe and ripe,
And then from hour to hour we rot and rot;
And thereby hangs a tale.

—Shakespeare, *As You Like It*

I should have known better, with all the mysteries I'd read and watched on TV. The heroine finds the secret pressure point behind the bookcase, and the whole thing swings out to reveal a secret passageway, but she never thinks to stick something in the opening so that she can get out when she wants to, because these things never ever open from the inside.

I would sit complacently in my recliner, shaking my head and saying, "Stupid! Stupid!" while Hal looked over from his own recliner and told me to take it easy. "Let's just wait and see what *you* do the next time you find a secret passage," he'd say, and since I had no reason to believe I'd ever be in that position, I'd just shrug and let it go.

And now, here I was, in the exact same situation. It's not that I didn't think to stick something in the door. I was just about to do that when the door closed on me so fast that I didn't have a chance. That in itself was worrisome, because on TV, secret doors always close slowly and silently, and this door closed so suddenly that somebody had to have pushed it. Slammed it, actually.

Who?

Was there somebody else in the house? Or was it just the wind?

I didn't recall it being particularly windy that day. Plus, all the doors and windows were closed, so it wouldn't matter whether it was windy or not.

Well, at least I was armed. If anyone had it in mind to harm me, I knew I could inflict some serious damage with the tools at hand. If all else failed, I could call 911 on my cell phone, which was in my pocket, assuming I still had service in there.

I stood still and listened for voices. I didn't hear any. So I turned around to see if there was any light coming from the other end, and as I did so, my foot slipped off the edge of the landing into thin air. I lost my balance and plunged down a flight of stairs, coming to rest up against something soft. In the process, I'd let go of my tools, which had come to rest on the steps above me.

I moved all my limbs experimentally and concluded that I hadn't broken anything, although I'd probably have a dandy set of bruises. Groaning, I pushed myself off the object that had broken my fall and crawled back up the stairs to retrieve my hammer and screwdriver and, most importantly, my flashlight. I sat down on the step and turned it on. I saw a short flight of stairs and a landing, from which another flight of stairs branched off to the right. The object on the landing looked like a pile of quilts.

My cell phone was still in my pocket and miraculously unbroken. I checked the screen and saw to my delight that I had full service and a fully charged battery, which would come in handy if I couldn't get out on my own.

So the secret room was a secret staircase. Where did it lead? It wouldn't make sense to have a secret staircase if it didn't lead to a secret room.

I got up, brushed myself off, and made my way back down the stairs. I lifted a corner of a quilt and peered underneath. As I did so, the all-too-familiar odor of decomposing flesh assailed my nostrils.

There was, indeed, someone else in the house with me.

And he was dead as the proverbial doornail.

Could this possibly be Dick?

There was only one way to find out.

Thank heaven I was wearing gloves. I pulled the quilt aside, trying not to breathe too deeply, to get a closer look at the face with my flashlight. Naturally, the head was turned into the quilts beneath it, which obliged me to turn it toward me in order to see the face. Then I wished I hadn't.

There wasn't much of a face left. The head had been smashed flat and was covered in dried blood.

Clearly, this was the person who'd been killed by the dumbwaiter. But his own mother wouldn't recognize him by what was left of his face.

A maggot crawled out of his nose. With revulsion, I threw the quilt back over his head. Then it occurred to me that his wallet might still be in his pocket, so I pulled the quilt back again, willing myself not to look at his face again, to access his back pants pockets. Sure enough, there was a wallet, and his driver's license was in it.

It was Dick, all right.

Or at least someone with Dick's wallet in his back pocket. Never assume.

Now what?

My first priority was to get out of there and call the police. It seemed logical that this staircase had to lead somewhere. So I picked up all my tools and gingerly picked my way down until I came to a dead end.

I put the flashlight down and felt around the wall in front of me. Maybe there was a secret entrance at this end too, but my efforts were in vain. So I picked up my hammer with the thought of pounding on the wall until it crumbled enough that I could escape, but an unwelcome thought stopped me.

That secret door on the second floor had closed so quickly that someone else had to have been in the house and slammed it behind me. I hadn't heard anyone come in, but I did have that sneezing fit, and if anyone had come into the house while that was going on, I wouldn't have heard them.

Was that person still there?

Anybody who had trapped me in this space with the intention of leaving me here to die wouldn't exactly have my best interests at heart if I managed to pound my way through this wall.

Maybe I was safer in here than out there.

Maybe when the police got here, I could ask them to pound on this wall while I prowled around downstairs to listen for where the sound was coming from.

But for now, I was stuck here, and since I'd disturbed Dick's quilts, the smell of decomposing flesh was getting pretty strong.

What to do, what to do ...

Then it occurred to me that with service on my smartphone as well as a fully charged battery, I didn't need to get out of here to call the police. I could call them from right here. So I dialed 911 and reported that I was trapped in a secret passageway in the MacTavish House on Country Club Drive.

The dispatcher informed me that there was a pretty stiff fine for prank calls to 911.

I assured her that this was no prank, and besides, there was a dead body in here with me.

She reiterated her previous statement and hung up on me.

Now what? Should I call back and hope for a different dispatcher?

Mental head slap. Idiot, I told myself. *You should call Mark or Tyrone.* So I did that. I called both of them. Neither of them was available. I left messages.

I had to admit that what I told the dispatcher and the messages I left sounded like something right out of a Nancy Drew mystery. I'd loved those as a child and had collected all of them. They were still right there in a bookcase in Mum and Nigel's house. I ought to pack those up and ship them home so that my granddaughters could enjoy them when they got old enough.

My phone rang, startling me. Had the dispatcher had a change of heart? Or was it Mark or Tyrone calling me back?

"Hello?"

Hal said, "Where the devil are you? Because Fiona's here, and you're not. I thought you two were going shopping."

I told him where I was.

He sighed. "Please don't mess with me, Toni; I've just had the afternoon from hell with my parents."

"I'm not messing with you. I'm really trapped, and what's more, I found Dick."

"He's in there with you?"

"His body is, and it really stinks."

"Are you sure it's Dick?"

"He had his driver's license in his wallet, so either he's Dick or someone else is carrying his wallet."

"You mean you couldn't recognize him?"

"I don't see how anybody could," I said. "Apparently he's the victim of the dumbwaiter."

"Oy gevalt!"

In the background, I heard my mother's voice saying, "What's wrong, Hal dear?"

"Don't tell her I'm trapped!" I said in alarm.

"Toni's found Dick's body," I heard Hal say, "in a secret staircase."

"What secret staircase?" Mum asked.

"I don't know," Hal said. "It's a secret."

I giggled in spite of myself, but apparently Mum didn't find that amusing. "That's quite enough, Hal dear," she said. "Let me talk to her. Kitten," she continued, her voice much louder now that she was speaking into the phone, "call the police and get out of there straightaway."

Jane Bennett Munro

Oh, if it were only that easy. "I called 911, Mum. They accused me of making a prank call and hung up on me."

"Oh, surely not, kitten."

I heard Hal in the background asking, "What'd she say?"

Mum told him.

"They can't do that!" Hal said. "Let me talk to her. Toni," he continued, "what exactly did you say to them?"

"I told them I was trapped in a secret staircase in the MacTavish House with a dead body."

"Hmm. That does sound a bit far-fetched. It sounds like something out of a Hardy Boys book. Okay then. I'll call Homicide and talk to Kincaid and your buddy Tyrone."

"I already did that," I told him. "I had to leave messages."

"Shit," Hal said. "Why don't those guys ever answer their phones? I'm coming over there. You sit tight."

"Okay," I said, although I don't know what he thought I might do instead. "By the way, I found a bunch of passports and driver's licenses with Dick's picture and different names in the desk in the kitchen."

We disconnected, and I sat on the lowest step staring at the display on my smartphone with all the apps, including the camera app, sitting there big as life, just begging me to use it. So I did.

I climbed back up to the landing and threw the quilt back to expose Dick, holding my breath against the smell. I photographed the body and the head from different angles with the flash. I even photographed his driver's license. Then I pulled the quilt back over him, hoping it would alleviate the smell, after which I picked up all my tools and went back to the top landing.

I sent all the pictures to my email address and then sat there on the top step and gave in to boredom.

I considered passing the time by playing solitaire on my phone, but that would use up the battery. While I sat there rationalizing that just a couple of games wouldn't hurt, my phone rang.

Hal said, "I'm here. Nigel's with me. Hey, who drives a neon-green Volkswagen?"

"I don't know. Who?"

"There was a neon-green Volkswagen coming out of the lane leading up to the gate. I didn't recognize the driver."

I hadn't seen any other cars besides Mum's on the grounds, and I'd had a panoramic view from the fourth-floor tower.

"Did you get a license number?"

"No. I suppose I should have, but I was too busy dodging. She obviously wasn't watching where she was going, and she was going way too fast for that road."

"It was definitely a she?"

"I think so. Where are you?"

I gave him directions. "There's a switch just to the left of the fireplace. Flip it on and flip it off. That's what I did, and the door opened. I'm on the top landing just inside it."

"Okay." He hung up. Soon I heard a door slam and Hal's voice. "Toni? Can you hear me?"

"Yes! Can you hear me?"

"Yes. I'm flipping the switch."

Nothing happened. Hal said, "This switch doesn't seem to do anything." I said, "Flip it off."

Suddenly the wall shifted and nearly knocked me off the landing. Hal began to step through the opening, but I stopped him. "You need to find something to prop it open, or else we'll both be trapped in here."

"Already thought of that," he said. "Nigel? Hand me that piece of four-by-four, would you?"

"Right here," Nigel said and handed Hal a three-foot-long section of lumber. Hal wedged it between the door and the rest of the wall. "There! That should do it. Come here, sweetie. Are you okay?"

He wrapped his arms around me, and I buried my face in his shirtfront. "I'm fine," I mumbled. But no sooner had I said that than Hal let go of me, held me away from him, and sniffed. "You don't smell fine. Is that …"

Nigel stuck his head into the opening and recoiled. "Blimey! Is that Dick?"

"It certainly is," I said.

The doorbell rang. "That must be the police," Hal said. "I'll get it."

After he'd gone, Nigel said, "Toni, old thing, you're a sight for sore eyes, but if you smell like that body, I'm not going to hug you. How could you stand to be cooped up in there with that?"

I stripped off my gloves and looked around for a place to dispose of them. I didn't see one, so I held on to them. "I didn't exactly have a choice," I told him. "I think I've actually gone somewhat nose-blind to it. Did Hal tell you he was killed by the dumbwaiter?"

"He mentioned it on the way over," Nigel said. "Neither of us wanted to talk about it in front of your mother. I gather you don't want her to know you were trapped either. Is that right?"

"You can tell her now that I'm out," I said. "I didn't want her to worry. She'll be mad at me, but it's better than having her frantic with worry."

I heard voices from below, which reminded me of the opening in the ceiling. "Nigel, you need to see this," I said and showed him.

He got down on his knees and peered through the opening. He slid the shelf aside to widen the opening. Through it we could clearly hear Hal and the detectives conversing.

"You do realize," Mark Kincaid was saying, "that disturbing a crime scene is a crime in itself."

Uh-oh. Was I about to be rescued only to end up in jail?

CHAPTER 8

Tell that to the marines; the sailors won't believe it.

—Sir Walter Scott

Nigel and I looked at each other. He held a finger to his lips; *be quiet!* The conversation continued. "We didn't disturb anything," Hal was saying. "We didn't go near the dumbwaiter."

"Hey, boss, quit being such a hardnose," Tyrone said. "She found us a body, didn't she?"

"And probably disturbed the hell out of it," Mark grumbled.

At this point, a door slammed, and I couldn't hear them anymore.

"Toni, old girl," Nigel said, "what we have here is a laird's lug."

"What's that?"

"It's the way the master of the castle would be able to listen in on conversations and see what his guests were doing and saying when they thought they weren't being observed."

"Huh," I said. "How about that? Check this out." I pressed Play on the cassette recorder and watched Nigel's face as he listened to the cacophony of spooky noises that ensued.

At this point, Hal and the detectives entered the room. The look on their faces was priceless.

Hal said, "What the hell …"

"Blimey," Nigel said. "No wonder Doris thought this house was haunted."

"This house isn't haunted," Mark informed us, "but it doesn't belong to Dick. Dick probably rents it."

"You mean Dick didn't inherit it from his great-uncle?" I asked.

"No," Mark said. "Where did you ever get that idea?"

"That's what Doris told my mother," I said.

"Probably because Dick told her that," Hal said.

"How come you didn't tell us that this morning?" I asked Mark.

"I had to check the records and make sure," he said.

"Well, if Dick doesn't own the house, who did all the construction work?"

"Dick didn't hire the work crew," Mark said. "This house belongs to Bradley McNabb. All the repairs were done by his construction company."

The hair rose on the back of my neck. McNabb had been one of the names on the passports and drivers' licenses.

"I'll bet Doris had no idea," Hal said.

"So where's this body?" Mark demanded.

"Down there." I pointed to the open door to the stairwell.

"You better let me do that, boss," Tyrone said. "You stay up here."

Apparently, Mark was just as squeamish as his brother Bernie. His face had already taken on a slightly greenish tint just from what we could smell in the room now that the stairwell was open.

"Any lights in there?" Tyrone inquired.

"No," I told him.

"What's at the bottom of the stairs?"

"A dead end," I said. "The body is on the landing."

"Did you disturb it in any way?"

"Well, yes, I had to see who it was," I said defensively. "I took some pictures too."

At this, I expected a scolding from Mark, but he seemed to have disappeared. Tyrone picked up a nine-volt lantern and disappeared into the stairwell.

I called after him and asked him to pound on the wall at the bottom, so I could figure out where it came out.

"I'm not stayin' in here any longer than I have to," he called back.

"Shit," I said.

"Now then," Nigel said, "what about the fishing reel?"

"That's the poltergeist," I said. "Watch this." I picked up the reel and began to reel in the fishing line. Hal and Nigel watched in amazement as the chair to which it was attached began to move.

"How did you ever even think to look up here?" Hal asked in amazement.

"I was down in the library," I said. "I went around the table to get at Dick's computer, and I tripped on the fishing line. So naturally I had to follow it and find out where it was coming from."

"Naturally," Hal said dryly.

"The CSIs left the computer here?" Nigel asked in disbelief.

Nobody answered him.

"Dick could tie this fishing line to anything in the room, and nobody'd ever see it," I continued.

"Unless they tripped over it," Nigel said.

"Apparently nobody ever did," I said. "I imagine Doris never went over there. She'd be reading on the couch, and Dick would be on his computer. He'd know better than to get tripped up on his own fishing line. Then he'd leave the room, and furniture would move, or something would fall off the mantel, or there'd be a weird noise, and Doris would have no idea that it was her husband all the time."

"Ingenious," Nigel remarked. "And also malevolent. What kind of a man would do this to the woman he loved?"

"'Abusive' comes to mind," I said. "Right along with poisoning her."

"Which we haven't established yet," Hal reminded me.

Tyrone reappeared. "Man, that's *rank*," he said, wiping his brow with a handkerchief. "We gotta get that body outta there and then get a team of CSIs in. They gonna need *respirators*, man."

"Where does the body go from here?" I asked.

"City morgue."

"Who does the autopsy?" I persisted.

"Coroner's office."

"Here in Long Beach?"

"No, in LA. We don't have an ME here."

"Damn. I'd like to see the autopsy. Is there any way I could do that?"

Tyrone scratched his head. "Lemme see what I can find out, okay?"

"Okay, thanks. Where did your partner disappear to?"

"I'm guessin' the bathroom downstairs." He started toward the door, but I stopped him.

"Did Hal mention the passports and driver's licenses in the desk?"

"Yep. We didn't have time to look for them on the way in, though; we came right up here to rescue you. But how about you show me where they are, and we'll take 'em with us."

I assented, and we all went downstairs. Mark met us in the hallway. "We're gonna go get those passports now," Tyrone informed his partner.

"Good idea. I'll get the computer." Mark headed into the library.

"Don't trip on the fishing line," Hal called after him.

Mark stopped. "What fishing line?"

"That's right, you missed all the excitement," Nigel said. "It seems the late Mr. Campbell, or St. George or whatever his name is, was a bit of a practical joker. There's a laird's lug in that room, where he ran fishing line down through the floor and attached it to various objects in this room to make them appear to move on their own, thus conveying to the unsuspecting that there is a poltergeist in the house."

"Huh?"

"Just stay on the right side of the table," I advised him.

"I'll explain it to you later, boss," Tyrone said soothingly, which had just the opposite effect on his partner.

"I get it, I get it! And stop calling me boss!"

"Yassuh, boss."

Mark shot Tyrone a poisonous glare, walked into the library, taking care to stay on the right side of the table, and picked up the computer.

I felt like I'd walked into the middle of a *Lethal Weapon* movie.

"Let me show you where those passports are," I suggested. Tyrone assented, and we went into the kitchen, where I took the opportunity to dispose of my gloves. Then I pulled out the drawer with the false bottom.

The passports were gone.

The driver's licenses were too.

"Well, shit," I said.

Mark came into the kitchen, carrying the computer. "Well?"

"They're gone," I told him.

"Are you sure they were ever there in the first place?" Mark asked.

I pulled out my smartphone and showed him the pictures. "This isn't my first rodeo, you know," I told him. "I've learned the hard way to document everything."

"Did you take them?" Mark asked.

"No, I didn't," I told him, trying hard to hold on to my temper. "I took pictures and put them back. I know better than to tamper with evidence."

Mark clearly didn't believe me. "Then who took them? You were the only person in the house."

"No, she wasn't," Hal said as he and Nigel came into the kitchen.

"Here's the charger," Nigel said to Mark. "You might find that comes in handy down at the station."

Mark took it. "Who else was here? And how do you know?"

"We saw a neon-green Volkswagen coming out of the lane up to the gate," Hal said. "Where else would it be coming from?"

"That explains it," I said. "I thought someone must have closed the door on me up there because it closed so fast. The same person must have taken the passports."

"I don't suppose either of you got a license number," Mark said sourly.

"No, we didn't," Hal said defensively. "She was going too fast."

"She nearly ran into us," Nigel said. "She wasn't looking where she was going."

"Hmph," Mark said. "Were they at least California plates?"

Hal and Nigel both shrugged.

Mark sighed and shook his head. Tyrone asked, "Was it a new Volkswagen or an old bug?"

"It was of those new bugs," Hal said, "and it was neon green."

"Okay," Tyrone said. "We might be able to narrow our search down with that."

"What would anybody want with those passports, anyway?" Hal asked. "Who could use them?"

"You'd be surprised," Nigel said. "Obviously it was someone who didn't want us knowing about Dick's aliases."

"Yes," I said, "and now that we do know Dick's aliases, it should be easier to find out who."

"Speaking of that," Tyrone said, "can you email me those pictures?"

"Sure."

After they left, Nigel said to me, "Why don't you ride with Hal? I'll drive Fiona's car home."

"Oh, no you don't," Hal objected. "I'm not having her stink up the Mercedes."

"You guys are hurting my feelings," I protested. "How about if I wrap myself up in a towel and you drive with the windows open?"

They assented, and I ran back upstairs and fetched a bath towel from the master bathroom.

When we got home, Hal left the Mercedes in the driveway with the windows down. I took my clothes off in the garage and put them straight into the washer, along with the towel. Hal fetched me clean ones to change into before we went into the house. But I knew the stink would be in my hair, too, and insisted upon washing it before letting my mother smell me.

On my way back to the house from the apartment, I stopped in the garage, threw my underwear and the towel I'd dried my hair with into the washer, and started it. By that time, Hal and Nigel had brought my mother up to speed on what was going on, apparently, because she grabbed me the minute I walked into the kitchen and hugged me tight before I had a chance to put my laptop down on the ironing board.

"Oh, Antoinette!" she exclaimed. "Kitten, why didn't you tell me you were trapped in that horrible place? I would have been *frantic*!"

I disengaged myself and put down the laptop. "Well, my darling mum, that's precisely why I didn't tell you."

Mum sighed. "Really, darling, I wish you wouldn't do that."

"What, you *want* to be frantic?"

We'd had this conversation so many times I could predict what she'd say next. And she did, hands on hips. "No, dear, I just want to know what's going on. That's the least you could do."

"Well," I said, picking the laptop up again, "never let it be said that I didn't do the least I could do." And with that, I went on into the living room, where Hal lounged in Mum's pink brocade easy chair with a beer, and Nigel stretched out in his recliner with a Scotch. The Dodgers were playing on TV, with the volume down so low that I couldn't even hear it until I was actually in the room. I sat on the couch and opened up my laptop on the coffee table, with the intention of sending my pictures to Tyrone.

Hal stood up. "Fiona, you can have your chair back. I'm going to fix Toni a drink."

"Oh, no, Hal dear, not yet," Mum said. "I want her to come with me to see Doris."

"Again?" Hal asked. "You saw her this morning."

"It's okay," I told him. "Just let me finish sending these."

Dr. Connors and Vicky were at Doris's bedside when we got to St. Mary's. They came out to the waiting room while I went in. Doris was still on the respirator and looked no better; if anything, she looked worse. Her face looked gaunt, as if her jutting cheekbones were about to pierce the skin.

Dr. Connors, Vicky, and I came back out, and Mum went in.

"Does anyone know what happened to Dick yet?" Vicky asked me.

"We do now," I told her. "He's dead."

Dr. Connors looked up from his cell phone. "Dead? How?"

"Not sure yet," I said. "He had an accident with the dumbwaiter. It could just be an accident, but it could also be murder. Although why anyone would murder someone with a dumbwaiter is beyond me. Why go to all that trouble when you could just hit him over the head or something?"

"Is there going to be an autopsy?" he asked.

"Most likely. If so, it will be at the county coroner's office in LA."

Vicky's mouth twisted. "I'd never say this to Mom, but I'll tell you it couldn't have happened to a nicer guy."

Mum came back out in time to hear this remark. "How so, Victoria dear?"

"Maybe we ought to talk about this outside," I suggested. "Dr. Connors doesn't have time to hear about family matters."

"I do if they have a bearing on our patient's condition," he said.

"He was an absolute control freak," she said. "He wouldn't let Mom have anything to do with financial matters. He wouldn't even let her look at the bills, let alone pay them. When Dad was alive, Mom handled their finances, and he was fine with it. But Dick told her to stay out of his desk and off his computer or there'd be hell to pay."

"Hiding anything, much?" I murmured.

"That's exactly what I said! But Mom told me not to make waves. I think she was afraid of the guy."

"It sounds like an abusive relationship," Mum said.

"It sure does," Vicky said. "He was all sweetness and light when they were dating. He was always buying her flowers, giving her extravagant gifts, like that Mercedes, for instance. And jewelry! You should see her jewelry. It had to have cost thousands. But once they tied the knot, it all stopped."

"He swept her off her feet," I said.

"That's how it usually starts," my mother said.

A nurse came out and whispered something to Dr. Connors.

His eyebrows went up. "So soon? I wasn't expecting that for at least a couple more days." He started scrolling through something on his smartphone. "Holy cow!"

"What?" I stepped around the end of the bed to get a look at the screen.

"Her arsenic level is over two thousand."

"Micrograms per liter?"

"Yes." He looked at Mum. "She hasn't eaten seafood in the last forty-eight hours, has she?"

"She's been here for the last forty-eight hours," I pointed out.

"She never eats seafood in any case," Mum said. "She's allergic."

He nodded. "In that case, we need to get her on dimercaprol right away."

"Is there anything in there about my blood arsenic?" Mum asked anxiously.

"Fiona, your blood arsenic is 120," Dr. Connors said, "and fractionation shows that thirty of it is organic."

"So that leaves ninety that's inorganic," I said. "But that's still too high. Mum, when was the last time you took Metamucil?"

"Yesterday morning," Mum said, "around eight o'clock. Why?"

"And you had your blood drawn, when, about four yesterday afternoon?"

"Yes, dear. Why?"

"Because arsenic doesn't stay in the blood very long," I explained. "It's half-life in blood is four to six hours."

"What does that mean?" Mum asked, her voice trembling slightly. "That it was even higher?"

"There's eight hours between your last dose of Metamucil and getting your blood drawn, so if we use four hours as the half-life, that means it was 180 at noon and 360 after you took it. It's got to be the Metamucil," I stated. "It's the only way you could have gotten that much arsenic."

"Please," Vicky begged. "Would somebody please tell me what all this talk about arsenic means? Does Metamucil have arsenic in it?"

"Not as a general rule," I said.

"What this means, Vicky," Dr. Connors said, "is that Toni, here, may have just saved your mother's life."

"My mother's too," I said shakily.

"Great Scott, yes!" Dr. Connors exclaimed, still scrolling through the results. "That Metamucil must have been absolutely loaded. Whoever did this must have just simply dumped half of that bottle into it and shook it up."

Mum sat down heavily in the one chair at Doris's bedside. "Now what happens?"

"Now we get you both treated," Dr. Connors said, consulting his smartphone.

Back when I was a medical student and intern, I had to carry around a fat little notebook in my lab coat pocket that was crammed with information such as drug dosages, so that I could refer to it whenever I had to treat a patient. Now one could access everything on a cell phone.

"Toni," Vicky said, "thank you for saving Mom's life. But *how*? What's going on here?"

I explained about finding the half-empty bottle of Cowley's Rat Exterminator in the basement and putting two and two together. "But nobody believed me," I told her. "Not the police, not the doctors, not even my own husband."

"So if you hadn't convinced the doctors to test her for arsenic, nobody would ever know and she wouldn't get treated."

"That's right."

"How did you convince them?"

"I didn't. Dr. Connors did."

"Okay," Dr. Connors said. "I'm ordering dimercaprol for Mrs. Campbell, to be given IM every four hours. For you, Fiona, I'm prescribing DMSA, or succimer, which comes in an oral form. You'll be taking a capsule every six hours for three days, after which we'll have you collect a twenty-four-hour urine to see if your arsenic is back to normal."

"Normal!" Mum exclaimed in disbelief. "Arsenic has a *normal* level?"

"If your twenty-four-hour urine shows an arsenic level below fifty micrograms per liter, you will be out of danger," he explained.

"What about side effects?" I asked.

"There may be some nausea or loss of appetite," Dr. Connors said. "Also, diarrhea and possibly a skin rash. We'll have to monitor your liver and kidney function too. In fact, I'd like you to go down to the lab and get a baseline today, so we'll have something to compare to."

"Right now?"

"Yes. And I'll fax a prescription. Are you using the same pharmacy?"

"Yes."

So Dr. Connors went back to his office, while Mum went to the lab, and Vicky and I went to the cafeteria, which was just down the hall from the lab. We had no sooner sat down to enjoy our coffee when Dr. Seligman burst into the cafeteria and made a beeline for our table.

"Just who do you think you are, Doctor?" he demanded, his beady little eyes boring into mine like lasers. "You have no right to interfere with the care of a hospital patient. You don't have hospital privileges here. And if you're even licensed to practice medicine in this state, I'll eat my yarmulke," he added unwisely.

"Then you may as well sit down and enjoy it," I said. "Shall I get you a cup of coffee to wash it down with?"

Vicky snickered. Dr. Seligman flushed and glared at her momentarily, then turned his fury back on me. "What the hell are you talking about?"

"My California license is still active," I informed him. "I've got it right here. Want to see it?"

"That's not the point!" he raged. "You may think you can wrap my resident around your little finger and get him to order anything you want, but you've reckoned without me."

"What is your point?" I asked quietly.

"Ordering dimercaprol for Mrs. Campbell is not in your scope of practice. You're a pathologist, for God's sake. Do you have any idea how toxic that is? Mrs. Campbell's renal function is impaired. Did you even check her lab work?"

"I didn't order it," I said reasonably.

"Then who did?" he demanded. "Did you get young Parker to do it against my express wishes? You won't get away with it," he went on, not giving me an opportunity to answer. "I've cancelled the order."

Vicky was no longer snickering. Instead, she rose to her feet and faced Dr. Seligman. Actually, she towered over him so that he was obliged to look up at her, a fact that did nothing to assuage his rage.

"Then you had better un-cancel it," she said evenly. "If you don't, I'll be forced to report you to the California State Medical Board and sue you for malpractice."

Dr. Seligman backed up a step but didn't back down. "Who the hell are you?"

"Victoria Maxwell-Jones," she informed him. "Attorney at law. Here's my card. I'm also Mrs. Campbell's daughter, and for your information, Dr. Day didn't order that medication. Dr. Connors did."

"He did it because her twenty-four-hour urine arsenic was over two thousand micrograms per liter," I put in. "Did you even check her lab work?"

Vicky turned away with her fingers to her lips in an effort not to snicker.

Dr. Seligman was finally and mercifully speechless, but if looks could kill, Vicky and I would both be dead.

CHAPTER 9

You are not permitted to kill a woman who has wronged you,

but nothing forbids you to reflect that she is growing older every minute.

You are avenged 1440 times a day.

—Ambrose Bierce

The four of us met Vicky and her husband, Greg, at King Arthur's on Anaheim Avenue, a place that was familiar to me because I'd celebrated my twenty-first birthday there and had my first legal alcoholic drink in public.

Vicky's husband, Gregory Worthington Jones, was in the same law firm as Vicky; in fact, that's where they met. Where Vicky had maintained her youthful appearance, Greg had not. He was as tall as Vicky but quite a bit heavier and bald as an egg.

King Arthur's hadn't changed much: the red velvet upholstery on the high-backed wing chairs had become somewhat threadbare, and the tapestries depicting scenes of Camelot had faded, but the food was still good. Thanks to the tapestries and the high-backed wing chairs, it was possible to talk without being overheard or drowned out by the chatter of other patrons. In fact, it was difficult to even *see* other patrons unless you craned your neck around the back of your chair.

Jane Bennett Munro

Which was why, when I had occasion to visit the ladies' room, I was astonished to come face-to-face with my mirror image. As I was washing my hands, I looked up and saw two of me in the mirror.

They say everybody has a double. Mum was lucky; hers was Susan Hayward. Mine was apparently this stranger drying her hands on a paper towel and glaring at me. I might have introduced myself, but apparently the lady did not especially care to make my acquaintance, judging from her expression. She threw her towel into the trash receptacle with an air of disgust and flounced out, leaving me to wonder what I had done to offend her.

Unless I had more than one double, that was probably Sonia. We didn't look exactly alike, of course; her clothes were much more sexy and revealing than mine, and she wore more makeup. But other than that, we had the same build, the same facial features, the same olive complexion, the same green eyes, and the same curly black hair, except that mine was streaked with silver and hers wasn't.

I wondered who she might have thought I was.

I wondered if Bernie Kincaid had ever told her about me.

I wondered if the two of them ever talked to each other. Pete had told me that their divorce was pretty acrimonious.

I wondered if Mark Kincaid had mentioned me. Did Mark and Sonia ever talk to each other?

I wondered if Sonia even lived in Long Beach. Just because Mark mistook me for her didn't mean she lived here.

On the other hand, just how many doubles of me were there in this area?

Things that make you go *hmmm* …

This was getting me nowhere. People were going to start wondering if I had fallen in and flushed myself.

When I got back to my table, my mother said, "Where did you go, kitten? Did you see somebody you know?"

"I didn't go anywhere," I said. "You must have seen my doppelganger."

"You mean Sonia?" Hal asked.

"Who's Sonia?" asked Vicky.

"The ex-wife of a cop I know in Twin," I said. "Remember Bernie? He told me once that I was the spittin' image of her."

"And her brother-in-law," Hal put in, "is one of the homicide detectives on this case."

"He mistook me for Sonia when he first saw me," I said, "and he wasn't happy. He must not have liked her very much."

"Well," Mum acknowledged, "I can see that the person I saw isn't you, kitten. Her clothes are different, for one thing. And the expression on her face! She looked if she were on her way to kill somebody."

She had no sooner completed that sentence than a disturbance broke out right behind me. A woman's voice rose above the buzz of other patrons talking. "It's her, I tell you! Go see for yourself if you don't believe me. She's sitting right there."

"Darling, please sit down," a male voice urged. "You're making a scene."

Far from placating the woman, his words only seemed to inflame her more. "You don't understand! That woman broke up my marriage, and all you care about is whether I'm making a scene or not. What kind of a man are you?"

"One who loves you very much," the man said soothingly but to no avail.

"The hell you do!" The woman's voice grew more strident. "You're a fucking coward. Grow a set, why don't you!"

The buzz of the other patrons talking grew louder, and I heard hurrying footsteps.

"Sonia, don't do this!" The man's voice grew louder. "You're going to get us both kicked out of here."

So it *was* Sonia! I wondered who she was talking about. Was it her marriage to Bernie that she was referring to, or a subsequent one? In any case, it had nothing to do with me. Or so I thought.

I heard the maître d' saying, "Sir, madam, I'm afraid I'm going to have to ask you to leave. You're disturbing the other patrons."

"I don't give a flying fuck!" Sonia shouted. "I'm going to give her a piece of my mind if it's the last thing I do."

"Madam," the maître d' remonstrated. "Please leave immediately, or I'll be forced to call the police and have you forcibly removed."

"I'm sorry," the man said. "My wife is a little upset. She seems to think she saw someone whom she holds responsible for her divorce from her former husband. It's all right. We're leaving. You don't need to call the cops. Come along, dear. We can continue this discussion at home."

"A little upset, my ass!" Sonia argued. "Try fucking pissed. It's not me you should ask to leave; it's her!"

At this, Hal, Nigel, and Greg shoved back their chairs and stood up, just as Sonia yanked my chair back and slapped my face.

For a moment, I was too stunned to react.

My mother, however, had no such inhibition. She was on her feet, arm drawn back as if to return the slap. "How dare you!"

Jane Bennett Munro

I jumped up and grabbed her wrist. "Mum, don't!"

"She assaulted you, kitten," she protested, but she dropped her arm, no doubt realizing that retaliation would only make things worse. But Sonia wasn't finished.

"That's right. Run to Mommy," she sneered. "What are you—afraid to fight?" And with that, she made a lunge toward me as if to grab my arm and let loose a blast of alcohol-soaked breath. Nigel, in a lightning move akin to legerdemain, stepped between us, grabbed Sonia's hand, and got her in some sort of thumb lock that effectively immobilized her.

Unfortunately, it didn't have the same effect on her mouth. "You fucking bitch!" she screamed at me. "You stay away from my husband if you know what's good for you, or I swear I'll kill you!"

Hal stepped between us. "Don't you threaten my wife," he said quietly, "or you'll have me to deal with."

Sonia turned her fury on him. "You'd hit a *woman*?" she demanded.

Hal put his hands on his hips and leaned closer to her. "Why not? *You* did."

Meanwhile, Greg had pulled out his cell phone and dialed. He moved away from the table to talk so that I didn't hear the conversation, but I hoped that he was calling 911.

All around us, people were getting up and leaving.

Sonia's husband, now that I could see him, proved to be a tall, mildly handsome individual with a mullet and an exceedingly embarrassed expression. He stood apart from Sonia and appeared disinclined to have anything more to do with her. As I watched, he put a hand over his face and turned away.

"Just who do you think I am?" I asked her. "I don't even know your husband."

"Don't play innocent with me," she sneered. "You took my first husband away from me. You're not going to get this one too, if I have anything to say about it."

"You mean Bernie?"

"Yes, as you know perfectly well."

"I didn't even meet Bernie until he was already divorced," I pointed out. "Don't go putting that on me. And as far as breaking up this marriage is concerned, I think you may have just done that."

At that, Sonia's face crumpled, and she burst into tears.

I could almost feel sorry for her, but my face hurt too much for me to say no when the maître d' asked if I wanted to press charges. I tasted blood. The

84

inside of my cheek must have been cut. The police arrived just then and took Sonia away.

The expression on her face when she looked back at me made my blood run cold.

"Well!" my mother exclaimed. "I must say I didn't expect dinner theater. It's quite taken my appetite away."

"Mine too," Nigel said. "I believe I'll skip dessert."

Everyone else agreed, and the maître d' told us that there would be no charge for our dinners under the circumstances.

As we were leaving, Sonia's husband approached us. "Please allow me to apologize for my wife's behavior," he said. "I can't imagine what got into her."

"I can," Hal said brutally. "She was drunk."

"I know," the man said. "Could I possibly talk you out of pressing charges against her? I can assure you that it won't happen again."

I put a hand to my sore cheek and shook my head.

"In my experience," Greg said, "it always happens again."

"It was extremely unwise," Vicky said, "for her to threaten to kill someone in front of witnesses."

The man looked from Greg to Vicky and back again. "What are you, lawyers?"

They nodded.

The man shrugged. "Well, all I can say is I'm sorry." He turned and walked away. We stood and watched as he got into his car and drove out of the parking lot.

In a neon-green Volkswagen.

Which was either the biggest coincidence on the planet, or Sonia had already had a go at killing me.

And there were no coincidences where murder was concerned.

CHAPTER 10

Litigious terms, fat contentions, and flowing fees.

—John Milton

"What now?" I asked of the group in general.

"Now," Greg replied, "we go downtown to the police station to file assault charges against that woman."

"The best part being," Vicky added, "that you already have lawyers."

The police station was located on First Street, just west of Long Beach Boulevard. Its serene exterior belied the chaos we could hear just inside the door. The female sergeant at the desk shook her head and jerked a thumb in that general direction. "Full moon," she commented. "It never fails. Now, how can I help you folks?"

There was a full moon, as it happened, and I knew that things got crazy in hospitals too, particularly in the emergency room, when the moon was full. "We're here to press charges," I told her.

Vicky put a hand on my arm. "Toni, let Greg talk. That's what he's here for."

"Your face can speak for you, sweetie," Hal said. "It's already turning purple, and you're gonna have a hell of a shiner."

Terrific, I thought sourly. But I shut up and let Greg do his job.

Sonia, on the other hand, had no such inhibitions. Somehow, she managed to break free of her captors and came running out to the lobby, where she stopped short upon seeing all of us at the desk. I held my breath, waiting to see what she'd do next, when Mark Kincaid, clad in casual clothes, burst through the front door with a face like a thundercloud and headed straight for her.

"Sonia, goddamn it, what have you done now?" Then he saw me, and his shoulders drooped visibly. "Oh, no. You didn't."

Meanwhile, two police officers took charge of Sonia, handcuffed her, and led her away. Mark shook his head. "Who the hell uncuffed her in the first place?"

Nobody answered. The female sergeant at the desk looked at me and said, "Well, I'll be damned. You never told me Sonia had a sister."

"She doesn't," Mark growled.

"Well, then, who's this?"

I opened my mouth to tell her, but Greg shushed me again. "No relation," he said. "This is the victim of the attack, and she's here to press charges. I'm her lawyer."

At this point, Vicky suggested that we all, including Mark, go sit in the waiting room and let Greg handle the legalities. She gently herded us all in that direction while Greg remained at the desk.

"Victoria dear," my mother said, "doesn't the leftenant have to go deal with this?"

"No," Vicky replied. "Since he's related to her, he can't have anything to do with this. It would be conflict of interest."

"But that doesn't stop them from calling me every time she gets arrested," Mark said sourly.

"So this isn't the first time she's done this sort of thing," Hal said.

"Not hardly," Mark said. "She gets drunk and disorderly on a regular basis. It's one of the reasons my brother divorced her. This is the first time she's ever assaulted anyone though."

"Nice of her to start with me," I said sotto voce.

"I'm not condoning her behavior, you understand," Mark said, "but I'm not surprised. She's been threatening you for years."

Startled, I said, "She doesn't even know me!"

"She's been threatening 'that bitch who stole her husband' for years," Mark said, making air quotes. "She's got a real bee in her bonnet about it. She goes on and on about it when she gets drunk. Apparently, my brother was the love of her life."

"Her present husband must really enjoy that," Hal commented wryly. "Who is he, anyway?"

"Bill Matthews. He teaches at Poly High. History or social studies, something like that. Coaches basketball, too, sometimes."

"Do they have kids?" I asked.

"No," Mark said. "They haven't been married that long, and in any case, Sonia doesn't want them. She doesn't want to spoil her figure."

"Time will do that for her," Mum said tartly, "whether she has children or not."

"She must have known who I was the minute she saw me in the ladies' room," I pointed out. "How? Did Bernie tell her about me?"

"He told me," Mark said. "I might have mentioned it to my wife. She might have mentioned it at a family gathering or something."

"Sonia came to family gatherings?" I asked in surprise.

"At first," Mark said, "but then she married Kevin and stopped coming."

"Kevin?" I asked.

Mark sighed. "Yes, and then there was John, and then Tyler. None of them lasted very long. This guy won't either."

At that moment, "this guy" walked into the waiting room, saw us, and went over to the other side of the room and sat down. He leaned forward, elbows on his knees, and put his face in his hands.

I felt sorry for him, a mild-mannered teacher having to deal with a wife who got drunk and disorderly on a regular basis, and now with a wife who had assaulted someone and would have to pay the consequences. This might affect *his* career. I began to regret my decision to press charges.

But not for long. Greg put his head in the door and said, "Toni? They want you in the interrogation room."

"What about the rest of us?" Nigel demanded. "We were all there."

"Maybe later. Right now, they just want Toni."

With trepidation, I followed Greg down the hall to the interrogation room, which was now quiet. A balding, middle-aged plainclothes detective in a brown tweed sport coat, blue shirt, and yellow tie waited for us. He stood when we entered, and I saw that he had a belly as big as Greg's. Actually, he looked a lot like Greg too. I wondered if they were related.

"Mrs. Shapiro?" He stuck out his hand, and I shook it. "Detective Sergeant Ernest Jones."

Greg settled his bulk into a chair and gestured for me to do the same. "My big brother Ernie," he said.

"Nice to meet you," I said politely. "What happens now?"

Jones shuffled some papers on the table in front of him. "Just a few questions, ma'am."

Ma'am? Seriously? "Could you possibly call me Toni?" I asked. "I hate 'ma'am.' It makes me feel old."

Jones cracked a smile for the first time. "Okay, Toni it is. Now, could you tell me, in your own words, of course, what transpired tonight at King Arthur's between you and the suspect?"

"You mean Sonia?"

"Yes. What happened?"

"I was just sitting there, eating my dinner and minding my own business, when she pulled back my chair and slapped my face."

"Did you know the suspect well?"

"I never saw her before tonight."

"When she slapped you?"

"No, I saw her in the ladies' room a few minutes before that."

"What happened in the ladies' room?"

"Nothing much," I said. "I came out of the bathroom stall to wash my hands, and there she was, looking back at me in the mirror. I suppose I did a sort of double take, because she does look just like me, but she looked daggers at me and stomped out without saying a word."

"Do you know why she did that?"

"I do now, but I didn't at the time."

"What do you mean by that?"

"Well, now I know that she thinks I'm responsible for her divorce from her first husband—wait, *was* Bernie her first husband? I don't even know. She could have been married to someone else before that. Anyway …"

Greg stopped me. "Let's get back to what happened tonight, shall we?"

"Oh, I don't know," his brother said. "This sounds kind of interesting. Before what? Who are we talking about?"

Greg sighed. "Let's stay on point here. We were talking about what happened at King Arthur's."

"Okay," Jones said, "but we're not done with this subject. So, Toni, what happened after you left the bathroom?"

"I went back to our table and sat down and ate my dinner."

"And where were Sonia and her husband sitting?"

"At a table behind me."

"Did you know she was sitting there when you went back to your table?"

"No. I couldn't see her."

"You couldn't? How come?"

Greg interrupted. "Ernie, you've been to King Arthur's. You know how those high-backed chairs …"

"Okay, okay, I get what you mean. So, Toni, when did you first know that she was behind you?"

"I heard a woman's voice say, 'It's her, I tell you. She's sitting right there. Go look for yourself if you don't believe me.' And then a man's voice telling her to sit down and not make a scene, and then she really got mad and started yelling at him."

"What was she yelling about?"

"She called him a coward, told him to grow a set, said that I had ruined her marriage and that she was going to give me a piece of her mind."

"And then she slapped you."

"No, then the maître d' came over and asked them to leave, and *then* she slapped me."

"What did you do?"

"Nothing. I was too stunned. Then my mother jumped up and was going to slap her back, but I stopped her."

"Then what?"

"Well, then she tried to attack me, but Nigel—my stepfather—got her in some kind of hold so that she couldn't move, and she called me a fucking bitch and threatened to kill me if I didn't stay away from her husband."

"Her present husband?"

"Yes. Then she said that I'd ruined her marriage to Bernie, and she wasn't going to let me ruin this one as well. I told her that I hadn't even met Bernie until he was already divorced, but she didn't care."

"Then what?"

"Greg called the police, and they came and took her away."

"That's all?"

"No. Then her husband asked if we'd consider not pressing charges. He said he could guarantee that it wouldn't happen again, but Greg and Vicky got all lawyerly on him, and he just shrugged and got into his neon-green Volkswagen and drove away. And by the way, about that neon-green Volkswagen …"

Greg stopped me again. "Toni, he doesn't need to know about the neon-green Volkswagen."

"What about the neon-green Volkswagen?" his brother asked. "And exactly who is this Bernie you keep mentioning?"

"He's a cop in Twin Falls, Idaho, where I live," I said, "who was in the process of divorcing Sonia when I first met him, and he disliked me on sight. Later I found out that it was because I look just like Sonia." I saw no need to add that Bernie had later done a complete volte-face and decided he wanted to have an affair with me. That would just muddy the waters.

I didn't have an affair with him, by the way. Just saying.

"What's his last name?" Jones asked, making a note.

"Kincaid."

Jones looked up, startled. "Mark's brother?"

"The very same."

"So are you that pathologist he's always talking about that drives his brother crazy?"

I smiled. "The very same."

Jones gave me an embarrassed grin. "Well, shit, then, I should be calling you Doctor. Sorry about that."

"That's okay," I told him. "Toni is fine."

"Now, what about the green Volkswagen?"

Greg sighed again. "Ernie, the green Volkswagen has nothing to do with this case."

"It might," I objected, "if Sonia has already tried to kill me."

Greg groaned. "I sympathize with Bernie. Are you trying to drive me crazy too?"

"It will all make perfect sense when I tell you about it," I assured him. "That is if you want to hear it."

"Do I have a choice?"

"No, you don't," his brother said, "because I want to hear about it too. Go ahead, Toni."

So I told them about being trapped in the secret staircase at the MacTavish house with a dead body and about the neon-green Volkswagen that had narrowly missed colliding with Hal and Nigel when they rode to my rescue.

"Who was the dead body?" Jones asked.

"Richard Campbell."

"Who the hell is Richard Campbell?"

"The husband of my mother's best friend," I told him, "who is in St. Mary's trying not to die of arsenic poisoning."

Detective Jones groaned and put his head in his hands.

"Mark will tell you all about it," I said soothingly.

"I get it," Greg said. "That's how you got involved?"

"Yes."

"So how come the police weren't told about this? It sounds like attempted murder to me."

"And murder too," I said. "And the police do know. Mark and Tyrone are all over it."

Detective Jones threw up his hands, rather like Hal does when he yells, "Oy gevalt!" to the ceiling. "Why didn't you tell us that in the first place?"

"I thought you knew," I retorted. "Don't you guys ever talk to each other?"

"Oh, a smartass, huh?" Jones leaned across the table. His eyes had turned hard. "Well, don't get too cocky, because your buddy Sonia told us that you attacked her, not the other way around. Her husband backed her up."

That figured. "All you have to do is ask the people that were there with me," I countered.

"Oh, right, your husband, your parents, and your lawyers," he sneered. "Of course they're gonna stick up for you."

"All right, then, how about the maître d' at King Arthur's? The wait staff? The customers? Besides, who's the one with the shiner and the purple cheek?"

"Oh, we'll get around to asking them, maybe tomorrow. In the meantime, it looks like both you and Sonia are gonna spend the night right here, courtesy of the city of Long Beach."

The thought of sharing a confined space with Sonia for twelve hours scared me rigid. I had no doubt that I'd be dead by morning.

I turned to Greg in dismay. "Can he do that?"

"He can, but he won't," Greg said. "He's gonna release you on your own recognizance. Sonia's the one with a record, not you. Isn't that right, big bro?"

Crap, I thought. *I'm in the middle of a pissing contest between two brothers.* But I'd misjudged Detective Ernie Jones.

"That's right, little lady," he agreed in an execrable John Wayne imitation. "That'll teach you to fuck with the Long Beach Police Department."

"Did you know he was going to do that?" I demanded of Greg as we walked down the hall back to the waiting room.

"Ernie was always a practical joker," Greg replied. "Sometimes he goes too far. But one thing he said was true; Sonia did try to turn it around on you, and her husband did back her up, but ol' Ern didn't believe it for a second."

"What about Sonia?"

"She'll be in a cell tonight, and she'll be arraigned in the morning, and bail set."

"What about me?"

"Nothing. You're free as a bird. Except that you'll have to appear at the arraignment."

I stopped walking. "Why? I didn't do anything."

Greg stopped and faced me. "You're the one who pressed charges," he pointed out. "But you're right; normally you wouldn't have to appear. I want you to. Your face is evidence."

"Why can't you just take a picture of me?"

We were standing just outside of the door to the waiting room, within earshot of everyone in it. Hal stuck his head out the door. "What are you two arguing about? Everyone can hear you."

"Guess we'd better get inside," Greg said, gently shepherding me ahead of him as we rejoined our spouses and my parents. Sonia's husband had disappeared.

"Greg wants me to be at Sonia's arraignment tomorrow morning, and I don't want to," I informed the group.

"Why can't they just take a picture of you?" Hal demanded.

"That's what I said," I told him.

"That time your arms were so bruised, remember?" Hal went on. "You went to Dave Martin, and he took pictures and put them in your medical record."

My heart sank. "I really don't want to go to the emergency room. I want to go home and sleep on an ice pack."

"We can take pictures of you here," Mark Kincaid said, startling me. He'd been so quiet that I'd forgotten he was still there. "In fact, we should, for evidence. By the time the trial rolls around, you won't look like that anymore. I'm surprised Ernie didn't think of that. We do have a police photographer. Let me see if he's here." He took out his cell phone and dialed.

I didn't blame Ernie for not thinking of photographs. I'd given him a lot of information to deal with.

I turned to Greg. "Now I don't have to be at the arraignment, right?"

"I can't force you," Greg said, "but I have an ulterior motive."

"Do tell, old boy," Nigel urged.

"I also want to see how Sonia reacts to Toni being there. If she acts anything like she did tonight, they might set bail higher than they would otherwise—maybe so high that there's no way she can pay it. I think she's a danger to Toni in her present state of mind, and I don't want her out of jail until you folks go back to Idaho."

Which was exactly how I felt when Detective Ernie Jones said that both Sonia and I would have to be incarcerated overnight.

"I don't either," I said with feeling.

"On the other hand, she'll probably be sober by then," Hal pointed out. "She could be nice as pie."

"I don't think so," Greg said. "She'll be hungover and blaming you for it."

Oh God, I hadn't even thought of that. When she wasn't attacking me, she'd be puking her guts up. I've got a pretty strong stomach, but I really hate being around people throwing up. It makes me want to join right in, and I'd rather die.

The police photographer was available and photographed me from several angles with lighting designed to show every aspect of my injuries. Since the images were digital, I could look at the pictures right away. They were impressive. I had no idea I looked *that* bad.

"So can we go home now?" Hal asked. "They don't need us for anything?"

"No, they don't," Greg said. "Go home and get some sleep. Toni, I'll pick you up at eight fifteen in the morning."

"I'll be ready," I said. "Death mask and all."

CHAPTER 11

Simply by being compelled to keep constantly on his guard, a man may grow so weak as to be unable to defend himself.

—Friedrich Wilhelm Nietzsche

"Toni, you look awful," Greg said the next morning when he arrived to take Hal and me to court. Hal insisted upon accompanying me in the event that Sonia attacked me again.

My face looked even worse than it had the night before, even though I'd slept with an ice pack to keep the swelling down. Nearly half my face was purple, and I looked like a negative image of the Phantom of the Opera.

I was also wearing the same outfit I'd worn the night before, which didn't smell very good, but I'd only brought one dressy outfit with me; everything else was tank tops and capris, which I didn't think were appropriate for court.

It comforted me somewhat to know that Sonia, too, would be wearing the same clothes as the night before—and she'd had to sleep in them.

But she wasn't. When they brought her into the courtroom, she was clad in an orange jumpsuit like an ordinary prisoner. Her curly black hair was disheveled, and her makeup smudged, and she still looked better than I did.

Greg and I sat in the front row on the left side of the courtroom, and Sonia's husband sat with Mark Kincaid on the other side. Sonia sat with her lawyer at a table facing the stand. The lawyer looked about sixteen, with long blonde hair, long, slender legs, and a little black suit with a tiny skirt. She fidgeted. I wondered if this was her first case.

In contrast, Sonia seemed utterly calm. I wondered if she'd been sedated. She sat so close to me that I could have reached out and touched her, and to my dismay, she was neither shackled nor handcuffed. She hadn't yet seen me, but I knew she would eventually, because Greg was dangling me as bait, to see if she'd bite.

And I was afraid she would.

"All rise!" the bailiff called. "His Honor Judge Raymond Toussaint presiding."

We all stood as the judge entered and took his place behind the stand. Judge Raymond Toussaint was a white-haired, heavyset black man with wire-rimmed glasses. He looked like someone's kindly old grandpa, and probably was, but Greg told me not to be deceived, because Judge Toussaint was nobody's fool and he could be tough.

The judge banged his gavel. "This court is now in session," he proclaimed in a deep southern accent, and we all resumed our seats. "First on the docket today is the matter of city of Long Beach versus one Sonia Marie Matthews. The defendant will please rise."

Sonia stood up, along with her teenage attorney.

"Ms. Matthews, you have been charged with assault and battery upon one Antoinette Day Shapiro. Is Ms. Shapiro present in the courtroom?"

Greg stood up and gestured to me to do the same. "She is, Your Honor."

I stood up. Sonia turned around and glared at me.

Judge Toussaint shook his head. "My, my, my. Look at that face. Ms. Shapiro, you may be seated. Ms. Matthews, how do you plead?"

"I didn't do it. She attacked me!"

Sonia's baby lawyer placed a hand on her shoulder and whispered urgently in her ear. Impatiently, she shook her off.

"Ms. Lookingbill," the judge intoned, "kindly control your client. Ms. Shapiro is not on trial here. Now, Ms. Matthews, when I ask how you plead, I want to hear only one of two things: guilty or not guilty. Nothing else. Are we clear on this?"

"Yes, Your Honor," the attorney answered.

"Now, Ms. Matthews. How do you plead?"

"She attacked me, I tell you! Just ask my husband! He'll tell you!"

The judge folded his hands in front of him and leaned forward. "Ms. Matthews. This is an arraignment. At an arraignment, there is no testimony allowed. An arraignment is simply to review the charges and determine whether this stays in municipal court or gets remanded to district court, to assign counsel, and set bail. Do you understand?"

"She does, Your Honor," Ms. Lookingbill answered.

"I was asking Ms. Matthews," Judge Toussaint said reprovingly.

"She attacked me," Sonia insisted. "I keep telling you."

Judge Toussaint leaned back in his chair and stretched his arms out. "Ms. Matthews. You are now in contempt of court. Do you care to go for two counts of contempt?"

"Not guilty, Your Honor," the lawyer said.

"Very good. This case will remain in municipal court. Trial will be in two weeks. Bail will be set at $250,000." The judge banged his gavel.

Bill Matthews gasped audibly. I didn't blame him. He would have to come up with 10 percent, $25,000, not easy for someone on a teacher's salary, which he wouldn't get back. Mark patted his shoulder and whispered something, and Matthews relaxed somewhat.

Judge Toussaint wasn't through. "And now, Bailiff, please take the defendant into custody."

"No!" Sonia screamed. "Bill, tell him you can pay! Tell him!"

Matthews silently shook his head.

"That may be, Ms. Matthews," the judge said, "but there is still the matter of two counts of contempt of court. You just earned yourself another one."

The bailiff, stone-faced, handcuffed her, while the baby lawyer tried to calm her, to no avail. As the bailiff started to lead her out of the courtroom, she turned back to glare at me with enough venom to kill an entire regiment. "I'll kill you, you bitch. Just wait. You're a dead woman."

Well, now. That was clear enough.

Hal had risen to his feet, but Greg pulled him back down lest he, too, be charged with contempt of court.

I wondered if Sonia's bail would be increased after that little outburst, but I doubted it.

"Are you okay?" Greg inquired as we all filed out of the courtroom. "That was pretty rough."

"It was scary," I agreed. "How long is she going to be in jail?" *Meaning, how long will I be safe?*

"It depends," Greg said. "If she can't pay her bail, until the trial. If she can pay it, she goes free until the trial. But there's the matter of contempt of court.

She'll have to be tried on that too, and she'll stay in jail until that trial can be held. The judge in that case can sentence her to a jail term or a fine or both."

"How long does it take to schedule a trial for contempt?" Hal asked.

Greg shrugged. "Hard to say. It could be either before or after the trial for assault and battery."

"You're not much help," I told him. "What do you suggest I do? Go home?"

"That would be my choice," Hal said.

"You can do that, but you have to be back for the trial. The assault trial, that is."

"Really? Even though you have pictures?"

"You're the chief witness."

Well, I couldn't really argue with that, so I changed the subject. "You know what I don't get? What was Sonia doing at the MacTavish house that day? What's her connection there? She couldn't have gone there to kill me, because she didn't know I was there. I mean, she knew someone was there, but she didn't know who. So why was she there in the first place?"

Greg opened the courthouse door for me, and we went out onto the courthouse steps. "You don't really know it was her that day. You only know it was someone in a neon-green Volkswagen. There have got to be other neon-green Volkswagens around here."

"Can we find out?"

"I can't help you with that, but here comes someone who might." Greg pointed off to the left where Mark Kincaid and Bill Matthews were descending the steps. "Lieutenant? Might we have a word?"

Mark and Bill parted at the bottom of the stairs, and Bill walked away, hands in his pockets, shoulders slumped. He looked utterly defeated, and I had to remind myself that he'd abetted his wife when she lied about who attacked whom in order to stop myself from feeling sorry for him.

Mark came up to us. "What's up, Counselor?"

"Toni wants to know why Sonia might have been at the MacTavish house," Greg asked.

Mark looked at me with skepticism. "Who says she was?"

"The neon-green Volkswagen," I contributed.

Mark laughed shortly. "That can't be the only neon-green Volkswagen in town. Besides that, Sonia drives a convertible. The Volkswagen is Bill's car."

"Okay then, what would *Bill* be doing there? Why would *he* want to lock me in a secret staircase with a dead body?"

Mark shrugged, palms up. "I'm sure I don't know. I'm sorry to run, but I really need to get back to work."

"Just one more thing," I begged. "Who was Sonia before she was Mrs. Bernie Kincaid? What was her maiden name?"

"I don't know. Furthermore, I don't care. Why don't you ask Bernie?"

Now, there was an idea. Why on earth hadn't I thought of that myself?

I planned to do that as soon as I got home. But when I got home, I found Mum in her chair, still in her bathrobe, looking like death warmed over. An untouched cup of tea sat on the end table next to her.

"I feel awful, kitten," she said weakly when I asked. "I'm nauseated, and I've been having diarrhea all morning. I must have picked up some kind of stomach flu."

I stopped short. No way was I going to expose myself to a gastrointestinal virus.

"You need to drink your tea, my love," Nigel said gently. "You can't let yourself get dehydrated."

Mum groaned. "I'm afraid to. I'm afraid it will just come right back up."

"Have you eaten anything this morning?" I asked her.

"Just my pills, dear."

Pills. Aha! "Mum, you don't have stomach flu," I told her. "You started taking those pills for arsenic, didn't you?"

She nodded weakly.

"Dr. Connors said you might have nausea and diarrhea as side effects. I can fix those. Just wait a minute."

I ran out to the apartment, where I found Hal poking around in my suitcase. "What are you doing?"

"Looking for your traveling pharmacy," he said. "Where do you keep it?"

I always kept a bag full of pharmaceuticals packed for travel. It contained things such as Tylenol, ibuprofen, Maalox, seasick pills, Benadryl, Imodium, and injectable Compazine, just in case. I also carried Ace bandages, Band-Aids, triple antibiotic ointment, and cortisone cream.

"In my carry-on," I told him. "Here, let me."

I fetched the Imodium and a syringe of Compazine, and we went back to the house, where I dosed Mum. "Is there any Coke in the fridge?" I asked Nigel.

"Let me look."

He went out to the kitchen and returned with a can of Coca-Cola. "You want her to drink *this*?"

"Pour it into a glass and let it go flat," I told him. "Flat Coke will settle her stomach. She used to do that when I was little and was sick to my stomach. Works like a charm if you just sip it."

"I never heard of that," he said.

"I think Mum got it from Doris, as a matter of fact. Which reminds me. We need to go and see how she's doing."

"Nothing doing," Nigel said. "We want to hear how it went in court."

So I told them: all about Sonia's baby lawyer, her behavior in court, and her contempt charges.

Mum laid her head back and looked up to the ceiling. "The girl must be mental to act like that in court," she murmured. "What was she thinking?"

"Did she see you?" Hal asked.

"Oh, yes. The judge asked if I was in court, and Greg had me stand up, so everyone could get a good look at me."

"How did she react to that?" Nigel asked.

"She just glared. But later, when she'd been charged with two counts of contempt, and the bailiff was taking her away, she turned around and threatened to kill me."

Mum sat up straight. "Antoinette!"

"Fiona, calm yourself," Nigel said. "She did the same thing in the restaurant, in front of God and everybody. How is this so different?"

Mum flopped back in her chair. "Well, I just hope they send her away for a long, long time."

"Apparently, that's not a given," I said. "Greg told me that contempt of court can be punished with a jail sentence or just a fine. And there needs to be a separate trial for that too."

"But what about assaulting you?" Hal asked.

"The judge set the bail at $250,000. If her husband can come up with 10 percent of that, she goes free until her trial, which is in two weeks."

"Antoinette," said my mother severely, "go home. Go home right now. If you don't, I won't sleep for worry until that woman is behind bars."

"How likely is it that she'll come up with bail?" Nigel inquired.

"Well, he's a teacher, so unless he has another source of income, not very. But we don't know, do we? Maybe Sonia has money of her own."

"If she has it, he has it," Hal said. "California is a community property state."

"Not necessarily," Mum said. "If the money was hers before she married Bill, it can stay hers. She can have it in an account in her name only. But if it's money she earns while married to him, *that* is community property."

"I don't know if she works," I said. "I could ask Mark Kincaid. Or I could ask Bernie. I was going to do that anyway as soon as I got here, but then Mum …"

"I actually feel a lot better now," Mum said. "I think I'll go get dressed." She got up and went into the master bedroom, closing the door behind her.

I took my cell phone out into the screened patio and stretched out on a chaise longue. I had Bernie's cell number programmed into my cell phone, as I did Pete's. Bernie answered after only two rings.

"Hi, this is Toni," I said.

"Hi. Are you sure you've got the right number? You never call me."

"I know, but this is different. I'm in trouble. Is this a bad time?"

"Not if you're in trouble. Does Pete know about this?"

"Not yet. I need to talk to you about Sonia."

Dead silence.

"Bernie, it's important. She threatened to kill me. She assaulted me. She's been arrested, and she was arraigned this morning. If her husband can raise the bail, she'll go free."

"How much do you know about Sonia?" he asked me.

"Nothing, except that she wants to kill me and used to be married to you."

"Okay. I'll tell you about Sonia. It may help explain what's going on with her."

Whatever I was expecting, it sure wasn't this.

"Okay," I said.

Bernie went on to tell me that Sonia was born in Long Beach to a rich girl named Susan Mary Worthington and a plumber named Frank Caligari. They divorced shortly after Sonia was born, and Susan's parents married her off to a rich friend of theirs named Winston Welles. He was the only father Sonia had ever known, and he died when she was sixteen. Then a man showed up and swept Susan off her feet, and she married him a couple of months later. Sonia didn't like him, and she ran away from home. Her mother died mysteriously a few months later.

"What was this guy's name?" I asked.

"Carter, Cartwright, something like that."

The hairs rose on the back of my neck. Cartwright was the name on one of the passports.

"Bernie, why are you telling me all this? I know you hate to talk about Sonia; what changed your mind?"

Whatever I had been expecting Bernie to say next, it wasn't anything like what he said.

"Actually, I've been kind of expecting you to call. If you hadn't, I would have called you."

"Why?"

"My brother called me and told me all about what happened with you and Sonia."

"Seriously?"

"He also told me about your mother's friend in the hospital with arsenic poisoning."

"Oh."

"And the passports."

"Oh," I said again. "That might explain why she was at the MacTavish house yesterday."

"Now you've lost me."

I told him what had happened at the MacTavish house and Hal and Nigel riding to the rescue. "On their way up the lane to the MacTavish House, they saw a neon-green Volkswagen coming down. It nearly collided with them. And Bill and Sonia have a neon-green Volkswagen."

"I'm sure it's not the only neon-green Volkswagen in Long Beach."

"Well, *somebody* slammed that door on me and took the passports. It makes sense for it to have been Sonia, if she thinks that Dick and Cartwright were the same person. Now that she has the passports, she *knows* they are."

"Cartwright?" Bernie still sounded confused.

"Cartwright was one of the names on those passports."

"Oh. So you think—"

I interrupted him. "When Sonia's mother died, was there an autopsy?"

"I don't know. Why?"

"Because I think she may have died from arsenic poisoning. And if Sonia thinks that Dick killed her mother, she may have killed him."

"So my brother was right."

"About what?"

"According to him, the relationship between you and me isn't Sonia's only problem with you."

I waited, but he didn't say any more. I grew impatient. "Well? Are you just going to leave me in suspense?"

"You just said it yourself. You think she's a murderer, and she knows it. She's scared of you."

Well, now. This was worse than I thought.

"If she slammed that door on me with the intention that I would die in there, that's attempted murder."

"Someone would have to file charges, and the intent would be hard to prove," Bernie said.

"Wait a minute," I said. "If Sonia didn't want the cops to find out, why did she tell Mark?"

"She didn't. Bill did. She doesn't know."

We ended the call after a bit more small talk.

My hand shook as I disconnected.

CHAPTER 12

The jury, passing on the prisoner's life
May in the sworn twelve have a thief or two
Guiltier than him they try.

—Shakespeare, *Measure for Measure*

I took a few deep breaths and tried to calm myself before I went back inside. I wasn't ready to tell Mum about this new development; it would just upset her.

When I went back inside, Mum was dressed and ready to go visit Doris. "We'll take my car, dear," she told me. "I wouldn't dare drive that Mercedes."

"You're not driving anything," I said. "You've had Compazine; it acts like a sedative."

"Really, dear? I don't feel the least bit sleepy."

"It'll hit you when you least expect it. Don't worry; I know the way to St. Mary's."

To our surprise and delight, Doris had regained consciousness. Dr. Parker was in the process of extubating her when we got there. We stayed out in the waiting room until he was finished. Even so, we could hear Doris coughing up a lung in there, and I grimaced in sympathy, knowing exactly what that felt like, since I'd once had occasion to be intubated myself some years ago. Jeff came out to tell us we could go back in.

"It's like a miracle," he declared. "I didn't know it would work that fast. She won't be able to talk much, though; her throat will be too sore for the next couple of days."

I remembered that part too. "Does Dr. Connors know she's awake?"

"I certainly do," boomed a voice behind us, and we turned to see the good doctor walk into the waiting room. "I guess there's no question about what was wrong with her now, is there?"

"Does she know about Dick yet?" my mother asked anxiously.

"She hasn't asked," Jeff said. "I'm not sure how much she remembers. I didn't want to bring it up right away, because she's still pretty fragile. Maybe when she gets some of her strength back …"

"I'll tell her," a new voice announced, and Vicky walked into the room. This was turning into a convention. We couldn't have managed it better if we'd called everybody and told them when to be there. "She has a right to know. Somebody's bound to mention it, and she shouldn't be blindsided by it."

Seeing Vicky reminded me of the name Worthington and why it sounded so familiar. It was Greg's middle name. Could Greg be related to Sonia? I made a mental note to ask Vicky about it later, after we broke the news of Dick's death to Doris. I didn't know how Mum felt about it, but I was quite happy to let Vicky be the bearer of bad news.

"You go tell her, Victoria dear," my mother said. "We'll wait out here until we see how she takes it."

"I'll go with you," Dr. Connors said, and they left. Dr. Parker remained with us and informed us that Doris had regained consciousness during the night and by morning was breathing on her own, although still intubated, with the ventilator off.

So he called Dr. Connors and asked about taking the endotracheal tube out, and Dr. Connors had concurred. "We don't like to leave people intubated more than three days because the tube can ulcerate the trachea," he said. "After three days, we generally do a tracheostomy. We would have had to do one on Mrs. Campbell if she hadn't started breathing on her own today."

Vicky came back out with a quizzical expression. "Well, I told her about Dick, but she didn't seem to know what I was talking about."

Dr. Parker frowned. "That's not good. Maybe she has some brain damage from the arsenic."

Vicky, clearly upset, put her fingers to her mouth. "Oh no."

"She just woke up today, and she's already extubated," I pointed out. "Give her time. Tomorrow she may be completely compos mentis."

Vicky sighed. "God, I hope so."

"Not to change the subject or anything," I said, "but is Greg related to Sonia?"

"Good heavens, no. Why do you ask?"

"Sonia's ex-husband told me that her mother's maiden name was Worthington, and it's Greg's middle name."

"I don't know," Vicky said. "Worthington isn't such an unusual name. It could just be a coincidence. He certainly didn't seem to know her at the restaurant."

I remembered that Greg had stepped away from the table with his cell phone when the kerfuffle broke out. I assumed he'd been calling 911. I also remembered him telling Sonia's husband he couldn't be sure Sonia wouldn't attack me again, because in his experience, it always happened again.

I wondered if the experience Greg was referring to was more than just professional.

It also occurred to me that if Sonia was in jail for murder, she wouldn't be able to kill me.

Unfortunately, she might get out on bail before she could be charged, because although everything I'd found out seemed to hang together in my mind, none of it had been investigated, and it could all be a series of coincidences.

In my head, I could hear Commander Phil Harris of the Twin Falls Police Department telling me that there is no such thing as coincidence in a murder. Too bad he couldn't be here to talk some sense into Mark Kincaid, who was just as skeptical as his brother Bernie when it came to putting two and two together and convincing himself that the right answer really was five.

So I guessed I'd have to do it myself.

When we got home from the hospital, Hal and Nigel were relaxing on the screened patio with beers in their hands and listening to the Dodgers on the radio. I decided to do a little research at the dining room table with my laptop while Mum emptied the dishwasher, which she'd run that morning. I figured I'd start with Sonia and go from there. But then I realized that I was missing a vital piece of information.

I hit redial. Bernie answered after only two rings. "What is it now, Toni?"

"What's Sonia's date of birth?"

Bernie must have figured he'd get off the phone faster if he just gave me what I wanted, because he didn't object; he just answered the question. "July 4, 1964."

I objected, however. "Oh, come on. Quit kidding around. You know that's my birthday."

"I'm not kidding you," he said. "That really is Sonia's date of birth."

"Next you're going to tell me she was born in England too."

"No, she was born right there in Long Beach, at Memorial."

After we rang off, I called to Mum. "Sonia and I have the same birthday. Are you sure you didn't have identical twins and give one up at birth?"

Mum came to the doorway, dishcloth in hand. "No, kitten. I'm quite sure I'd have known if I had two of you. It isn't the sort of thing one forgets, dear."

Then it occurred to me that Sonia, like me, was swiftly approaching the big five-O, and I was willing to bet she was a lot more pissed off about it than I was.

Mum said, "What are you doing, kitten?"

"I'm just trying to find the people in the passports online, and I thought I'd start with Sonia, since she's an actual person who really exists. So now that I know Sonia's birthdate, maybe I can trace her parents and find a record of her mother's marriage to someone named Carter or Cartwright."

"Or," Mum said, "you could look up Samuel Tobias and come at it from that direction."

At this point, I had an epiphany. Or maybe it was an apostrophe.

In order for Dick to impersonate someone, there had to be someone with the same name around the same age who had died so he could use the same birthdate and Social Security number and show a birth certificate. So all of those names had to be of dead people. We'd have to look at death rolls to find them. And had all of them died in California? It would seem to be statistically impossible for a man to impersonate three other people in the same area without *someone* recognizing him.

I could Google people and get some of that information, but Dick couldn't have done that, because Samuel Tobias Cartwright's passport had been issued in 1980, and the earliest, under the name John Harold McNabb, had been issued in 1968. Google wasn't around until 1998 and wasn't nearly the powerful search engine then that it is now.

Or maybe Mark could just simply ask Sonia what her stepfather's name was and what happened to him. I certainly couldn't do that, but maybe he could.

Then I could find out where the late Susan Mary Carter, or Cartwright, was buried and talk Mark into getting a court order to exhume her to see if she died of arsenic poisoning.

If she was, we'd need to find out who John Harold McNabb and Quentin St. George had married and get them exhumed too.

This was getting spooky. I was having flashbacks to another person I knew who stole the identity of a child who died at age three, killed her entire family, and nearly burned down my house.

"What's the matter, kitten?" my mother asked. "You look as if you've seen a ghost."

"I was just thinking of Tiffany Summers, nee Mary Bernadette Kowalski."

Mum shuddered. "Whatever made you think of her?"

"All of the names on these passports have to be people who have died as children and had their identity stolen. I'd Google them, but they were all born between 1947 and 1952."

"Try," Mum said. "What can it hurt?"

So I started with Richard Alexander Campbell, moved on to Quentin St. George, then Samuel Tobias Cartwright, and finally John Harold McNabb. I didn't find Dick anywhere. I couldn't find Susan Mary Worthington either.

This puzzled me because Quentin St. George actually had a police record. He'd been arrested on suspicion of murdering his wife. Therefore, his wife's name would be in that record. All I had to do was ask Mark Kincaid. Easy-peasy, as Hal said.

This was getting old. Would I ever find a real person in all this mess? What if I Googled Sonia? She had a police record too. But nearly every reference was about the 1920 silent horror film *The Cabinet of Dr. Caligari* and the semi-remake in 1962, *The Cabinet of Caligari.*

I had better luck with Frank Caligari. I found numerous references to a Frank Calegari, a mathematics professor at the University of Chicago.

I also found a website for McNabb Construction, owned by a Bradley D. McNabb. *That must be the construction company that Mark said owned the MacTavish house*, I thought, and then I wondered why in hell they hadn't repaired the dumbwaiter and the cellar stairs.

The website featured a picture of a bright yellow McNabb Construction truck and a head shot of Bradley McNabb himself, bald as a billiard ball, with a truly pissed-off expression on his face. If that was what he looked like while posing for an advertising photo, what must he be like in real life?

I hoped I never had to find out. He might not be too pleased to find me snooping around his property.

By this time, the game had ended, and Hal and Nigel came in to see what I was doing.

I closed out Google and shut the lid of the laptop with a sigh. "Time to go to the library," I announced. "Clearly I'm going to have to resort to newspaper accounts on microfiche. What a horrible thought."

"Wait a minute," Hal said. "Aren't newspaper archives online now? The *Clarion* is. I know that much."

I opened my laptop back up again. "Of course. I can start with the Long Beach *Press Telegram* and branch out to the Los Angeles *Times* if I need to."

I Googled the *Press Telegram* and found a number of sites containing archives. But sadly, every site I tried required me to have a subscription.

"Well, that's a nonstarter," I complained.

"Darling kitten," my mother said, "aren't you forgetting something? *We* have a subscription."

"Of course you do. Why didn't I think of that?" I said. "Okay, what's your username and password?"

"My what, dear?"

"Don't you have digital access to your newspaper? We get digital access to the *Clarion*, and it's included in the cost of a regular subscription."

Mum shrugged. "I have no idea what you're talking about, kitten."

"Would it be okay if I establish a digital account for you?"

"But we don't even have computers, kitten. We'd never use it."

That wasn't strictly true. Mum and Nigel both had smartphones, like Hal and me. But the very thought of trying to read a newspaper article on a cell phone screen made my eyes cross, so I didn't even mention it.

"It won't matter. You'll still get your paper same as you do now."

"Just do it," Nigel said.

So I set up the digital account and wrote down the username and password on a sticky note, which Mum stuck on the bulletin board in the kitchen.

Unfortunately, that was as far as I got. No reports of births, marriages, or deaths prior to 1995 were available.

I consulted my photos of the passports and driver's licenses again.

Dick's latest passport, issued in 2012 under the name Richard Alexander Campbell, gave his date of birth as April 1, 1952—April Fool's Day, which made me I wonder if we were the fools, just chasing our tails.

Samuel Tobias Cartwright's passport, issued in 1980, gave his birthdate as October 15, 1948.

Quentin St. George's passport, issued in 2003, showed that he had been born July 2, 1950.

John Harold McNabb's passport, issued in 1968, gave his birthdate as December 23, 1947.

This was all well and good, but passports don't give Social Security numbers, nor do they give place of birth. They give the state but not the city. All four passports showed California as the place of birth. This was minimally helpful, by virtue of ruling out the other forty-nine states and countless foreign countries, but it still left an awfully large area to cover.

Driver's licenses, on the other hand, contain actual street addresses where these folks lived when they were issued. I already knew that Samuel Tobias Cartwright had lived in Bel Air, but now I knew that John Harold McNabb and Richard Alexander Campbell lived in Long Beach, and Quentin James St. George lived in Huntington Beach.

Which reminded me that I also needed to Google Derek Buchanan, who had pressed charges against Quentin St. George for murdering his mother for her insurance.

If he was still in this area, he could also have somehow found out that Dick was formerly Quentin St. George and killed him, and then stolen all the passports and driver's licenses to cover his tracks.

I found countless Derek Buchanans in every state of the US as well as the UK and Ireland. I found none who were in Long Beach, but on LinkedIn, I found two in the Greater Los Angeles area. One was too young to be the one I was looking for, but the other looked to be about the right age and was listed as a financial professional. Unfortunately, I couldn't find out any more about him without "connecting" with him, and I thought I'd best not do that. Maybe at the library in the morning, I'd find out more.

Dutifully, I entered all this information into the Word document on my laptop. I saved it but didn't log off.

"Mum, did Doris bring any files with her when she moved in?" I asked.

"I don't know, kitten. Why don't you look in her room?"

Mental head slap. Why hadn't I thought of that myself?

Mum stood up and picked up her now-empty wineglass. "Whilst you're doing that, I'll go get dinner on the table."

Hal and Nigel went into the kitchen to get another beer, and soon I heard the television go on.

Doris's room was just the way she left it. Aside from my looking for her pills in her luggage, nothing had been touched.

Doris had hung some clothes in the closet, but her suitcases still lay open on the floor. Their contents were a jumble of underwear and personal items. There was a jewelry box in one of them. It didn't look like she'd had a chance to put anything away.

Maybe I could make up for invading her privacy like this by putting things away for her, so she wouldn't have to do it when she came home from the hospital.

The room Doris occupied had once been mine. Mum and I had moved into the main house after my grandparents died. There was a chest of drawers that should have been empty, and I checked to make sure they were before putting Doris's things neatly into them. I put the jewelry box on top.

I kept going until both suitcases were empty, and I hadn't found any papers.

I closed the suitcases and put them in the closet. That's when I noticed two shoeboxes on the top shelf.

Another mental head slap. Of course!

I lifted them down, set them on top of the dresser, and opened them up. They were full of photographs. No papers.

I put them back up on the shelf. They were probably of Doris and Bob as young marrieds and Vicky as a child, but there might be some clues to be had. Now that I knew they were there, I could look through them later. Maybe I could get Doris to look through them with me when she got home.

When we moved into the main house, Mum had bought me a desk for my room, so I wouldn't have to do my homework on the kitchen table anymore. The desk was still there. It had a file drawer.

Nothing ventured, nothing gained. I opened the file drawer.

Bingo!

It was full of papers. In nice, neat Pendaflex folders. I leafed through some of them and saw that there were insurance policies among them.

We'd hit pay dirt.

I gathered them up, Pendaflex folders and all, and brought them out to the dining room table. "Mum, I found something."

Mum came into the dining room wiping her hands on her apron. "What is all that, kitten?"

"I don't know, but I did see some insurance policies in here; want to go through them with me?"

"Not right now, kitten; dinner's almost ready. You'll have to put that somewhere else for now. Would you set the table for me?"

Once the table was cleared and the dishwasher started, we all gathered to go through Doris's papers. "There are eight folders here," I said. "Why don't we each take two and see what we can find?"

"This seems like a waste of time," Hal said. "If these are Doris's papers, there won't be anything in here she doesn't already know about."

"Because these may be the folders that were in Dick's desk," I said. "The file drawer in Dick's desk is empty. Dick told Doris to stay out of his desk or there'd be hell to pay. What if Doris grabbed the whole contents of that drawer when she left the house?"

"Okay, whatever. Give me two," Hal said, holding out his hand.

"I assume we're looking for insurance policies," Nigel said.

"Among other things," I said. "There might be other legal documents too."

But the only thing of note we found was Doris's life insurance policy from Bob's company—a whole life policy for $500,000.

The beneficiary was Richard Campbell.

Which answered only one of our many questions.

CHAPTER 13

Nothing succeeds like success.

—Alexandre Dumas

The Long Beach Library was on the corner of Thirty-Sixth Street and Atlantic Avenue, just an eight-block walk from the house. When I was in high school, I'd spent hours there, looking through countless references for material with which to craft term papers that would earn a decent grade from Mr. Long, my extremely picky sophomore social studies teacher. They had to be complete with footnotes, which were really difficult when you had to type the whole page over again if you didn't leave enough room for them at the bottom of each page in the first place.

Thanks to Mr. Long, college term papers had been a snap.

Since it was such a nice morning, I decided to walk. I loaded my laptop into my backpack, along with a yellow legal pad and several pens, covered up my bruised face with makeup, and set out. I walked up Lemon Avenue to the corner at Thirty-Sixth, where my friend Sharon used to live, and along Thirty-Sixth to California Avenue, where my friend Annette used to live, to Olive Avenue, where Doris, Bob, and Vicky had lived, and kept going until I reached the side door of the library and slipped inside.

I didn't recognize the librarian, which didn't surprise me. I didn't really expect Mrs. Cole to still be there after all these years. What did surprise me was that the librarian recognized me.

"Toni Day, is that you?"

I racked my brain as I approached the desk, but for the life of me, I couldn't place the shapely blonde who stood behind it with a big, welcoming smile.

"You don't remember me, do you?" she said. "I used to sit next to you in homeroom."

Okay, that would be at Hughes Junior High. Hmm. Who sat next to me in homeroom? Other than that pimply boy who thought it was cool to snatch my purse and paw through it ... Suddenly light dawned. "Diane? Diane Rogers?"

Diane Rogers had been plump, freckled, and mousy brown in seventh grade. She'd had braces on her teeth and worn glasses. No wonder I hadn't recognized her.

She giggled. "It's not Rogers anymore; it's Seligman. I don't blame you for not recognizing me. I've changed a lot. Now, *you*—you haven't changed at all."

"Is that bad or good?"

"Oh, good, of course. I always wished I could have been cute like you. What can I do for you?"

"I need to look at back issues of the *Press Telegram* and the *Los Angeles Times*."

Diane's smile faded. "You know, we're not supposed to let you do that unless you have a library card."

Damn. "I don't. But I used to. Does that count?"

Diane nodded. "Let me look you up." She sat down, pulled the keyboard closer, and began typing. "Let's see. Day. Lots of Days in here. Can't be too many Tonis, though. Hmm. You're not in here."

"How far back does that thing go?"

"We've digitized every library card ever issued here. All the way back to 1888."

"Wow, there have to be thousands of names in there."

"Try millions."

"Try looking under A."

Diane looked up. "A? A for what?"

"I might be in there as Antoinette."

"Antoinette, seriously? I never knew that was your real name."

"I didn't exactly advertise it."

"Here you are. How about I just update this? You don't still live at 3548 Lemon, do you?"

"My mother does. I live in Idaho now."

She looked up again, with a quizzical expression. "Idaho? Whatever for?"

"A job."

"What do you do there?"

"I'm a pathologist at the hospital in Twin Falls."

"Pathologist? You're a doctor?"

I nodded.

"You always did say that was what you wanted to be. So you actually did it, huh? I didn't, obviously, but at least I married a doctor."

Seligman? No, that would be *way* too much of a coincidence. Besides, Dr. Seligman was young enough to be …

"My son's a doctor too," she went on. "He's at St. Mary's." She went back to the keyboard, while I struggled to keep my expression neutral. "If we put on here that you live in Idaho, you'll need to pay sixty dollars a year for this card."

I started to tell her that was okay, as a doctor I could afford that, but then she said, "So I'll just leave your mother's address on here. Are you married? I mean, is your name still Day?"

"I still use my maiden name professionally. My married name is Shapiro."

She glanced up again. "You're Jewish? I never knew that about you either. You didn't go to our temple."

"I'm not. Hal is, but I'm not."

Her eyes narrowed. "Hal Shapiro? That name sounds familiar. What does he do?"

"He's a college professor. He teaches chemistry. I met him at Long Beach State."

"Omigod. You married Dr. Shapiro? That man was a serious hunk."

"He still is."

"Wow. You lucky bum." She hit Enter, and a nearby printer began humming. Diane reached over and extracted a laminated card. "Here's your new library card. Now let me show you how to get at these archives."

She left me with explicit instructions on how to access both the *Press Telegram* and *Times* archives. I was delighted to learn that both newspapers had been archived and digitized all the way back to their inception, which was 1888 for the *Press Telegram* and 1881 for the *Los Angeles Times*.

According to Diane's instructions, all I had to do was type in a name, and every article that contained that name would come up on the screen. I soon discovered that if I did that, I'd get pretty much what I'd gotten with Google. So I narrowed it down by adding dates or locations and what section of the paper it was likely to be in. That worked much better.

By the end of three hours, my eyes were burning, and my neck ached. But I had accumulated a treasure trove of information. My pen was out of ink, and my legal pad was *smoking*.

From the *Press Telegram*, I learned that Sonia Marie Caligari had been born to Susan Mary Worthington and Francesco (Frank) Caligari, July 4, 1964, in Long Beach, which I already knew, but one does have to check.

Richard Alexander Campbell had been born to Jeannette and Alexander Campbell, April 1, 1952, in Lakewood, California, and died at age three of leukemia on December 16, 1955, survived by parents and grandparents, no siblings.

Richard Alexander Campbell and Doris Faye Maxwell had been married at St. Luke's Episcopal Church in Long Beach on February 14, 2014, and would be making their home in Long Beach.

I'd already heard from my mother that Doris and Dick had tied the knot on Valentine's Day and how cloyingly sweet she thought *that* was.

In other news, Quentin James St. George, born to Catherine and Joseph St. George in Burlingame, California, July 2, 1950, had accidentally drowned in the ocean off Mendocino on June 27, 1953. Parents were said to have been distraught. Police found no evidence of foul play. Again, no siblings.

But he magically reappeared fifty years later to marry wealthy widow Gloria Jean Buchanan at St. Barnabas Catholic Church on June 15, 2003. If the pictures on the society page were any indication, it had been a lavish wedding. The bride wore a Balenciaga wedding dress. The happy couple was to honeymoon on the French Riviera and make their home in Huntington Beach.

Gloria Jean St. George passed away after a short illness on November 5, 2005. A lavish funeral was held at St. Barnabas. Friends and family were interviewed and tearfully testified to how sad it was that their idyllic marriage was so tragically cut short. The one discordant note was from the deceased's son, Derek Buchanan, who said there was more to it than met the eye.

As Mark had already told me, it was Derek who had communicated his thoughts to the police, resulting in the grieving widower being questioned by the police, and briefly held on suspicion of murder, in 2006. Quentin St. George disappeared shortly after that, having taken his boat out with the intention of sailing it to Catalina, but he never arrived, and neither the body nor the boat was ever found.

Derek Buchanan had been born May 10, 1969, which made him five years younger than I was. The brief mention of his stepfather being held on suspicion of murder and ultimately released occupied a mere paragraph among the police news in the local section of the *Press Telegram* of November 23, 2005.

Unfortunately, that didn't help me to find out where he was now, but the *Los Angeles Times* of January 13, 2003, contained an ad for the investment company he worked for, which listed all the financial consultants by name. Besides Derek, the list included one Jennifer Buchanan, to whom he may or may not have been related.

From the *Los Angeles Times*, I learned that Samuel Tobias Cartwright, aged three, drowned off the coast of Redondo Beach, California, in a boating accident on July 4, 1951. The Coast Guard had investigated but concluded that it had simply been an unfortunate accident. There had been no other casualties.

Susan Mary Worthington Caligari was wed to wealthy industrialist Winston Welles on Christmas Day 1964 in one of the biggest society weddings of the year. They honeymooned on a privately owned island in the Caribbean before returning to make their home in Beverly Hills. The picture of the happy couple suggested that Winston Welles was old enough to be her father.

That made sense. Bernie had mentioned that Susan's parents had married her off to some friend of theirs who was even wealthier than they were.

Sadly, Winston Welles passed away from lung cancer on April 11, 1980, just in time for the reincarnation of Samuel Tobias Cartwright to rush in and comfort grieving widow Susan Mary Worthington Welles. They were married on June 15, 1980, in Malibu Beach. They were to honeymoon in Tahiti and then make their home in Bel Air.

Susan Mary Worthington Cartwright died at home after a short illness on November 29, 1980, aged thirty-six, survived by her husband, Sam, daughter, Sonia, and her parents. No other children were mentioned.

Samuel T. Cartwright disappeared on January 20, 1981, a suspected suicide, as the decedent had been depressed over the death of his wife.

Sonia would have been only sixteen in January 1981. A junior in high school.

Poor Sonia, I thought. All alone in the world at sixteen. She'd lost both parents within a very short time. Winston Welles had been the only father she'd ever known, but he hadn't seen fit to adopt her. I knew that because her name had still been Caligari when she married Bernie.

Then she lost her mother and was left with a stepfather she didn't know very well, who disappeared less than two months later. Talk about your abandonment issues!

Or maybe she'd abandoned him. Hadn't Bernie mentioned a stepfather she didn't like and that she'd run away from home? Gone to Hollywood to become an actress and had to supplement her income as a prostitute.

I'd been assuming that Sam Cartwright had no use for Sonia once he collected the insurance money and whatever else Susan had left him, but maybe I was wrong. Maybe he did have a use for her. If that was the case, no wonder she ran away.

Jeez. Abandonment issues. Sexual abuse. No wonder Sonia was such a seriously screwed-up individual.

I hadn't been able to find a birth notice, marriage, or obituary for John Harold McNabb.

I did, however, find an article in the *Press Telegram* about a huge health insurance fraud that had bankrupted hundreds of unsuspecting families in the Long Beach area back in 1974. By the time insurance investigators had traced the origins of the scheme back to a certain J. H. McNabb, the man had mysteriously disappeared. His wife, Frances, who had reported him missing, denied any knowledge of the scheme and claimed she had no idea where her husband could possibly have gone.

Some weeks later, a body was found in a cabin up in Big Bear that had burned to the ground. The cabin had been owned by a John H. McNabb. Frances McNabb had denied any knowledge of the cabin. She didn't know her husband had ever purchased one.

The body had never been identified, but since police had been unable to locate Mr. McNabb, the San Bernardino County Sheriff's Department had assumed that the body was his and closed the case. Dental records had been no help since apparently the deceased had never seen a dentist. DNA matching techniques of the present day hadn't been available back then.

I wondered why I'd never heard anything about it until now. I lived here in 1974. Of course, I had been only ten years old at the time, and the case was probably eclipsed by all the hoo-hah about Nixon and Watergate going on at the same time.

Obviously, if he'd recreated himself as Samuel Tobias Cartwright, Quentin James St. George, and Richard Alexander Campbell, he could not have died in that cabin fire, which raised a whole host of other questions.

I returned home with my backpack bulging.

I'd downloaded everything of interest onto my thumb drive and also printed off copies of them so that everyone could read them—especially the wedding articles with pictures of a gradually aging Dick with yet another blushing bride.

Mum had prepared lunch, a delicious crab salad, and we had it with rolls and iced tea at the table in the screened patio since it was such a nice day. While we ate, Hal paged through my legal pad. "So John Harold McNabb disappears in 1974 to avoid prosecution for insurance fraud, and Samuel Tobias Cartwright appears in 1980, disappears in 1981. Then Quentin St George appears in 2003 ... wait a minute. What happened between 1981 and 2003? That's twenty-two years unaccounted for."

"Not only that," Nigel said, "but St. George disappeared in 2005, and Dick didn't show up until this year. That's another nine years unaccounted for."

I reached for a roll. "There were six years between John McNabb and Samuel Cartwright," I said as I buttered it. "It probably took that much time to establish himself in each of his identities, create a background, and acquire the proper documentation, etcetera. He couldn't just appear out of nowhere, as if he was raised in the jungle by wolves."

"So who really died in that fire?" Hal demanded. "Do you think John McNabb killed someone to fake his own death?"

I held up a finger while I swallowed some salad and washed it down with iced tea. "He would have had to," I said, "unless someone just happened to be in the cabin at the time."

"Like who?" Hal asked.

"Like a homeless person trying to keep warm," I said. "Maybe he tried to light the stove or fireplace or something and ended up starting a fire."

"That would be the biggest coincidence in the universe," Hal said. "It would never happen. Unless John McNabb offered the use of his cabin to someone like that and then set the place on fire, which would amount to the same thing."

"Same as what, Hal dear?" Mum asked. "I'm getting confused."

"Same as killing someone," Hal said. "Only it would be someone nobody would miss."

"P'r'aps he had more than one reason to fake his death," Nigel said, buttering a roll. "He was an insurance man, after all. P'r'aps he had his own life heavily insured and hoped to collect."

"Do you suppose maybe that's what his insurance scheme was all about?" Mum suggested. "Funding his own life insurance policy?"

"But who actually got the money?" I asked. "Who was the beneficiary?"

"His wife, most likely," Hal said.

"Okay," I said. "Suppose his wife got the money. Say the insurance company sent her a check. How'd he get it? He couldn't collect it himself. He was supposed to be dead."

"Obviously, his wife would have had to be in on it," Nigel said. "Didn't the police talk to her?"

"I don't know," I said. "Maybe I should ask Mark to look into it."

Hal sighed. "Toni, my dearest love, leave the poor man alone, can't you?"

"I wonder what she'd be doing now," Mum mused. "Assuming she's still alive, that is."

"Why shouldn't she be?" Hal asked. "She'd only be in her late sixties."

I finished my salad and took my plate to the pass-through. "She might not be," I said. "If she was in on the fake death, Dick, or rather John, would have had to share the money with her. What are the chances?"

"You think he killed her so he could have it all?" Mum asked. Her plate was empty, so I picked it up and added it to mine. "Thank you, kitten."

"You're welcome. They couldn't actually live together on it as husband and wife," I said. "Besides, she was a loose end. He couldn't risk having her inadvertently let something slip and blow his cover, could he?"

"Decidedly not," Nigel said. "I think it's much more likely that he did away with her."

Hal refilled his iced tea. "Especially if he'd insured her for the same amount he'd insured himself for."

"That won't work," I objected. "Either he fakes his own death to collect the insurance on his life, or he kills his wife to collect the insurance on her life. He couldn't have it both ways."

"Good point," Nigel said. "Since he had to fake his death to escape the long arm of the law, he couldn't collect his wife's insurance."

"Clearly, he would have had to sneak back and collect the money from his wife before he killed her and morphed into Samuel Tobias Cartwright," I said. "Maybe Mark can look into whether Frances McNabb was killed, or whether she's still alive."

"If she's still alive, she may not be Frances McNabb anymore," Mum said. "She could have remarried. She would have been quite young back then."

Mum got up and cleared the table. "We have some cookies for dessert," she said.

Nigel said, "I'll get them, Fiona. You sit down and relax." He went into the kitchen and moved the dirty dishes from the pass-through to the sink before coming back with the cookies.

I did a quick calculation in my head. If John McNabb had been born in 1947, he would have been only twenty-seven years old in 1974. His wife was probably younger than that.

If Frances McNabb was still alive, she'd only be in her sixties now, like Doris and Dick.

I needed to Google her, I realized. I hadn't done it before because I didn't know her name.

"It's interesting," Mum said, helping herself to a cookie, "that this started out as insurance fraud and segued into killing people for their insurance. I wish I could talk to Doris about it."

"Doris?" Hal echoed. "Why Doris?"

The cookies were chocolate chip, soft and chewy, just the way I liked them, not like anything that comes out of a box. "Mum, did you make these?" I asked.

"Yes, dear. I baked them this morning."

"They're wonderful," I said through a mouthful of crumbs.

"Don't talk with your mouth full, kitten," she said automatically. "When Doris and I were working, Doris's job was in the insurance department. Also, Doris's late husband, Bob, owned an insurance company. Victoria worked there too, during the summers when she was in high school. They both know quite a bit about how insurance works. Doris would have been very interested in this article about the insurance scam. She may even remember when it happened."

I washed down my cookie with a swig of iced tea and reached for another. "Who owns the insurance company now?" I asked.

"Bob's partner," Mum said, "Larry Murphy. Why, dear?"

"Maybe he knows how Dick found out how well insured Doris was."

"Blimey!" Nigel exclaimed. "Spot on, my girl. We hadn't even considered that angle. How did this bloke find his victims in the first place?"

"What company insured the others?" I asked. "Maybe Bob's company insured them all, and somebody in the office was in cahoots with Dick, or John, or whoever he was at the time and gave him a heads-up about well-insured widows."

"Oh dear," Mum said. "I do hope you're wrong about that, kitten. Larry and Louise are such nice people. We've known them for years. We're insured with them ourselves. Would anyone like more iced tea?" She picked up the pitcher and waved it suggestively.

"Me, please," I said and held out my glass. Hal and Nigel did the same, and she filled them before filling her own, emptying the pitcher.

"I'll have to make some more," she said.

"I'll do that, Mum. You've done enough. How old is Larry?" I asked.

"Younger than Bob," Mum replied. "Late fifties, early sixties, perhaps."

"Which insurance were they agents for?" Hal asked.

"Advantage," Mum said. "They deal in all kinds of insurance—life, homeowners, liability, auto, everything but medical."

"Then they couldn't have been involved in this scam back in the seventies because that was medical insurance," I said. I picked up the pitcher and took it into the kitchen with the intention of making more iced tea. I knew exactly how she made it because she'd taught me as a child as soon as I was tall enough to reach everything. Luckily, I could hear everything that was said through the pass-through.

"Thank heavens for that," Mum said. "For a moment there, I thought you were actually going to accuse them of complicity in that dreadful affair."

I filled Mum's teapot with water and put it on the stove to boil. "Did Bob and Larry start that insurance company together?" I asked.

"No, dear. Bob went into partnership with Carl Johnson originally, and when Carl died, it was just Bob and the secretary for several years, and then Larry joined him, I think sometime in the early eighties."

I got a lemon out of the fridge. "Is the secretary still there?" I persisted.

"Oh, yes. Gladys has been there almost as long as Bob. She practically runs the office. Why, she must be getting close to retirement age by now."

"We need to go talk to them," I said.

"Whatever for, kitten?"

I fetched the cutting board from over by the sink, put it on the kitchen table, closer to the pass-through, and sliced the lemon. "Maybe they remember the scam," I said. "I'd love to know more about it. Why don't we go together, and you can introduce me to them?" I started picking seeds out of the lemon slices.

"We have to have a pretext," she told me. "One can't simply waltz into an insurance office and begin interrogating the employees."

"Well, our insurance man is always nagging us to update our homeowner's insurance," Hal said.

"That's true," Nigel said. "We got a letter just this morning to that effect."

"We did?" Mum asked. "Why didn't you tell me?"

I rinsed out the pitcher and put the lemon slices into it.

"We've been a trifle busy, love," Nigel said. "It simply slipped my mind until just now. I'll just go and get it." He rose, came into the kitchen, and retrieved a business-sized envelope from the pile of mail on the ironing board. He took it back out to the patio. Extracting the contents, he went on, "It says something about the replacement value of the contents of the house, that people often underestimate what it would cost to replace everything in one's house if it were to burn down or otherwise be totally destroyed."

"There's your pretext," Hal said.

"Do you need to make an appointment, or can you just walk in?" I asked. "Because if you do, the sooner, the better."

"Yes, dear," Mum said. "I suppose I'd better, if I expect to talk to Larry. Otherwise, we might have to deal with one of the other agents who probably don't know us. That would never do." She rose and came into the kitchen, just as the water began to boil.

I took it off the heat, put six teabags in it, and covered it. Mum smiled her approval, retrieved her cell phone from her purse on the ironing board, and went into the dining room to make the call. I put a quarter-cup of sugar and a tray of ice cubes into the pitcher on top of the lemons.

Mum came back into the kitchen smiling. "Larry can talk to us first thing in the morning, nine o'clock sharp."

I didn't have a chance to respond to that, because my cell phone rang. It was Tyrone.

"Toni? You still want to see that autopsy?"

"Of course," I said eagerly.

"Well, they're doing it at nine tomorrow morning. They're expecting you." He gave me directions to the Los Angeles County Morgue, and we rang off.

I turned to Mum. "Well, this is a fine how-do-you-do," I said. "If I want to see Dick's autopsy, I can't go with you tomorrow."

"No worries," Nigel said comfortably. "I'll go with her. I know how to ask questions too, you know."

That was probably the best solution anyway, I thought, since I tend to piss people off when I ask them questions, something my stepfather was too diplomatic to say.

The tea was ready. I removed the teabags, poured the hot tea over the ice cubes, and put the pitcher in the refrigerator.

Then I Googled Frances McNabb.

I found two likely entries for Frances McNabb, which left me totally confused, because both of them could not possibly be true.

"Well, this is no help," I said in exasperation.

"What isn't?" Hal asked.

"Look at this. Here's an article in the *Santa Cruz Sentinel* about a Frances Diane McNabb, age twenty-six, and Bradley David McNabb, age four, who died when their car went off Pacific Coast Highway and plunged into the ocean just south of Big Sur, on August 29, 1974," I said. "She was predeceased by her husband, John. And here is an obituary from the *San Jose Mercury News* about a Frances Diane McNabb who passed away at age fifty-nine in San Jose, predeceased by husband, John, and survived by son, Brad, who lives in Long Beach."

"Obviously, they can't be the same Frances McNabb," Hal said.

"I know. But what a coincidence that they both had husbands named John and sons named Brad."

"One of which died at age four in 1974, and the other is alive and well and living right here in Long Beach."

"And possibly owns a construction company that probably worked on the MacTavish house, because he owns it," I said. "I wonder who owned it before him."

"That's a good question. How would we go about finding out?" Hal asked. "In Twin, you'd go to City Hall and make a formal request."

"Then you'd have to wait," I objected. "We don't have time to wait."

"Maybe Victoria could help with that," Mum said. "She's the city counsel."

"I didn't know that," I said. "I thought she was in practice with Greg."

"She is, but she does this too."

"That's a terrific idea," I said. "You know what else I'd like to do is look at blueprints for the MacTavish house. That secret staircase has to go somewhere. The house was built right around Prohibition, so there could have been all kinds of secret rooms and passageways for transporting and hiding hooch. Maybe it even has a speakeasy in it."

"Now you're letting your imagination run wild," Hal said.

"I think she's got a point," Nigel said. "Why don't you give Vicky a call?" So I did.

"That's easy," she said. "All that stuff's been digitized, and I can access it on the computer; you don't have to bother with City Hall. I've got some time around four; why don't you just drop by then?"

"Perfect," I said. "Thanks!"

She gave me directions, and we disconnected.

Vicky and Greg's office was on Linden Avenue, not too far from St. Mary's. All we had to do was go down Atlantic past the hospital, turn right on Tenth, turn left on Linden, and go two blocks.

All four of us went because Mum's idea was to visit Doris after we were done with Vicky.

A severe-looking woman with iron-gray hair piled on top of her head and a stiff, high-necked white blouse greeted us at the reception desk and haughtily informed us that Ms. Maxwell Jones was very busy today and would be unable to see us.

"But she told me she had time at four," I protested.

"And you are?"

"Dr. Toni Day."

With that, her demeanor changed as if she had flipped a switch. "Oh, Doctor, of course she has time for *you*," she gushed. "Please, take a seat, and I'll tell her you're here."

We sat down in a group of roomy chairs tastefully upholstered in blue-gray tweed. We only had to wait about thirty seconds before Vicky came out and said, "Come on back."

Vicky's office was nearly as big as Mum's living room. My office at the hospital in Twin would have fit into it four times. The carpet and walls were beige, and the furniture a rich mahogany. Bookcases filled with imposing law tomes lined the walls. Two large windows looked out on Linden Avenue and were shaded by large trees from the afternoon sun. Vicky's desk was L-shaped and large enough for all of us to sit around it and see the two computer monitors at right angles to each other.

"Please, sit," she invited as she walked around the L and sat down in front of the computer. "I did a little research and found out who has owned the house since Dougal MacTavish. Here's a printout you can keep."

"Cool!" I said, accepting it.

"There were only three owners," Vicky said. "Dougal Alexander MacTavish owned it from 1920, when it was built, until he died in 1991. His son, Dougal Jr., commonly known as Doug, inherited it and couldn't pay the taxes, so the county took it over in 2009. Bradley David McNabb bought it at county auction in 2010."

"What happened to Doug?" I asked.

"He was an alcoholic," Vicky said. "Either he died or moved away. Nobody really knows."

"Was he married?" I asked. "Did he have a family?"

"He was married and had a daughter. His wife divorced him and moved away, taking the daughter with her."

"What were their names?"

"Kitten, why are you asking all these questions?" Mum asked. "What difference does it make what their names were?"

I shrugged. "I don't know. I'm just curious."

"His wife was Shirley, and the daughter was Linda," Vicky said. "I really don't know any more about them. I've also accessed the blueprints. Shall we look at them now?"

I folded up the printout and stuck it in my purse, then pulled my chair up as close as I could without blocking everybody else's view. Vicky hit a few keys and made a few mouse clicks, and the blueprints came up, filling both screens.

"Now," Vicky said, "I can move this around any way you want, but it might be hard to stay oriented with it moving on both screens at once. Did you all take your seasick pills?" She turned her head to look at our reaction.

"Uh-oh," I said.

"Oh, dear," Mum said.

Hal and Nigel shrugged.

Vicky laughed. "It won't be that bad. I was just teasing. Now, was there any particular part of this you wanted to see?"

"I need to see where the secret staircase goes," I said. "I was on the second floor in the bedroom directly over the kitchen, and the staircase goes down to the first floor, I think, but it's a dead end."

Vicky clicked a box at the edge of the screen, and the blueprint changed. "Here's the second floor," she said. "Is this the bedroom you were in?"

"Yes," I said. "The staircase is just to the left of the fireplace."

"Here it is," she said. "It shows a door to the left of the fireplace, and a hallway ... no, wait, there are stairs and a landing."

"The stairs turn right off the landing," I said.

She squinted. "I don't see it. Maybe if we go back to the first floor ..." She clicked another box, and the screen changed.

Now I could clearly see the kitchen, with its chimney and a staircase behind it. From the staircase, a door led into a long room behind the fireplace, running the length of the kitchen.

I looked around at my companions. "Do you all see that?"

"There's no room behind the kitchen," Mum said.

"There is according to this," Vicky said. "I'm sure Mom had no idea it was there."

"I know why I couldn't find a door at the bottom," I said. "I was pushing on the wall right in front of me. This looks like the door is in the wall on my right. I need to get in there and find it."

"Oy vey," Hal groaned.

"How big is that room?" Nigel asked.

Vicky peered at the scale. She clicked a box with a plus sign in it, and the picture doubled in size. "According to this scale, it's twelve by twenty-four feet," she said.

I pointed to something I hadn't seen at the previous magnification. "Isn't that another door?"

"Where?"

"Right there. Right opposite the door from the stairs."

"I see it," Hal said. "Hey, it looks like there are stairs leading from it too. Where do they go?"

I was beginning to see, in my mind's eye, a scene developing. "I'm guessing they go to the cellar. The part we can't get into."

Vicky clicked on a box with a minus sign, and the picture returned to its original size. She clicked another box, and the cellar came up—one big empty space, with no wall dividing it.

"I knew it!" I said. "That brick wall isn't original. It was added later."

"Why?" asked Hal.

"I don't know, but there are the stairs and the door."

"You're right," Nigel said. "That is the part blocked off by that wall."

"We've got to get in there," I said. "If we can cut back some of those branches, we can open those cellar doors on the outside."

"It's got to be safer that those stairs," Nigel said.

My mental picture was nearly complete. Bootleggers would bring in the liquor through the cellar doors and take it up the stairs to the speakeasy on the first floor. It's too bad they didn't figure out an easier way to get it up there. Or did they?

"Hey," I said suddenly, "does that dumbwaiter open from the other side?"

"She's right," Nigel said. "We bloody have to get back into that house. I'll give the leftenant a call and arrange it."

CHAPTER 14

As someday it may happen that a victim must be found, I've got a little list, I've got a little list. Of society offenders who might well be underground, And who never would be missed, who never would be missed.

—Sir William Gilbert

Neither Nigel nor Mum nor I felt comfortable driving the Mercedes, so while Mum and Nigel went to see Larry Murphy in Mum's Chevy, Hal offered to drive me into Los Angeles to the county morgue.

I suspected Hal just wanted an excuse to drive the Mercedes on the freeway.

When we arrived, an elderly receptionist greeted us. I told her who I was and whose autopsy I was interested in. There was a computer on her desk, but instead of using it, she took her own sweet time nearsightedly perusing a large ledger on her desk. She finally told me that Dr. Magruder was expecting me in autopsy suite 2, down the hall to the left.

I paused. "Dr. Magruder?"

"Yes," she said, somewhat impatiently. "Dr. Patricia Magruder."

"I wonder if it's Patti," I said to Hal as we walked down the hall toward autopsy suite 2.

"Patti?"

"You remember Patti," I went on. "We were residents together at St. Mary's."

"Oh, that Patti," Hal said.

When I rang the bell outside autopsy suite 2, a young man in scrubs answered the door. "I'm Dr. Day," I told him.

"Toni, is that you?" a voice called out. A tall redhead in the process of tying a plastic apron around her white Tyvek jumpsuit came around the corner. It was indeed Patti Magruder, her luxuriant auburn locks now cut short and showing more than a few strands of white. Otherwise, she didn't seem to have changed at all. She threw her arms around me, hugged me, and then held me away from herself and peered into my face. "What the hell happened to you? Hal, you didn't do that, did you?"

"Not me," Hal said. "Her doppelganger did."

"Who?"

"It's a long story," I told her. "We can talk about it later."

"Okay, if you insist, but I'm not letting you out of here until we do. Do you two want to suit up?"

"Sure, why not?" I said.

"I'll pass," Hal said. "I'll just watch."

"You should at least put on an apron, just in case," I told him. "And some gloves."

"And shoe covers," added Patti. "You never know what's going to drip."

The young man in scrubs, whom Patti introduced to us as Josh, showed us where all the PPE, or personal protective equipment, was located, and showed us where to change. "You both really should suit up with everything," he advised. "You never know what's going to drip, but you also never know what's going to spray or splatter."

Hal made a face but said nothing.

When we emerged from the changing rooms in our Tyvek jumpsuits, plastic aprons, shoe covers, head covers, and face shields, Patti led us into the autopsy room itself, where a sheet-covered body lay on the stainless steel table. We all donned gloves.

Patti pulled back the sheet. There lay Dick, looking worse, if such a thing were possible, than the day I found him. He was also naked.

Hal recoiled. "Oy gevalt!"

Hal was no stranger to autopsies, having helped me with them on occasion at the old hospital, Perrine Memorial, where I had no morgue and was obliged to do them in funeral homes. But this was no ordinary autopsy, and unlike me, Hal hadn't seen the body before today.

Dick's head was completely flattened. His facial features were unrecognizable. The skin over what had once been the forehead was split, and shards of bone protruded from it. One cheek was actually torn away from the cheekbone. More shards protruded from the back of the head, along with some brain matter and blood clot that had become detached and lay on the stainless steel table next to it. A rim of gray hair encircled his head just above the ears, which were also smashed flat and split.

"What did that?" Patti asked.

"A dumbwaiter," I said.

Patti grimaced and turned away.

There were no marks on the rest of the body. Also, he didn't smell nearly as bad as he had in the stairwell.

"We went ahead and retrieved what evidence we could from him and his clothes and bagged everything," Patti said. "He's not embalmed, but he's been refrigerated since he's been here. That's why he doesn't smell."

"I bet he will when we open him up," Hal said.

"Luckily, we have the best ventilation system there is," Patti said. "This room is negatively pressurized. It has to be. We get bodies in here that smell a lot worse than this one, and he was pretty ripe when he got here. We estimated from the amount of skin slippage that he'd been dead about ten days to two weeks."

"When did you get him?" I asked.

"The same day you found him," Patti said. "They brought him straight here, and I took it from there."

"How did you know she found him?" Hal asked.

"These things get around," Patti said with a chuckle. "It's rather unusual to have a body discovered in a secret stairwell by having someone fall on him."

"Toni doesn't do things like anybody else," Hal said, with a wink in my direction.

"You mean *you* were the one who fell on him?" Josh asked in disbelief. "What did you do?"

"I went back up the stairs to get my flashlight so that I could see what I'd fallen on."

"She took pictures," Hal said, "with her cell phone."

"I saw those," Patti said. "Lieutenant Kincaid forwarded them to me. They were surprisingly good, considering the lighting conditions." She propped the head up on a headrest, and with a scalpel made the vertex incision, extending it down behind both ears, just as I always did. Since Patti and I had been trained together, we did everything the same way.

She pulled the skin forward over the forehead and backward down to the neck, using the scalpel to divide any soft tissue attachments to the skull. Josh handed her the Stryker saw, and she made the cut through the bone, making a little tab in front so that she could put the skull cap back on the same way it came off.

The average person wouldn't realize it, but it's surprisingly difficult to get the skullcap back on properly if you don't create a landmark by which to orient it. It's even harder when the skull is damaged as badly as this one was.

She divided the cranial nerves, transected the spinal cord, and lifted the brain free.

The entire posterior aspect, what was left of it, was covered in blood clot, and there were bone fragments sticking into it and into the rest of the brain. Josh photographed it and the inside of the splintered skull before placing it in a bucket of formalin.

The rest of the autopsy was pretty anticlimactic and typical of a somewhat overweight American white male in his sixties. Patti and Josh collected urine and blood and liver tissue for toxicology and tied off the stomach and duodenum to preserve the contents for analysis. Samples of all the organs were placed in formalin for processing later.

After the autopsy was finished and we had removed our protective gear, Patti took us to her office, where she offered us coffee and we accepted.

"Okay, Toni," she said in a tone that brooked no refusal, "give."

"Give what?"

"Don't give me that innocent act, girlfriend. Who gave you that shiner?"

"Her name is Sonia Matthews, and she looks exactly like me. I ran into her in the ladies' room of a restaurant. It turned out she and her husband were seated at a table next to us, and the next thing I knew, she and her husband were fighting about someone who had ruined her marriage to her first husband, and guess who that was?"

"Hmm," Patti said. "I'm guessing that would be you."

"You would be right. So she slapped my face."

"Did you slap her back?"

"No, but I had to physically restrain my mother."

"Attagirl! Then what happened?"

I told her what happened at the restaurant and at the courthouse.

"My God," Patti said. "What on earth did you do to her first husband? Who was he, anyway?"

"Lieutenant Kincaid's brother, Bernie. He's a homicide detective in Twin Falls."

"Did you have an affair with him or what?"

Not quite. "No. He was already divorcing her when I first met him. I had nothing to do with it."

Since I had not yet told Hal what Bernie told me about Sonia's other motive to kill me, I didn't tell Patti either.

"But she thinks you did."

"She's a troublemaker," Hal put in. "She's got quite a rap sheet for drunk and disorderly conduct."

"What does Lieutenant Kincaid think about that?"

"He hates it. Every time she winds up in jail, they call him to deal with her."

"The first time he met Toni, he thought she was Sonia," Hal said. "He was all ready to tear her a new one until his partner convinced him otherwise."

"His partner knew me from high school," I said.

Patti blew out a breath. "Wow. I hope they put her away for a long time."

"Long enough for Hal and me to get back to Idaho, anyway," I said.

"Now tell me how you got involved with this case."

"Okay," I said and gave her the *Reader's Digest* condensed version of what happened to Doris.

"Apparently," I said, "the whole story was a tissue of lies. The cops told us that the house is owned by a Bradley McNabb and that Dick was renting it from him. Doris knew nothing about it. She thought the house was haunted, and she refused to stay there alone, so Mum and Nigel let her stay with them."

"Nice of them," Patti said. "Is she still there?"

"No, she's in the hospital."

"She's being modest," Hal said. "We found a bottle of old rat poison in the basement that was pure white arsenic, and she immediately decided that Dick was poisoning Doris with it."

"Uh-huh," Patti said, "and I'll bet she turned out to be right."

"Well, I had some background to fit that into, because Mum said Doris had been ill with gastrointestinal problems since shortly after they were married. Also, it was a very sudden wedding. Mum said that Dick swept Doris off her feet."

"That's usually how abusive marriages start," Patti said sourly.

Uh-oh, I thought. "Are you and Syd having problems?"

Patti and her life partner, Sydney, an ICU nurse, had been together since residency.

Patti waved a hand negligently. "Oh, no, we're fine. I was just thinking of some of our past cases where men beat their wives to death or women kill their husbands in self-defense. So did Dick abuse Doris that way?"

"No, he just poisoned her," Hal said.

I went into a bit more detail about the psychological and verbal abuse Dick had inflicted upon Doris.

"I see," Patti said. "Why do you think he was poisoning her?"

"For her insurance," I said. "Doris's late husband owned an insurance company and left her very well off. He insured both Doris and himself for a lot of money, and I'm sure that Doris made Dick beneficiary as soon as they tied the knot."

"Tell her about the passports," Hal said.

"Passports?" Patti echoed.

"I found four passports under four different names in Dick's desk," I said, "and three driver's licenses." I gave her the abridged version of the research I'd done. "Not only that, but the earliest one, John McNabb, was involved in a big medical insurance scam back in 1974 and disappeared. As far as the police know, he died in a cabin fire up in Big Bear."

"But ..." Patti began.

"Exactly," I said. "It couldn't have been John McNabb who died in that fire, because he came back as Samuel Cartwright and Quentin St. George and finally as Dick Campbell."

"Well," Hal said, "at least we know he's dead now."

"Maybe," I said. "We still don't know about the DNA."

"Yes, we do," Patti said. "Lieutenant Kincaid told me that the DNA from Dick's personal effects and the blood from the dumbwaiter and from the body match, and the dental records confirmed his identity."

"As Dick Campbell or as one of the other guys?" Hal asked with more than a trace of sarcasm.

"As Dick Campbell, of course," Patti said with a smile.

"I don't imagine he used the same dentist as Quentin St. George or any of his other identities," I said.

"And didn't you say," Patti interjected, "that the wives all died shortly after the wedding from a 'mysterious illness'?"

"Well, at least Mrs. Cartwright and Mrs. St. George did," I said. "But Doris is on the mend, and we don't know what happened to Mrs. McNabb."

Patti pulled a notepad closer and clicked her ballpoint pen. "Tell me again what the wives' names were."

I did so.

"Can you email me the stuff you found?"

"I can do better than that," I said. I rooted around in my purse until I found the thumb drive and handed it to her. "You can download it all off of this right now."

"Girl, you rock." Patti fired up her computer and proceeded to do just that.

"Now you know as much as I do," I said.

"With all this information, we can find out where they're buried, whether they had autopsies, and what the findings were," Patti said.

"I know that Gloria St. George had one," I said, "because her son told the police he thought there was something funny about her death. But the drug screen was negative."

"Didn't they test for heavy metals?" Patti asked. "If they didn't test for them, they'd never know they were there. We'd have to exhume them and test them."

"I know."

"Have you mentioned this to the Long Beach police?"

"She tried," Hal said.

"I showed them the bottle of arsenic," I said. "I told them I thought Doris was suffering from arsenic poisoning."

"They blew her off," Hal said.

I narrowed my eyes at him. "You did too, sweetie."

Hal had the grace to look embarrassed. He cleared his throat and shifted in his chair. "I'm afraid I did," he said, "but now I think she might be on to something."

"Well, since then, Doris ended up in the hospital with very high arsenic levels, and the police are supposed to be testing the Metamucil, but we haven't heard anything. So now we know for sure that at least Dick was trying to poison Doris."

"At least *somebody* was," Patti said. "So who killed Dick?"

"Well, it couldn't have been Doris," Hal said.

"Why couldn't it?" I asked.

"Because she was in the hospital," Patti suggested.

"She wasn't in the hospital when Dick disappeared," I countered. "He'd been gone at least a week when we got here, and she didn't go into the hospital until the day we got here. Which was three days ago. It's not outside the realm of possibility that Doris killed Dick and then reported him missing and moved in with Mum and Nigel."

"She would have needed help," Hal argued. "He was a big guy. No way she could haul him up to the second floor and throw him down the stairwell by herself. Not to mention getting his head into the dumbwaiter in the first place."

"Which begs the question," I said, "of why anyone would go to all the trouble of killing someone with a dumbwaiter in the first place."

"Unless it was an accident," Patti said.

"The fact that the wall panel was put on backward to hide the blood suggests it was murder," I said.

"Or to hide his identity," Patti said. "It would mess up dental identification. Of course, there's always DNA, so why bother?"

"Well, if Doris couldn't kill Dick by herself, Sonia couldn't have either," I said. "She's no bigger than I am."

"Well, at least she has a husband," Hal countered. "He could have helped."

"Wait a minute," Patti said. "What's Sonia got to do with this case?"

"Sonia," I said, "is Samuel Cartwright's stepdaughter. Susan Cartwright was her mother. Sonia was the product of her first marriage."

"But why do you think she had any reason to kill Dick?" Patti asked.

I gave her a brief synopsis of the abandonment and sexual abuse scenario.

"I see that Sonia would have a motive to kill Dick," Patti agreed, "but why would she come after you? How would she know you were there in the first place?"

"She'd know somebody was there because she'd have seen Mum's car," I said. "Maybe she came back to clean up evidence and panicked. She probably had no idea who it was that she shut up in the secret staircase. All I know is that Hal and Nigel saw a neon-green Volkswagen coming down the lane from the MacTavish house when they were coming to get me out of the stairwell, and Sonia's husband drives a neon-green Volkswagen."

"So you think Sonia and her husband were in the house while you were there?"

"I think *somebody* was in the house with me. I think somebody pushed the door shut on me and locked me in the stairwell with the corpse, and I know for sure that somebody stole the passports and driver's licenses."

"Luckily she took pictures of them," Hal said.

"I should say so," Patti said. "What are you going to do now?"

We didn't get a chance to answer that question because Josh stuck his head around the door to tell Patti that another body had come in.

Jane Bennett Munro

So we left, after retrieving my thumb drive and vowing to keep each other posted.

In the car, Hal turned to me and said, "So what are we going to do now?"

"Go home and see what Mum and Nigel found out."

"I need a drink and a shower," Hal said. "Not necessarily in that order."

"And we should go see Doris," I said. "Maybe she's more alert today."

"In that case," Hal said, "the drinks can wait."

CHAPTER 15

Much water goeth by the mill
That the miller knoweth not of.

—John Heywood

Mum and Nigel were still not home when we got there, so I called Mum's cell. "We're home, and you're not."

"We're having lunch at the Foster's Freeze right across from the library. Can you join us?"

I covered the receiver and looked at Hal. "They want us to join them for lunch."

"Right now?"

"Yes, right now."

"Okay," he said. "I guess we don't smell *that* bad."

"We shouldn't. We were covered from head to toe." I uncovered the receiver. "Okay. We'll be right there."

By the time we got there, Mum and Nigel had already gotten their orders. They were sitting in a corner booth by the windows. The same jukebox that had been on the table when I was in eighth grade was still there, but the vinyl on the seat was new. We slid into the booth with them. "So how'd it go?" I asked without preamble.

"And hello to you too, kitten," my mother said reprovingly.

"Sorry. Hello, Mum. Hello, Nigel."

The waitress came over to take our orders. Hal ordered a bacon cheeseburger with fries, and I ordered the same thing I had always ordered ever since Mum and I had gone there every Friday night for supper when I was in school; a Swissburger and a hot fudge sundae made with soft ice cream.

After the waitress left, I said again, "So how'd it go?"

"We upgraded our homeowner's insurance," Mum said with a twinkle in her green eyes.

"And?"

"We put an inflation rider on it so that it would upgrade itself along with the inflation rate."

"Mum!"

By now, Mum was laughing. Nigel took over the narrative. "Your mother is just teasing you, old dear. We also learned more than we ever wanted to know about insurance scams."

"Do tell."

"Insurance companies have to be licensed by the state in which they operate," Nigel said. "They have to comply with consumer protections, such as having standards by which they are solvent enough to pay the claims of the people who are insured with them. They also have state guaranty funds as a safety net in case of insolvency."

"That makes sense," Hal said.

"But insurance scammers don't worry about such mundane things," Nigel went on. "They offer a low-priced comprehensive plan and don't worry about preexisting conditions or physical examinations. They claim they have group purchasing agreements and can negotiate lower prices from insurance companies. They also claim that their plans are exempt from state insurance laws. And they use marketing techniques that look legitimate. And they actually pay promptly on their small claims so that people will be lulled into a false sense of security. But they delay or deny payment on the large claims."

"So people would be on the hook for their medical bills out of pocket," Mum said. "They could lose their homes. They could be forced into bankruptcy. That's what happened with the McNabb scam."

"So did Larry actually know about that scam by name?" I asked. "Interesting."

"Not really, dear," Mum said. "People who deal with insurance have to know their history."

"But aren't there regulations for preventing such things?" Hal asked.

"There are now, but there weren't back then," Mum said. "The Employee Retirement Income Security Act was passed in 1974. That's ERISA for short. Its purpose was to provide federal regulation of employee benefits, which includes medical insurance. In 1982, Congress gave it authority to regulate group purchasing arrangements, and that got rid of most of the scams."

Our food arrived. We suspended the conversation until the waitress had served us and gone back to the kitchen, after which we busied ourselves with making sure everybody got what they had ordered and that we all had napkins and utensils with which to eat it.

I took a giant bite of my Swissburger and moaned with pleasure. Hal did the same with his cheeseburger and wiped ketchup off with a napkin.

"Antoinette, you don't have to eat that whole thing in one bite," my mother said reprovingly.

"Sorry," I said, as soon as my mouth was empty. "Where were we?"

Mum delicately dabbed at her lips with a napkin. "McNabb, dear. ERISA. 1974."

"Right," Hal remarked. "McNabb disappeared in 1974. By then, all the damage was done."

"Did Bob or Larry ever actually meet John McNabb?" I asked.

"Larry said that Bob may have, but he never did," Nigel said. "He didn't join Bob Maxwell until the early eighties sometime."

"Did he know what happened to Mrs. McNabb?"

"No, but Gladys did," Mum said. "Gladys said she actually knew Frances McNabb. She moved away right after her husband died and remarried. She died a few years ago."

"Did she and Gladys stay in touch all those years?" I asked.

"Well, they must have," Mum said. "How else would Gladys know these things?"

How else indeed. "So who told Gladys she had died?"

"Her son."

"Frances McNabb had a son?"

"Yes. I think Gladys said his name was Brad."

"We already knew that," Hal said.

The door behind us opened, startling me. I turned to see who had come in. A man with a mullet and a woman with short, curly black hair were being seated in a booth on the other side of the room. I tensed.

Hal noticed. "What's wrong, sweetie?"

"I think Sonia and her husband are here," I hissed.

Jane Bennett Munro

"What are you two whispering about?" Mum asked.

"Toni thinks Sonia and her husband just came in," Hal told her.

From where she was sitting, Mum could see the booth across the room without turning around. "That's not Sonia, kitten. Why are you so upset?"

I couldn't tell her, not now, not here in a public place. "I just don't want another scene like the last one," I said.

"Well, it's not Sonia, so let's not worry about it," Hal advised. "Now, where were we?"

"Mark Kincaid told me that the owner of the MacTavish house is Bradley D. McNabb, who owns a construction company," I said.

"But if she remarried," Hal said, dipping a fry in ketchup, "her name wouldn't be McNabb anymore." He popped it into his mouth.

"Oh, dear," Mum said. "I don't think Gladys mentioned Frances's new married name."

"Where did she move to?" I asked, before taking another bite of Swissburger.

"She said somewhere in Northern California, near San Francisco," Nigel said. "San Jose? Does that sound right, Fiona?"

"I think so," Mum said.

That explained why there was no wedding announcement or death notice for Frances and no birth notice for Bradley in the local papers. There wouldn't be if she moved to Northern California. And it went along with one of the two funeral announcements we found online.

"When did Gladys come to work for Bob?" I asked.

"Larry wasn't quite sure," Nigel said. "It was before his time, but he thought it was in the mid-seventies. Gladys said she'd been in that office nearly forty years and knew where all the bodies were buried. Her words."

"That sounds like 1974 to me," I said. "Did she specify which bodies she was referring to?"

The man in the booth behind me coughed.

Hal said sotto voce, "Maybe you better keep your voice down. People are listening."

I shivered in the warm restaurant.

"Whatever are you talking about, kitten?"

"Well, I know they insured Doris," I said, keeping my voice down, "but what about Susan Mary Cartwright and Gloria St. George?"

"I asked about that too," Nigel said, "but they have these pesky privacy policies that prevent them from telling us. Rather like your HIPAA, y'know. So the police will have to get a warrant if they wish to get that information."

"Well, that pretty much takes care of the insurance angle," Hal said. "What do we do now?"

"Talk to Doris," Mum said. "We haven't visited her yet today."

Doris was sitting up in bed when we got there, having just finished her lunch. She greeted us with a smile, clear eyes, and pink cheeks. The gray look was gone.

"I'm feeling so much better," she said. "You have no idea! Dr. Connors says my arsenic levels have come way down and I can go home tomorrow."

"Darling, that is such good news," Mum said, giving her a hug.

Nigel harrumphed and said, "Jolly good."

"Doris, can we talk about insurance?" I asked her.

"Geez, sweetie, nothing like cutting right to the chase," Hal said. "Give her a chance to catch her breath, why don't you?"

"It's okay, honey," Doris said. "What is it about insurance you want to know? Is it about my insurance, because I did change the beneficiary when I married Dick, you know."

I pulled a chair up to the bedside and sat down, endeavoring to maintain a straight face, because I already knew that from snooping in her private papers. "I found an article about a big insurance scam back in the seventies," I began. "Medical insurance."

Doris's eyes narrowed. "That wouldn't happen to be the McNabb case, would it?"

"How did you know?" I asked.

Doris laughed. "What else could it be? That was the biggest insurance scam to hit California in the last hundred years. You know, John McNabb worked for Bobby and Carl way back in the day when they first started out. Good-looking devil. Quite the ladies' man with the girls in the office. He was a less-than-satisfactory employee, Bobby said. Wouldn't do things by the book. Always taking shortcuts. Failed his licensing exam. They fired him. He threatened to start up his own company and put them out of business."

"Wow. Good riddance," I said.

"You got that right. We didn't hear any more about him until all hell broke loose over that scam. Then we heard he'd died, and that's all I know."

"Actually, he didn't," I said.

Doris frowned. "But the papers said ..."

"He died but not back then," I explained. "He died just a couple of weeks ago when a dumbwaiter fell on his head."

Doris was momentarily speechless.

"Antoinette, really!" Mum exclaimed

"That's our Toni," Nigel said. "Always rushing in where angels fear to tread. Couldn't you just sort of ease into it instead of bashing her over the head with it?"

Doris burst out laughing.

A nurse came in. "What's going on here?"

"She's had a bit of a shock," I said, "and I'm afraid it's my fault."

The nurse looked at the monitor, checked the IV, and looked at Doris's pupils with a penlight. "Everything seems to be all right," she said, "but maybe you folks better leave and let her get some rest."

Doris was still laughing.

"What is so funny?" Mum asked her.

Doris controlled her mirth with difficulty. "It couldn't have happened to a nicer guy," she said when she could get her breath.

I giggled all the way down the hall. In the elevator, Mum shook her head and said, "I'm not sure how I was expecting her to react, but it certainly wasn't like that!"

"I do hope she won't do that at the funeral," Nigel said. "It wouldn't be seemly."

"Toni, stop it," Hal said. "What's the matter with you?"

"Do you remember that episode of the *Mary Tyler Moore* show when Chuckles the Clown died?"

"You mean the one where Mary laughed herself sick at the funeral?"

That was it; but I wasn't feeling so amused when we got out to the car.

As I was getting into the back seat with Mum, I noticed a petite woman with short, curly black hair getting into a neon-green Volkswagen one row over and felt a frisson of fear. I slammed the door and hunkered down, hoping she hadn't seen me.

That absolutely had to be Sonia. What was she doing here? Was she following me?

"Kitten, what are you doing?"

"Sonia's here," I said.

Hal looked back as he backed out of the parking space. "Toni, you're seeing things. That was the same woman that we saw at Foster's Freeze."

Mum put her hand on my arm. "Kitten, you're shaking. What are you so scared of?"

I sighed. "Sonia. I think she's trying to kill me."

"She was drunk when she said that," Hal said.

"She said it at the arraignment too."

"She was probably hungover," Nigel said. "Besides, you don't really think she'd kill you over that business with Bernie, do you? That would be a bit much."

There was that British understatement again. The time had come. I had to come clean with my family and damn the consequences.

"That's not all there is to it," I said. "When I talked to Bernie, he said that if I hadn't called him, he would have called me."

"I'll believe that when I see it," Hal scoffed.

"He would have called me," I continued, "because his brother called him. Mark told Bernie that Sonia had figured out that I suspected her of killing Dick, and she's trying to prevent me from telling the cops. That's why she locked me in the staircase and stole the passports."

"So how'd Mark find out about it if she didn't tell the cops?" Hal asked. "*He's* the cops."

"She didn't. She told her husband."

"Who told Mark," Nigel said. "Well. That does make the cheese more binding. And by the way, locking you in that staircase could be construed as attempted murder."

"That explains why you're seeing Sonia everywhere," Hal said. "She has a real motive to get you out of the way."

"Don't worry, old girl," Nigel said. "We'll soon be home and dry."

At home, Hal and I finally got our showers and our drinks, in that order. While Hal, Nigel, and I relaxed on the screened-in patio, Mum went into the kitchen and began to prepare dinner.

"Right, then," Nigel said. "What have we learned today?"

"I was just thinking," I said. "When you accused me of bashing Doris over the head, it made me wonder why it was necessary to go to all that trouble with the dumbwaiter when all one needed to do was bash Dick over the head."

"Have you forgotten our Caribbean cruise?" Hal asked. "Why our killer went to all the trouble to crush the body on the roof?"

"To hide a ligature mark," I said.

"A very recognizable ligature mark," Nigel said. "Are you suggesting that Dick was first bashed in the head with something that would leave a recognizable mark on the skull?"

"It's possible, isn't it? Maybe I should call Patti and suggest that she take a closer look at the scalp and the skull fragments just in case."

"We should also look in Dick's basement for some kind of tool he could use to do that," Hal said. "Maybe it still has Dick's blood on it."

"It would make more sense to wait until Patti finds a mark and then try to find something to match it," I said.

"Then I suggest you call her straightaway," Nigel said, "and get her going on that, eh what?"

I allowed as how that made a lot of sense and went into the kitchen where I'd left my purse on the ironing board. Mum appeared to have dinner preparations well in hand. Four steak filets lay defrosting on the drain board by the sink. A head of lettuce, a tomato, a red onion, and an avocado sat on the cutting board next to a salad bowl. Mum looked up from putting the finishing touches on a baking dish of macaroni and cheese. "What now, kitten?"

I extricated my smartphone from my purse. "I need to call Patti," I explained. "I want her to take a closer look at Dick's head and see whether he was bashed over the head before it was flattened by the dumbwaiter."

Mum made a face. "Really, darling, I do wish you could be less graphic. It's terribly off-putting."

"Sorry," I said and went back to the patio.

Patti was still at the morgue when I called. "What's up, Toni?"

"We're trying to figure out how someone could get Dick into the dumbwaiter in the first place. He'd have to be subdued first, wouldn't he?"

"I'm way ahead of you," she said. "I got our bone expert to reconstruct the skull, and she found an area on the back of the head where the bone was depressed and fragmented, as if it had been hit with a blunt object."

"You mean like a hammer or an ax?"

"It was a rectangular area about six centimeters long and maybe one centimeter wide, so it couldn't have been a hammer, and the skin over it was lacerated, not cut, so it couldn't have been an ax, unless he was hit with the backside of the ax instead of the sharp edge. But she said that the depression had rounded edges, not sharp like you'd expect from the back of an ax."

"Did she have any ideas on what it could have been?"

"She thought maybe a golf club or a hockey stick, something like that."

Suddenly I had a flashback to the day we looked for blood in the trunk of Dick's car. "Dick had a golf bag in his car. We need to look at the clubs! Thanks, Patti! You rock."

"I've sent the report to Lt. Kincaid. He can take care of that. And I sent you pictures. Don't let your mom see them."

"Thanks," I said again, and we rang off.

"Now what?" asked Hal.

"Patti got their bone expert to reconstruct Dick's skull, and they found a mark on the bone showing that he'd been hit on the head with something like a golf club before he was put into the dumbwaiter."

"Jesus," Hal said. "What for?"

"Dick was a pretty big guy, and our suspects are all women. Not only would Dick have to be subdued somehow, but there would have to be at least one other person involved. They'd need help getting Dick's head into the dumbwaiter and holding him in place while someone else released the car so it would fall on him."

"They might need two more people to do all that," Hal said. "But why do you say 'all our suspects'? We only have Sonia."

"What about Doris?"

"You were serious about that?" Hal asked.

Mum came out onto the patio with a glass of wine in her hand. "Kitten, you can't be serious about suspecting Doris. As sick as she's been, she couldn't possibly …"

"She could if she had help," I said.

"Who would help her do such a thing?" Mum demanded. "The only people who would *possibly* want to do that would be Victoria and …"

"Don't say it, Fiona," Nigel said. "Don't even go there."

"Okay," I said. "We won't even consider Doris."

Mum lay back in her chaise longue with a sigh. "Thank you, kitten."

"We won't consider Vicky either," I said. "Although she would have help. She has a husband."

"Nonsense, dear," Mum said. "They're both lawyers."

"Lawyers commit crimes too," I argued. "Although they're usually not quite this messy."

"So I guess we're back to just Sonia," Hal said. "She has a husband too."

"We're forgetting something," I said, stricken by a sudden thought. "What about Derek Buchanan?"

"Who?" Hal asked.

"Gloria St. George's son," I explained. "You know, the one who accused his stepfather of murdering his mother. He's got a motive too, especially because the police couldn't put the guy away."

"You don't know that he's even still in this area," Hal objected.

"He's in Los Angeles," I said. "He's a financial consultant for an investment company."

"Then he probably doesn't know anything about this," Hal said. "So we're right back to where we were."

"Unless," I mused, "Frances McNabb is still around."

"Whatever made you think of her, kitten?" Mum asked. "Surely she's dead. Didn't you say that her husband would have had to kill her because she's a loose end? And what about those funeral announcements you found?"

"They could both be false, for all we know."

"So what do we do now?" Hal asked. "Go to the police?"

"Speaking for Scotland Yard," Nigel said, "the police would probably tell you to hire a private detective."

"Well, this is pure speculation," I said, "and you're all going to tell me I'm reaching, but what if Frances McNabb is working right now in Bob's office under an assumed name?"

"You're reaching," Hal said.

"That is a bit of a stretch," Nigel agreed.

"Well, think about it," I said. "John McNabb worked for Bob."

"Surely Bob would have met Frances at some point," Mum said.

"Maybe he wasn't married at the time," I said. "Didn't Doris say he was always chasing the office girls?"

"For some men, it would make no difference whether they were married or not," Nigel said.

"It might make a difference to the office girls," Mum said tartly.

"Okay, so let's assume for the purpose of this discussion that either John McNabb wasn't married or that if he was married, nobody in the office knew it. So nobody in the office had ever met Frances."

"Okay, let's assume that," Hal said, "for the purpose of this fantasy of yours."

"Okay," I said. "So John McNabb was said to have died in 1974, but we know he didn't because he reincarnated himself as Samuel Tobias Cartwright for the purpose of marrying wealthy widow Susan Mary Worthington Welles. How did he know when and where to make his appearance?"

"Are you suggesting that he had an accomplice with inside information?" Nigel asked. "Such as a secret'ry in the insurance office that insured her?"

"Aren't you forgetting something, kitten?" my mother asked. "She was his wife. And she was trying to marry him off to another woman? I find that incomprehensible. How could she do that?"

"Well, if he had life insurance, his wife would have to get the insurance money for his supposed death," I continued.

Hal interrupted. "After which he killed her so she couldn't squeal on him."

"Or," I said, "maybe she pulled a Scheherazade act on him."

"A what?"

"Scheherazade, Hal dear," Mum said. "From *1001 Arabian Nights*. She was a slave girl who told stories to the sheik so that he wouldn't kill her."

"What I'm suggesting," I said, "is that maybe this whole conspiracy was her idea. Since he was supposed to be dead, they couldn't actually live together, so she proposed that she would go to work in an insurance office under an alias, and he would reinvent himself as somebody else, and whenever some heavily insured man passed on, she would hook him up with the widow. They'd get married, and then after a couple of months, he'd poison her, collect her insurance, and disappear."

Hal stood up and applauded. "Bravo, sweetie. I'm impressed. What an imagination you have. You're also out of your ever-lovin' mind." He sat back down. "Are you seriously suggesting that she just sat by while he married and poisoned three different women?"

"Okay, maybe it's a little far-fetched," I conceded, "but if she made herself indispensable to him in some way, he wouldn't want to kill her. Especially if it meant getting even more money."

Hal turned up his palms. "How long was this supposed to go on? Because they're both in their sixties now, assuming she's still alive."

"They're retirement age. Maybe it would have stopped with Doris," Mum said.

"Possibly," Nigel said. "It's stopped now in any case."

"Because he died, and she didn't," I said. "If Frances McNabb is still around, she's probably royally pissed at being cheated out of Doris's insurance by whoever killed Dick."

"She's probably pissed at you too," Hal said, "for finding out about the arsenic before it had a chance to kill Doris."

"Thanks a lot, bub," I retorted. "Now how am I supposed to sleep at night?"

"Wait a minute, kitten," Mum said. "Bob and Doris had their insurance with Bob's company. Whoever told Dick that Doris was a wealthy widow had to work in Bob's office."

"But we don't know who insured Susan Cartwright or Gloria St. George," I said.

"And we won't, as long as they have those privacy policies," Hal said.

"Right then. So if we suppose that they were all insured by different insurance companies," Nigel said, "there would have to be somebody who worked in all three companies at the right time. Is there anyone at Bob's company who was hired between Gloria St. John's death and Bob's?"

"When did Gloria die?" Mum asked.

I sorted through my notes. "She died in November 2005."

"So all we have to do," Hal said, "is ask them who was hired after that."

"Not so fast," Nigel said. "What makes you think they would tell you?"

"What you're saying," I said, "is that we need a warrant."

"Back to square one," Hal said with disgust. "You know, if we knew who insured Susan and Gloria, we wouldn't need to know who's been hired since 2005. But we can't find out who insured them without a warrant either."

"If we were to find out that Susan and Gloria were both insured by Bob's company," I said, "then we'd know. There's only one person who's worked there for all that time."

"Who?" asked Hal.

"Gladys."

"Surely not," Mum objected. "Kitten, you can't possibly suspect Gladys. Why, I've known her for years. She couldn't possibly kill anyone."

"I'm not suspecting her of being the killer," I said. "I'm suggesting that perhaps she introduced her husband to Doris. He did the rest."

"But the fact remains," Nigel said, "that without knowing who insured the other two victims, we're dead in the water."

"Besides," Hal said, "she'd need help to kill Dick too. Not only is she a woman, but she's getting on in years."

"I wish I'd taken Dick's computer before the police got there," I said ruefully.

"It's a good job you didn't," Nigel said. "That would be tampering with evidence. You could go to jail for that."

CHAPTER 16

Heaven has no rage like love to hatred turned,
Nor hell a fury like a woman scorned.

—William Congreve

I awoke just after dawn, my mind already focused on the case. I stretched, yawned, and got quietly out of bed to avoid waking Hal up. After I took care of business in the bathroom, I went into Mum's kitchen to make coffee. I was surprised to see that Mum's car wasn't in the carport.

A note pinned to the bulletin board in the kitchen said that they had gone to pick up Doris from the hospital. So I took my coffee and my book out on the screened-in patio to wait, either for Hal to get up or Mum and Nigel to return with Doris.

I'd gotten completely immersed in the escapades of Lord Peter Wimsey when two things happened simultaneously.

Hal came out on the patio with his coffee, and the car pulled into the carport.

"What's going on?" Hal asked.

"Doris is home," I said unnecessarily.

Nigel had gotten out of the car and was assisting Doris out of the back seat. When she stood up to her full height, I saw that she had lost a noticeable amount of weight. She hadn't been any too heavy to start with, and now she was practically skeletal. She walked slowly and clung to Nigel's arm as he guided her through the screen door.

Jane Bennett Munro

She sank into one of the chaise longues with a sigh. "Hey, you kids, what are you up to?"

"You don't want to know," Nigel said dryly. He went back out to the car, opened the trunk, and retrieved a large plastic sack. "Shall I put this in your room, Doris?"

"I suppose," she said. "I don't know as I need any of it; it's just the stuff from the hospital that I used. Since I paid for it, I may as well have it."

"How are you feeling?" I asked.

"I feel terrific," she said. "But I'm weak as a kitten after lying in that hospital bed for, what, four days?"

"Five," Hal said. "But who's counting?"

Mum poked her head out the pass-through. "Doris, would you like some coffee?"

"I sure would," Doris said. "I think I'm suffering from withdrawal. They wouldn't let me have anything but decaf in the hospital."

"We would too," I said. "Ours is all gone."

"Here's the pot," Mum said, "and some extra cups. We'll be right out." She placed the pot and three cups on the pass-through shelf, and I got up and retrieved them. By the time I'd poured five cups of coffee, Mum and Nigel had made themselves comfortable.

"Do you want something to eat?" I asked Doris.

"Oh, no, honey. I had breakfast at the hospital, such as it was. Now, please tell me what's been going on around here. I know that Dick is dead, and I know that you found him, Toni, but what's all this about John McNabb?"

"I tried to explain it to her," Mum said, "but apparently I didn't do it very well."

"First, let us express our condolences," Hal said.

"Oh, don't worry about that," Doris said, waving a hand negligently. "If Dick was the one making all those spooky noises and moving things around to make me think the house was haunted, and poisoning me with arsenic on top of that, I'm glad to be rid of him. My daughter tells me that you're the one who nagged my doctors into treating me for arsenic poisoning in the first place. She says you saved my life. Thank you, sweetheart."

"You're welcome."

"But now it seems that he wasn't really Dick Campbell at all. That's what I'm having trouble wrapping my head around."

I picked up my cell phone and moved my chair over next to Doris. "A picture is worth a thousand words," I said, "so here are some pictures I took inside your house. Oh, and by the way, turns out it isn't really your house. Lieutenant Kincaid told us that the MacTavish house belongs to Bradley McNabb, and Dick was only renting."

"So I could go back there if I wanted to," Doris said. "Not that I particularly want to. I don't have good memories of that place."

"Well, at least we know now that it's not haunted," I said.

"I wish I could just go back to my own little house," Doris said.

"We'll get a Realtor working on it," Nigel said. "Just as soon as you feel up to looking."

"The sooner the better," Doris said. "Not that I haven't enjoyed being here, but I'm sure I've worn out my welcome."

"It's all right, dear," Mum said. "Don't give it another thought."

Nigel stood up. "I'll get on it straightaway," he said and went into the house.

"Now that that's taken care of," Doris said, "what about those pictures?"

"Don't show her the ones of Dick, please, kitten," Mum begged.

"I'm not," I assured her. "Just the passports. Doris, I found four passports and three driver's licenses in the rolltop desk in the kitchen. They were all Dick but under three other names. This one here is John McNabb."

"Yes, I recognize him. You know, I always thought it was odd that Dick had no pictures of himself as a young man."

"That's because he wasn't Dick then. The newspaper article I read said he died in a cabin fire up in Big Bear, but obviously he didn't because here he is as Samuel Tobias Cartwright."

"Well, then, who was it that died up there instead?" Doris asked. "Did they recover a body?"

"They did, but it was burned beyond recognition. The police just assumed it was John because he owned the cabin. The dental records didn't help, and they couldn't do DNA back then like they can now."

"Could they do it now? If they exhumed the body?"

"Maybe, if the body was buried and not cremated," I said. "The problem would be finding anything to match it to, and we already know that it wasn't John McNabb. It could be anybody. What would be the point?"

"Yeah, I guess you're right," Doris conceded. "What did Samuel Tobias Cartwright do?"

"He married a wealthy young widow named Susan Mary Worthington Welles. She had a daughter by her first husband, whom she divorced prior to marrying Winston Welles, who was very wealthy indeed. The daughter ran away from home when her mom married Cartwright, and we now know her as Sonia Matthews. She's the one who gave me this black eye."

Doris looked sharply at me, eyes narrowed. She put her hands on either side of my face and turned it this way and that, trying to get the best light. Finally, she said, "By golly, you do have a shiner. I couldn't see anything at first."

"It's fading," I said.

"Yes, and your chin is green."

"I know."

"So what's this Sonia got against you?"

I decided not to tell Doris just yet what Sonia's real motive was. "She thinks I broke up her marriage."

"Did you?"

"No, of course not. Bernie was already divorced when I first met him."

"Now who's Bernie?"

"A cop I know in Twin Falls. He's my son-in-law's partner. He's Lieutenant Kincaid's brother."

"What Toni isn't telling you," Hal put in, "is that Sonia looks identical to her. They could be twins."

"I'm not sure if that has anything to do with it," I said. "The main thing is that Susan Cartwright died of a so-called mysterious illness just a few months after the marriage."

"Something like *my* mysterious illness?"

"Probably exactly like it."

"What happened to Samuel?"

"He disappeared. A suspected suicide, they said, because he had been despondent over his wife's death."

"But there was never a body," Doris guessed.

"Well, no, because otherwise he couldn't morph into Quentin St. George."

Doris peered at the passport picture. "He does look like a younger Dick—with more hair and a moustache."

"Quentin St. George married a wealthy widow named Gloria Buchanan, who also died mysteriously a few months after the wedding."

"And then he disappeared?"

"Not right away, because Gloria's son Derek Buchanan went to the police and asked them to investigate because he was suspicious that his mom had not died a natural death. So Quentin was arrested and held on a suspected murder charge while an autopsy was done, but it didn't show anything. Toxicology was negative. So Quentin was released, but now he has a rap sheet. He's in the system."

"How could toxicology be negative if she was poisoned with arsenic?"

"Because toxicology only tests for drugs. They didn't test for heavy metals, so they didn't find arsenic."

"Hmph. Sounds to me like those two need to be exhumed and tested," Doris stated.

Nigel, returning from the kitchen where he'd been on the phone through this whole conversation, said, "Good luck with that. The police hate exhumations. They cause a fearful kerfuffle with the family. The county medical examiner would have to request it."

"I bet she already has," Hal said. "She and Toni talked about it."

Nigel frowned. "When?"

"She did the autopsy on Dick," I said. "It's my friend Patti Magruder. We were residents together at St. Mary's."

"Toni has connections everywhere," Hal said.

As if she had heard me mention her name, Patti chose that exact moment to call me back. "Toni? We found something."

"You did? Just a minute while I get out of earshot." I excused myself and went into the living room, the one place where nobody on the patio could hear me. "Okay, shoot."

"We've found out where Susan Cartwright and Gloria St. George are buried. I've sent in a request for exhumation. Now it's up to the Superior Court of Los Angeles County. But I've gotta tell you—the chances aren't good. So far, the police aren't investigating the murder of either woman. They're investigating Dick's murder."

"What if they reopen the investigation of Gloria St. George's suspicious death that Derek Buchanan started?"

"Well, maybe," she said. "But don't get your hopes up."

We disconnected, and I came back to the patio just in time to hear Nigel say, "And I've also arranged for a Realtor to take you house hunting tomorrow."

"I don't know if I'll feel up to it tomorrow," Doris objected.

"You will after you've had a good hot meal and a good night's sleep," Hal said. "Nobody gets any sleep in the hospital."

"By the way, Nigel, do we have permission to be in that house?" I asked. "Because it's a crime scene."

"No worries," Nigel said again. "Mark and Tyrone are going to meet us there."

Now that Doris was back home, some rather unwelcome thoughts were rising up from the clutter at the bottom of my mind.

Was it possible that Doris had killed Dick?

We'd discussed it before and dismissed it because she couldn't have done it herself and didn't have a husband or other strong male to help her, and besides, it was upsetting Mum.

But that didn't mean she couldn't have done it. The spouse or significant other is always the most likely suspect.

I couldn't even think about it here because Mum would know. She always could see right through me because my face gave it away.

"I need to clear my head," I announced. "I'm going to take a walk."

"Not in your pajamas, I hope," Mum said.

"Of course not. I'll get dressed first."

I went out to the apartment and put on my capris and tank top and a pair of sneakers, and waved as I went by the screened patio. Mum called out to me, "Do you want some company, kitten?"

Oh God, no. "No thanks, Mum. I just need to think."

My route took me up Lemon Avenue toward Bixby Road while my mind kept coming back to Dorothy Sayers's novel, *Strong Poison*, where the murderer had poisoned his cousin by putting arsenic in the food. They both ate it, but only the cousin sickened and died. There was quite a discussion about how it was possible to desensitize oneself by eating just a tiny bit of arsenic at first and then working up to larger and larger amounts. Rasputin was mentioned. If the murderer had done that beforehand, he would be able to eat the same amount of arsenic that he gave his cousin without even a twinge.

A mean-looking Chihuahua yapped at me from behind a picket fence, startling me. A woman's voice called out from inside the house, "Paco, shut up."

I walked on by, and Paco did eventually shut up.

So suppose Doris knew all about that bottle of white arsenic in the cellar, and suppose she had been desensitizing herself. Suppose her aversion to going in the cellar was just playacting. Suppose her plan was to kill Dick and distract everyone by making herself sick and making everyone think Dick was poisoning her. I mean, one can fake being sick, but when one ends up in the hospital, there had jolly well better be some arsenic in one's system when they finally get around to testing for it.

But wait—if that was her plan, why did it take us so long to come around to the idea that it was arsenic poisoning in the first place? I mean, the bottle of Cowley's rat and mouse killer was shoved way in the back of an ancient

154

apothecary cabinet covered in dust. Why would anybody even look there? We wouldn't have either, if the dumbwaiter hadn't malfunctioned, and that was on the opposite side of the cellar from where the apothecary cabinet was. It was only the merest chance that any of us would have ever looked in it. Mum certainly wouldn't have since she didn't like spiders any more than Doris did.

A car came down the street just as a ball rolled out into it right in front of me. I stopped. Balls are almost always followed by children.

Sure enough, a little boy ran right out in front of me without looking. The car screeched to a halt, but by then I had grabbed the child and dragged him out of harm's way. His screaming caused his mother to rush out of the house, yelling, "Frankie! Get back here! You bad boy! If I've told you once, I've told you a hundred times not to run into the street without looking. Now you're gonna get it." She grabbed him from me without a word and continued to rant as she took him inside, no doubt to give him a spanking.

"You're welcome," I called after her, but she ignored me. I walked on, crossing Thirty-Seventh Street. What an ungrateful bitch. No point in dwelling on it, though. It was none of my business. I had plenty to think about without that.

Then I had to practically beat the doctors over the head to get them to even consider the possibility of arsenic poisoning and test for it. Why would she take such a chance? Why wouldn't she bring up the possibility herself that she was being poisoned?

Well, duh. Because she was unconscious when she was taken to the hospital. Maybe she overdid it and gave herself too much. Perhaps she panicked when Mum told her we were coming to help solve the mystery of Dick's disappearance. It's pretty hard to fake a grand mal seizure and then fake unconsciousness for days and be intubated without so much as a twitch, and absolutely impossible to fake renal failure. No, I think the events leading up to her hospitalization were real and not part of her plan, assuming she had one.

I was now on Bixby Road, standing outside the grounds of Hughes Junior High. School was out for the summer, so nobody was around; just the memories were. I walked on toward Country Club Drive, which was nearly a mile away.

Once Doris got treated and regained consciousness, she found out that Dick was really John McNabb, whom she actually had met as a young man. She remembered that he was supposed to have died. So clearly, she didn't know about Dick's aliases.

Not until I told her John McNabb was killed by the dumbwaiter two weeks ago.

So what other reason would she have to want to kill him?

Maybe because he was abusive. He made it look as if the house was haunted and made her think she was losing her mind. He wouldn't let her have anything to do with their finances and told her to stay away from his desk and his computer—or else.

That would have been a deal breaker for Hal and me.

A bicycle bell jingled behind me, and I hastily stepped aside to let it pass.

So why couldn't she simply divorce him? Maybe because they'd only been married a few months and she just hadn't gotten around to it yet. Maybe because divorces, especially if there's a lot of money involved, take for-friggin' ever, and she didn't want to wait.

Could the blow to the head have actually been the cause of death? No, because he bled all over the hoistway and the wall panel when his head was crushed, but he was surely unconscious.

No matter how much I tried, I couldn't get past the problem of who might have helped Doris move Dick once he was unconscious—because somebody had to. Doris was a tall woman but not especially muscular, and she was in her late sixties. She couldn't possibly have done it alone.

Who would have helped her? Vicky and Greg? Mum and Nigel?

Absolutely no way. I couldn't even contemplate either of those possibilities.

I turned around and started back.

When I got back to the house, Nigel was pacing the patio. "It's about time you got back."

"And hello to you too," I said. "What are you so uptight about?"

"Had you forgotten that Mark and Tyrone were going to meet us at the house this morning?"

"You never said *when* they were going to meet us," I said defensively.

"I thought I did," he said.

Mum poked her head out the pass-through. "No, you didn't, lovey."

Nigel looked abashed. "My mistake. Sorry and all that. However, Mark and Tyrone are waiting for us, so I suggest we go."

Hal came out onto the patio with a toolbox and three flashlights. "Oh, good, you're back. Ready?"

"Would it be okay if I pee first?"

Hal and I allowed as that would be okay, so I did so, and then we were on our way. Mum and Doris elected not to go, so it was just me and the boys.

A police cruiser was already in the driveway when we drove up in Mum's Chevy. Nobody was inside. We went up the front stairs and knocked.

Mark swung the door wide. "Welcome to our crime scene."

"Did your CSIs find the speakeasy?" I asked.

"What the hell are you talking about?"

"Did they find the door at the bottom of the secret staircase?"

"They were all over the secret staircase," Mark asserted. "They didn't miss anything. There is no door."

"I've seen the blueprints," I told him. "They show a door, and another room, and another door leading to a staircase into the cellar beyond the brick wall. But they don't show the brick wall."

Mark put his hands on his hips. "How the hell did you manage that? It usually takes weeks to get that from City Hall."

"She didn't go to City Hall," Hal said.

"The city counsel and I were best friends as children," I said.

"Toni has connections everywhere," Nigel said.

"Apparently," Mark said. "So where do you want to look first? The secret staircase?"

"Please," I said.

We ascended the stairs to the second floor and went into the first bedroom on the left. The door to the staircase had been left open, and the windows were open too. The smell of decaying flesh was gone.

Mark went first, I assumed to make sure we didn't destroy anything before he could prevent it. Hal followed with the toolbox. I followed him, and Nigel followed me. Mark cast a jaundiced look upon the toolbox. "Just what do you think you're going to do with that?"

"The blueprints showed a door," Hal replied. "It may have been plastered over. I can't remove plaster with my bare hands, you know."

"There's no door," Mark reiterated. "The CSIs would have found it."

We reached the bottom. Mark extended a hand toward the end of the passage and said, "Okay. Do your worst. But bear in mind that Brad McNabb will expect you to pay for any damages."

Hal put the toolbox down on the landing. "The blueprint shows that the door is here." He indicated the right-hand wall. "Did the CSIs check out this wall?"

For the first time, Mark looked uncertain. "I don't know," he admitted.

Nigel aimed his flashlight at the top of the wall and at the bottom. He bent down and felt of something at the bottom, then ran his fingers along the bottom. "There's an edge here," he said. "And over here, there's a corner."

Hal parked the toolbox on the third stair, opened it, and took out a small pry bar. He handed it to Nigel. "See if you can get this underneath it."

Nigel took it and inserted the curved end under the edge. He pulled up on it, and a section of plaster came off. "Blimey. That was too bloody easy. I can't believe the CSIs didn't find this."

"Let's get the rest of this off," Hal said. He took a hammer and a chisel out of the toolbox and was about to set to work when Mark said, "Wait. You need masks and gloves. I left them downstairs. I'll go get them."

We all came back upstairs with him. I sat on the bed to wait. Hal objected. "Do you see how dusty that is? You'll be filthy."

"We're going to look a lot worse than that once we start working on that plaster," Nigel said, and he sat down too.

Mark came back with masks and a box of nitrile gloves. "Let's get back to work," he said. "I don't know if there's a door under there, but there's definitely another wall."

"Made of wood," Hal said. "Not stone."

We all donned masks and gloves and went back down. The dust had settled somewhat. Nigel and I parked ourselves on the stairs and watched as Hal and Mark removed the rest of the plaster.

There was a door, all right. A wooden door that looked like the same black wood the front door was made of, with a latch like the one on the front door, only smaller.

We all stood and looked at one another. Finally, Hal said, "What are we waiting for?"

"It's probably locked," I said.

"You won't know till you try," Nigel said.

Hal laid a gloved hand on the latch and said, "Here goes nothing!" He pushed the latch down, and the door moved. It didn't exactly open, but it clearly wasn't locked.

He pushed harder. Mark pushed too. They managed to get it open about three inches. "I think there's something behind it," Hal said.

"Like what?" Nigel asked, getting to his feet.

"Here, let me," Mark said. He squatted down and aimed his flashlight into the space. "I see hardwood floor, nothing else." He inserted his hand but couldn't get his whole forearm through, so he pulled his hand out.

"My arm's too big," he said and looked at me. "Toni, can you get your arm in there?"

"I'll try," I said. Mark got up, and I squatted down, reaching in with my left arm. I was able to get my whole arm inside and bend my elbow to feel what was keeping us from opening the door. "It's carpet," I said. "It's loose and bunched up behind the door."

"Can you move it?" Hal asked.

"I'll try," I said again. But the carpet was heavy, and I couldn't budge it. Not even when I stretched out full length on the landing, which allowed me to feel exactly what the problem was. The carpet was not only bunched up behind the door; it was bunched up *underneath* the door. I pulled my arm out. "Let me try the pry bar," I said.

Hal handed it to me. I stuck my arm back in there and tried to pry the carpet out from under the door, but no dice. It was wedged in too tight. "Can you pull the door to about an inch?" I asked.

"And crush your arm?" asked Hal.

"Just an inch won't hurt me," I said.

I was wrong. It did hurt. But the carpet came free, and I was able to roll it back on itself. "Try it now," I said.

Hal pushed the door open, and it opened far enough to allow me to actually enter the room. With my flashlight, I was able to see that the carpet was Turkish, or maybe Persian, like the one in the foyer, only smaller. I grasped it by the rolled-back corner and pulled it back far enough to allow the men to enter the room.

By the light of all our flashlights, I could see a long, skinny room with no windows. A bar ran almost its full length. There were a dozen barstools. Behind the bar were cupboards with glass doors, filled with dusty glassware. Several cocktail tables with chairs stood along the wall opposite the bar.

"Isn't there any light in this place?" Hal asked.

I aimed my flashlight at the opposite wall and saw another door. There was a light switch in the wall next to it. I walked over and flipped it.

Lights went on inside the cupboards, illuminating the glassware inside. Small, tasteful low lamps on the bar lit up, showing their Tiffany shades. I was now able to see sconces on the opposite wall, and a light switch on the wall by the door we'd come in. I flipped it, and the sconces lit up.

Now we could see that the bar was made of gleaming mahogany, with a brass rail for propping up one's foot while standing and drinking.

"Wow," Hal said, looking around in wonder, "this is amazing."

"Must have cost a pretty penny," Mark said.

"One could make pots of money on booze during Prohibition," Nigel remarked, "if one knew how to go about it without getting caught."

I noticed that there were no cocktail tables down at the other end of the room and wondered why. When I went over to look, I found out.

"Gentlemen, I've just answered one question."

"What's that?" asked Mark.

"The dumbwaiter does open on both sides."

"What?" Mark came hurrying over to look, just as Hal gave a holler from behind the bar. "Look what we have here! More boxes!"

While Mark changed direction and headed over to look behind the bar, I pushed the button on the dumbwaiter. The door opened to reveal the car, which we'd left on the first-floor level.

Then I noticed streaks on the wood paneling underneath the dumbwaiter. It looked like someone had tried to clean up a spill. Then I noticed the carpet beneath my feet had been shoved right up against the wall instead of out in the middle of the room, and when I pulled it back, I found out why.

The streaks on the wall were continuous with similar streaks where someone had tried to clean the hardwood floor. Under the streaks, the hardwood was stained dark.

I supposed it could be a spill of food or drink from taking it out of the dumbwaiter and then promptly dropping it. It could also be blood.

"Mark!" I called out. "You need to see this."

"What?" He came out from behind the bar and hurried over to me.

"See those streaks? See the floor?"

"Oh jeez," he said. "We need to get the CSIs back here."

"You'd need to get them in any case," Nigel said from behind the bar.

"Yeah," Hal chimed in. "These boxes are full of money."

CHAPTER 17

When you have eliminated the impossible, whatever remains, however improbable, must be the truth.

—Sir Arthur Conan Doyle

While the CSIs worked on the speakeasy, the rest of us moved on to the cellar.

The door leading to the staircase that led to the cellar opened easily, and the stairs were lit and had banisters. At the bottom, however, we came to a dead end.

"Now what?" asked Mark.

"According to the blueprints," Hal said, "this should lead to the cellar. We should be able to punch right through this wall here. It's just particleboard."

He put down the toolbox, took out a hammer, and punched a hole in the wall. "There!"

Mark peered through the hole. "I can't see anything. It's dark."

"According to the blueprints, this is the part of the cellar on the other side of the brick wall," I said. "There are no lights on, and the cellar doors are closed. At least they were the other day when Hal and I looked."

"I hope looking was all you did," Mark said in a warning tone.

"It was," I assured him. "We couldn't even get close because of the branches from the blue spruces around it. Somebody's going to have to cut those back if we want to get in that way."

"Well, we do need to get in that way," Mark said. "I'll give McNabb a call and ask if he minds."

He did so, and from the sound of the tinny voice emanating from his cell phone, McNabb was not exactly compliant. However, as Mark informed him, his house was a crime scene, and he was expected not to hamper a police investigation.

Mark pocketed his phone. "Well, he gave in grudgingly, but he gave in. He says there are pruning shears and a chainsaw in the barn."

We had to go back up the stairs and through the speakeasy to get out, and one of the CSIs called Mark over.

"This looks more like the killing scene than the one in the cellar," he said. "Look at that!"

By the light of his ALS, or alternate light source, the wall below the dumbwaiter and the stain on the floor fluoresced bright blue. "That's a blood pool," one of the other CSIs said.

"It certainly is," Mark said.

"That explains why we didn't find one in the cellar," the CSI said. "The victim was killed here."

"Hey," I said to Mark as we made our way up the stairs to the bedroom on the second floor, "I don't remember you asking McNabb if he minded you tearing off this plaster."

"I did that before you got here," he said smugly.

"Then he must have known you'd find the speakeasy."

"If he even knew about it," Mark said. "We don't know he did, now do we?"

"That's true," I said, "but whoever killed Dick certainly knew about it, and whoever killed Dick must have plastered up that wall, because why would he carry the body down to the cellar and up those rickety stairs and up to the second floor to throw the body down this staircase when he could just shove it out onto the landing?"

"You've got me there," Mark said.

When we went outside, another cruiser had parked next to Mark's, and Tyrone was getting out of it. "Hey, boss! Thought you might need some help. What's the CSI van doing here?"

Mark explained.

"What about the blood in the cellar?" Tyrone asked. "If Dick was killed in the speakeasy, how'd his blood get into the cellar?"

"I imagine that when the car came down on his head and smashed it, he bled into the hoistway," Nigel said. "Also, there would have been blood on the bottom of the car, and it would have splashed all over the bottom of the hoistway when it landed."

"Then it would also have splashed on the inside of the door," Mark said. "Also, there would be blood smeared on the side of the car as it smashed Dick's head and went on by."

"That must be how his cheek got torn off," I said.

Mark put his hand over his mouth and swallowed. "It seemed so simple when we thought the car landed on his head in the cellar. Now we're going to have to take that dumbwaiter apart. I'd better go tell the CSIs." He ran back up the stairs and went inside.

Tyrone looked at each of us in turn. "Why do you all look like you've been floured?"

"That's plaster dust," I told him. "The door to the speakeasy had been plastered over, and we had to rip it down."

"So what were you about to do when you came out here?"

I told him about the blue spruces. "We need to access the outside door to the cellar."

"I can help with that," he said. "In fact, I have to. Since it's a crime scene and all."

With Tyrone helping, we made short work of the branches covering the outside cellar doors.

Our first look at those doors was not encouraging. They were wooden and had once been painted white, but most of the paint had peeled away, and the wood was badly warped. Moreover, the hinges were badly rusted, and the hasp was secured by a huge padlock, also badly rusted.

Again, I wondered about the workmen. Shouldn't they have maintained that entrance to the cellar?

"Is there a key to that padlock?" Tyrone inquired.

"Probably on that big key ring in the kitchen," I said. "Want me to go get it?"

"Sure," he said doubtfully, "but it may not work with all this rust."

"We'll never know if we don't try," I said and ran back around to the front. I went into the kitchen to get Doris's keys and encountered a heavyset man in coveralls who had just come in through the outside door to the kitchen. I recognized him right away from his website photo.

It was Bradley McNabb.

I fought the desire to run. He looked every bit as pissy as he had on his website. I ignored him and went right to the junk drawer and grabbed the key ring.

He grabbed them away from me. "Who the hell are you? And what the hell are you doing in my house? You have no right to be here."

"I'm here with the police," I said. "What are you doing here? This is a crime scene. May I have those keys back, please?"

"Crime scene, my ass! This is my goddamn house!"

"Now, now, what's all this?" Mark inquired as he walked into the kitchen. "McNabb, what are you doing here? This is a crime scene. You need to leave."

"The hell I will. I have a right to see what you're doing in my goddamn house."

"Toni, what's taking so long?" Tyrone had apparently gotten tired of waiting for the keys. Then he saw McNabb and Mark, and summed up the situation immediately. He went right up to McNabb, grabbed his hand, and clapped him on the back like a long-lost brother.

"Bradley, my man! Don't you know better than to disturb a crime scene? Why, you could get in all kinds of trouble doing that. I'd surely hate to have to put you in jail for disturbin' a crime scene and interferin' with a *po*-lice investigation."

Tyrone was much larger than McNabb, and all the time he was talking, he was easing McNabb toward the outside door, and before McNabb knew it, he was outside.

Tyrone said, "Let me help you into your truck," and I heard McNabb say, "I don't need any goddamn help."

Tyrone said, "Oh, I reckon you do," and the next sound I heard was the truck starting up and leaving.

Tyrone came back in with the key ring. "Just a little misunderstandin'. Now then, shall we?"

Mark said, "Thanks, buddy," and we went back outside to meet Hal and Nigel, who had also gotten tired of waiting. I wasn't planning to tell him about the confrontation with McNabb, but Mark and Tyrone did.

"Just a little to-do with McNabb just now," Tyrone said casually.

"Tyrone took care of it," Mark said.

"Don't expect he'll be back," Tyrone said.

Hal's eyes narrowed, and his lips compressed, but he said nothing.

I caught Nigel's eye. He pursed his lips and shook his head minutely.

I was also not so sure McNabb wouldn't be back, but I said nothing to Hal because I had a feeling he wouldn't like what I was planning to do.

Tyrone managed to unlock the padlock with only the tenth key he tried.

"Okay," Hal said, "we've come this far, let's see if we can get it open." He flipped the hasp open, and he and Tyrone each tugged at a door. With a dreadful creaking noise, the hinges reluctantly yielded. Actually, one of them broke. Finally, we were able to see stairs going down into impenetrable darkness.

"Good job we have flashlights," Nigel said.

The stairs into the cellar from outside were built of stone and were much sturdier than the decrepit wooden ones leading upstairs into the hallway. The cellar appeared empty except for one thing.

A coffin.

It had been quite a nice coffin in its time, but now it was covered with dust and cobwebs.

"Oy gevalt!" Hal threw up his hands. "Now who the hell is *this*?"

Mark stood staring at it with his hands on his hips. "Any idea who this might be?" he asked finally.

"Your guess is as good as mine," I said. "Maybe it's the elusive Frances McNabb. Why don't we just open it and see?"

"It's probably locked," Nigel said.

"Maybe not," I said and went around to the other side, where the lid was secured by an ancient padlock, even more rusted and decrepit than the one on the cellar doors had been. I yanked on it, and it fell apart in my hands. "Here, help me get this open," I urged.

Mark objected. "Doctor, you know better than to open a coffin without the proper precautions. You don't know what the deceased died of. You could get sick. We could all get sick. I won't allow it."

By the time he'd finished his diatribe, I had managed to undo the clasps and shove the lid up far enough to see what was inside.

"This isn't going to make anybody sick," I said. "Except the person it belongs to."

"What do you mean?" Mark asked, hurrying around the coffin to see what I'd found. Hal was right behind him.

"Well, I'll be damned," Hal said reverently.

"So will I," Mark said. "Talk about evidence!"

Nigel simply said, "Blimey."

The coffin was full of money.

Mark groaned. "Now I need the CSIs to get this thing out of here. They're gonna need another van."

While Mark went to tell the CSIs about the coffin, the rest of us tried to locate the hole in the wall that Hal had punched from the bottom of the stairs. I was the first to find it, in the middle of a large piece of particleboard that had been crudely nailed up on a wooden frame.

It took Hal and Tyrone exactly five minutes to tear it down, exposing the stairway, just in time for Mark to come back and see it.

"Now," I said, "we need to find a way to get to the other side of the cellar."

"Good idea," Mark said. "How about you and Tyrone go around to the other side, and Hal and Nigel and I will stay here."

Tyrone and I went back outside and entered the house via the front steps.

"I sure am not looking forward to going down those steps again," he said as we went down the long hallway.

"You did before, and you were fine," I said. "You should be okay this time too. I'll go first."

I got down without incident. But Tyrone's progress down the stairs was accompanied by a loud creaking, followed by a ripping sound, a yell, and a horrific crash. I turned to see Tyrone rising like a phoenix out of a pile of rubble in a cloud of dust.

The stairs were gone.

I heard Nigel's voice from the other side of the wall. "What the bloody hell was that?"

"I'm all right, I'm all right," Tyrone grunted, sounding for all the world like Uncle Billy in *It's a Wonderful Life* after crashing into the garbage cans. He brushed himself off and stepped carefully out of the rubble. "Luckily I was nearly halfway down before that happened," he said. "I'm probably going to have a fine set of bruises, but nothing's broken."

"Except the stairs," I pointed out. "Now we absolutely have to find a way out of here. You start over there by the dumbwaiter, and I'll start over here by Dick's workshop."

"What's in those boxes?" he asked.

"I don't know," I said. "I assume it's Doris's stuff that she hasn't had a chance to unpack."

Tyrone reached up and took a box off the top. He blew the dust off it and tore it open.

It was full of money.

Tyrone groaned and leaned on the stack of boxes. It swayed alarmingly but didn't fall over. "Shee-*it*. If one is full of money, they probably all are," he said. "The CSIs are gonna have to take these too." He walked over to the brick wall and shouted, "Boss!"

Mark shouted back, "What?"

"More boxes of money," Tyrone said.

"Then we damn well better find a way through this wall," Mark said, "or we'll have to tear it down."

So Tyrone went over by the dumbwaiter, and I went to the other end. I followed it to the left, until it ended up against a solid stone wall. Then I followed it all the way back to the point where I'd started and kept on going. A shaft of light caught my attention after just a few steps, and I stopped to see where it was coming from.

There was a chink in the wall where a brick had been broken off at one corner. I pushed on the brick experimentally, and to my surprise, it fell out, landing on the stone floor on the other side.

Hal called out, "Toni? What was that?"

"See the hole in the wall where the brick fell out?"

"What hole?"

I stuck my hand through the opening and waggled my fingers. "This hole."

Hal took my hand. "Now I do."

"Why do you suppose they left a loose brick in this wall?"

"How should I know?" Hal asked irritably. "Nothing about this house makes any sense." Experimentally, he pushed on another brick. It moved.

And then the whole wall moved.

CHAPTER 18

Though this be madness, yet there is method in't.

—Shakespeare, *Hamlet*

"**L**ook out!" Hal shouted.

He meant well, but I couldn't really see what to look out *for* exactly, so I stood rooted to the spot while the entire right side of the brick wall slid three feet to the right, creating an opening through which one could walk.

Of course, I reasoned, once one walked through it, the wall would no doubt close again, just like in the movies, trapping us in a …

"Well?" Hal said impatiently. "What are you waiting for?"

I shrugged and stepped through the opening. The wall slid shut behind me, just as I expected.

I turned to look, and when I did, I could no longer see where the opening had been.

Mark joined Hal and said, "What just happened here? Toni, how did you get through the wall?"

"It moved," I said. "Didn't you see it?"

"No. I wasn't looking."

"Nigel?"

Nigel shrugged. "No joy, I'm afraid. I wasn't watching either."

"Which brick did you push?" I asked Hal.

He shrugged. "I don't know. Maybe this one?" He pushed one. Nothing happened.

We began randomly pushing bricks, to no avail. The wall stubbornly remained closed.

"So if you weren't looking," I said to Mark, "then you didn't see which brick Hal pushed."

"We have to find the brick you pushed," I said. "And I think I know how."

"Be my guest," Hal said with a mock bow.

"Tyrone," I called.

"I'm here. Where are you?"

"On the other side of the wall."

"How'd you do *that*?"

"Hal pushed a brick, and the wall moved. When I walked through it, it closed again."

"You're kidding."

"I'm serious as a heart attack. We're trying to find the brick that Hal pushed."

"Good luck with that," Tyrone said, "because otherwise you gonna have to haul me out of here with a *crane,* man."

A few feet away, I saw the brick that I'd pushed out of its space lying on the floor in pieces.

Directly above it, at eye level, I found the space where the brick had been. Then I started pushing the bricks around the space. When I came to the one on the right side of the space, the wall began to move.

"Hooray, she did it!" Tyrone said.

"Wait," Hal said. "When Toni walked through this opening before, the wall closed again."

"So what?" Mark said. "We can just push the same brick to open it again."

"Or," I said, "we can put something in it to keep it from closing."

"I know just the thing," Hal said, and he stepped through the opening. I heard him crashing through the debris around Dick's workbench. The wall began to close behind him, but I pushed the same brick and opened it again. He returned with a metal pry bar, which he placed on the floor. It fit the opening perfectly.

"Now we can come and go as we please," I said.

Hal walked through the opening, knelt down, and inspected the floor. "Ingenious," he said. "This part of the wall is on rails, like a toy train. That brick must be some kind of a switch. Now, why do you suppose old MacTavish put this contraption in?"

"I thought this wall wasn't part of the original construction," I said.

"Me too," Hal said, "but now I'm not so sure. Imagine, if you can, old MacTavish closing up after a busy night in the bar. What does he do with the money?"

"Takes it to the bank?" Mark suggested.

"He can't do that," I said. "It's illegal. So he puts it in a box, opens the wall, and puts it in here, so that customers coming and going from the speakeasy won't see it and try to steal it."

"He wouldn't be able to build anything like this with stone," Hal said, "so he used bricks."

"Well," Tyrone said, "I found something too."

"Where?" I asked.

"Come see for yourself." He led us back to the dumbwaiter and showed us a passageway between it and the wall. Beyond the passageway was a well-lit space containing an electric furnace, a water heater, and a chest freezer.

"Did you look in that freezer?" I asked him.

He stopped and turned. "What—do you think that's full of money too?"

"We'll never know if we don't look," I replied, and set about unlocking the lid. "Here, give me a hand. It seems to be stuck."

Tyrone flipped open both locks, squatted, and shoved upward on the edge of the lid. With a dreadful creaking noise, it moved upward a whole quarter inch.

Tyrone stopped pushing and scrambled to his feet, hand over his mouth. He pushed the lid back down.

"What are you doing?" I demanded.

"Christ, Toni, don't you smell that?"

"Smell what?" I asked, but even as I said it, I could detect an odor issuing from the direction of the freezer. It sure didn't smell like anything I'd ever smelled in a freezer before. At least not in one that was working. It smelled like decomposing flesh. It smelled like Dick. "Oh. You think there's something dead in there."

"There's definitely something dead in there," Tyrone stated, "and I'll bet it's not a side of beef. I'm not opening that, and neither are you. We're going to let the CSIs haul it out of here just as it is."

"I'm on it," Mark said and left.

"You know," I said, "if that freezer was working, it shouldn't smell at all. So it must not be working."

Hal peered at the floor on one side of the freezer, and then the other. "I don't know. I don't see a cord or an outlet, but obviously there's electricity down here, so it should be working. Maybe it's unplugged."

"That's going to take a third CSI van," Tyrone observed. "Man, I've never seen a case like this."

"Let's go home, honey," Hal said. "I'm beat."

"We'd better brush ourselves off before we get into the car," Nigel said. "Fiona won't appreciate plaster dust on the seats."

In the car, I said, "I wonder whose body that was."

"Not to worry," Hal said. "It'll end up with your friend Patti, and she'll tell you all about it."

I hoped Mum and Doris were resting at home and that someone had prepared dinner. I suddenly realized that none of us had eaten lunch. No wonder I was hungry.

When we got home, Mum and Doris were enjoying their drinks on the screened patio.

"Whatever happened to you two?" Mum demanded. "We were beginning to worry that the cops had arrested you or that you'd fallen down the stairs into the cellar."

"Fiona was about to start calling hospitals," Doris said. "So what were you doing all this time?"

"You want to tell them, or shall I?" Hal asked me.

"I want a shower first," I said.

"You all look like you need one," Mum said. "And after that, I want to hear all about it. Leave nothing out."

"We're having fried chicken for dinner," Doris said. "I'll get it going while you clean up."

When Hal and I came back to the main house after showering and putting on clean clothes, Nigel was preparing our libations, and the aroma from the kitchen was heavenly.

We relaxed on the screened patio with our drinks and took turns telling Mum and Doris about the speakeasy, the boxes of money, the coffin, the body in the freezer, the moving wall, and the incredible workload we'd dumped upon the CSIs.

"Tyrone said he'd never seen a case like this," I told them.

"Well," Mum said, "we have some news of our own that might interest you."

"We went shopping this afternoon," Doris said, "because I've lost so much weight that nothing fits me anymore. And after that, we took a little drive by my old house, and guess what?"

Mum didn't give us a chance to guess. "It's still on the market! All Doris had to do was take it off the market, and she can move right in."

"It's been on the market since January," Doris said. "I couldn't believe it hadn't sold. I just called the Realtor and asked her to take it off the market, and she said to give her a couple of days, and then I could move back in. Isn't that wonderful?"

I frowned. "Yes, it's wonderful, but I don't get it. When we moved to Idaho, our house didn't sell for months, and we had to continue to pay the mortgage, and the utilities, and the property taxes. It was a financial nightmare."

"How could you not know it hadn't sold?" Hal asked.

Doris shrugged. "Dick didn't want me to bother my pretty little head about money. He wanted to take care of all that."

"Yes, I know," I said. "Vicky told us."

Doris said, "I didn't particularly like it, but I thought it best to humor him, and then I got too sick to care."

"Oh." I hadn't considered that, but it certainly made sense. Doris had been sick for over three months, and during that time, Dick had had free rein with the proceeds from Bob's life insurance.

I hoped he hadn't cashed it and put it in a box in the basement of the MacTavish house.

It was barely light when I woke up the next morning. Hard as I tried, I couldn't seem to get back to sleep, so I got up, got dressed quietly so as not to wake Hal, grabbed my book and my cell phone, and slipped out of the apartment.

Something had been slipped under the door. I picked it up by a corner. I'd become more aware of fingerprints over the last few days, almost to the point of paranoia.

It was a plain white envelope, addressed simply Dr. Toni Day. *What the hell*, I thought. I closed the door as noiselessly as I could and carried the envelope into the kitchen, where I got a baggie out of a drawer and put the envelope inside, with only the top edge of it sticking out so that I could slit it open with a knife without actually touching it. Inside was a note. I got a pair of tongs out of another drawer and slipped the note out. It was typed and said:

Stay away from the MacTavish house or you'll be sorry.

My hands shook as I slipped it back into the envelope, closed the baggie, and called the police. I didn't really expect to get Mark or Tyrone at this early hour after the day they'd put in the day before, and I didn't.

The dispatcher said they'd send somebody out.

There was a fresh, hot pot of coffee on the kitchen counter. Mum, or Doris, had set it up last night and set the time for five in the morning, and it was now five fifteen.

I poured myself a cup and took it and my phone and my book out to the screened patio and settled into a chaise longue. I tried to read, but I couldn't concentrate. It was a relief when the doorbell rang.

I ran to the living room to answer the door before the ringing woke Mum and Nigel, but Nigel, in his pajamas, beat me to the punch. The uniformed policeman who stood on the stoop was a thin, balding, hatchet-faced individual whom I disliked on sight. His badge said BAKER.

"Come in, Sergeant Baker," Nigel said, opening the screen door. "What's this all about?"

"It's about this," I said, brandishing the baggie.

"Are you the one who called, ma'am?" he asked me.

"Yes."

"Did you touch the envelope or the note?"

"Only one corner of the envelope, when I picked it up."

"Where did you find it?"

"I'll show you," I said. "Come with me."

I took him out to the apartment. "It was under this door. I found it when I got up."

"What time did you get up?"

"About half an hour ago."

Sgt. Baker checked his watch. "So about five?"

"Yes."

"So you sleep in there?"

"Yes, and my husband is still asleep in there, so let's go back to the house before we wake him up, okay?"

"Yes, ma'am."

I took him back to the house, where Mum and Doris were also up and sitting at the table on the screened patio with their tea and coffee, respectively. I invited Sgt. Baker to sit, but he demurred. "I'd rather talk to you alone, if you don't mind."

"Okay," I said. "We can talk in the dining room. Can I get you some coffee?"

"No, thank you."

"Well, I'm going to have some," I said, picking up my cup. My coffee was now cold. I went into the kitchen and got fresh coffee, and then joined Sgt. Baker at the dining room table.

He had donned gloves and had a pair of tweezers in his hand. As I sat down, he extracted the envelope from the baggie and brandished it at me. "Is this you? *Doctor* Toni Day?"

He sounded angry. I wondered why. "Yes."

With the tweezers, he pulled out the note and read it. "Right. I thought that was who you were."

"What does it matter who I am? I'm a person who received a threatening letter shoved right under the door to where my husband and I were sleeping. That bothers me. Doesn't that bother you?"

"Just who do you think you are, telling the police what they should or should not be looking for? What do you take us for? Do you think we're a bunch of doofuses, just sitting around on our hands doing nothing? And where do you get off ordering exhumations?"

The tirade took me off guard. I couldn't possibly answer his questions as fast as he was firing them at me, so I just seized on the last one. "I didn't order exhumations," I protested.

"As good as," he raged. "You got your girlfriend, the county medical examiner, to do it …"

"And those bodies were full of arsenic. They were poisoned. Why are you attacking me?"

Nigel appeared in the doorway. "Sgt. Baker, I believe you owe my stepdaughter an apology."

Sgt. Baker looked up at Nigel. "And who are you?"

"Detective Chief Superintendent Nigel Gray, Scotland Yard, at your service." Nigel's British was so crisp it practically crackled.

It had the desired effect. Sgt. Baker nodded. "Dr. Day, I apologize. I don't know what got into me."

"Accepted," I said.

Sgt. Baker asked me a few more questions, put the note back in the envelope, and transferred it to an evidence bag. "Dr. Day, I can see that this is related to the MacTavish case, and so I will communicate with Lt. Kincaid about it."

"Thank you," I said.

He left. I heaved a sigh of relief, refreshed my coffee, and went back out on the patio to be met with a barrage of questions.

"Kitten, what was all that about?" Mum asked. "Why was that awful man yelling at you?"

"Why was he here in the first place?" Doris asked.

"The bloke seemed to have a problem with Homicide," Nigel observed. "I had a word with him about it. It seemed to do the trick."

Hal emerged from the apartment and came into the screened patio to join us. "What's going on?"

"I got a threatening note," I said. "I called the police about it, and they sent a sergeant to interview me."

"A threatening note?" Hal asked. "From who?"

"Whom, dear," my mother said automatically.

"What did it say?" Hal demanded.

"It said to stay away from the MacTavish house or I'd be sorry," I said. "And I don't know who it was from."

"Did it come in the mail or what?" Hal asked.

"No, it was shoved under the door to the apartment," I told him. "I found it when I got up at five."

"Under the door to the *apartment*?" Hal asked. "Do you realize what that means? Whoever did that not only knows where you're staying but where you *sleep*. I find that frightening."

"I find it appalling," Doris said. "It's so *invasive*."

"But why was the sergeant yelling at you, kitten?" Mum asked.

"I don't know. He seemed to have an issue with me being involved in a homicide case and getting preferential treatment," I said. "I called him on it, and then Nigel got all Scotland Yard on him, and he simmered down."

"I don't like it," Hal said. "I'm going to call Mark Kincaid about it."

"It's a trifle early for that," Nigel said. "It's just getting on to six. You might want to wait a bit."

"Sgt. Baker said he'd tell Mark about it because it's related to the case," I said.

"I have a feeling we'll be hearing from Mark before too long," Nigel said.

CHAPTER 19

And much of Madness, and more of Sin,
And Horror the soul of the plot.

—Edgar Allan Poe

Nigel was right. Shortly after breakfast, Mark called and wanted to compare the information he had with the information the police had; he wondered if he could come to the house.

Nigel and I thought that was a dandy idea. I went out to the apartment and gathered up my laptop and all my printouts from the library. I took them out to the screened patio where it seemed we were spending all our time lately. But it was June, and after the morning fog burned off every day, it had been perfect as far as the weather was concerned.

Mark and Tyrone arrived about half an hour later, parking their cruiser on the side of the street in front of the house. When the doorbell rang, Nigel answered it and instructed them to pull the cruiser right up in the driveway, as it would be more convenient, being right next to the screened patio.

They got out of the car wearing blazers but immediately took them off and threw them back in the car. Mark carried a notebook and a folder full of papers, and Tyrone carried a laptop.

They sat down at the table with Hal and Nigel. I went into the kitchen where Mum and Doris were preparing canapés and iced tea.

I started to say something about this not being a party and not requiring refreshments, but then I thought, *What the hell*. In Mum's world, it was time for elevenses, and the cops could just deal with it.

I came back out with iced tea glasses and set them in the center of the table. Mum and Doris came out right behind me with a tray of canapés and a pitcher of iced tea.

Mark said, "Mrs. Gray, you didn't have to ..."

"Nonsense," Mum said. "And please call me Fiona. This is my friend Doris Campbell."

Mark and Tyrone rose to their feet, shook hands with Doris, and sat back down again. "Do you feel up to answering a few questions, Mrs. Campbell?"

"Oh, for heaven's sakes, call me Doris," she said. "Sure. Fire away."

Mark opened up his notebook. "I understand that your late husband owned the first Advantage Insurance office in Long Beach," he began. "How long ago was that?"

"It was in 1969," Doris said. She poured herself a glass of iced tea and took a sip.

"Was he the only insurance agent?"

"No, he went into partnership with Carl Johnson originally."

Mark made a note. "When did John McNabb come to work there?"

Doris thought for a minute. "About 1970, I think. He didn't last long, though."

"Why not?"

"Oh, he didn't really want to work; he just wanted to chase the girls in the office. His work was sloppy, he was always taking shortcuts, and he kept failing the licensing exam. So Bobby fired him."

"I understand he threatened your husband."

"Yes, he said he was going to open his own company and put Bobby and Carl out of business. Well, he opened his own company, all right, but he didn't put them out of business, not by a long shot."

"Does anybody who worked back then still work there?"

"I don't think so."

"What about Gladys Pierce?"

"Oh, Gladys didn't come to work there until after John McNabb was long gone," she said. "It was about 1974, I think, after all the hoo-hah about the big medical insurance scam had died down a bit. She's been there ever since. I don't know what Larry would do without her."

"Who's Larry?"

"Bobby's partner, Larry Murphy. He joined Bobby after Carl died, sometime in the early eighties. He's the only agent in that office now."

"When did your husband die, if you don't mind my asking?"

"Last December, just a few days before Christmas."

"When did you meet Mr. Campbell?"

Doris explained that she'd met Dick at the office when she gone in to clean out her husband's desk. She described how he'd swept her off her feet and that they were married on Valentine's Day.

Out of the corner of my eye, I saw my mother make a face. It was gone so quickly I couldn't be sure I'd actually seen it, but I knew how she felt about Doris getting married so soon after Bob's death.

"Less than two months after your husband's death," Mark said. "Pretty sudden, wasn't it?"

Doris shrugged. "I guess it was."

"What happened after that?"

"We moved into the MacTavish house," Doris said. "He told me he'd inherited it from his great-uncle. Of course, now I know that wasn't true. At the time, I thought it was haunted." She went on to describe the supernatural manifestations she'd experienced in the house and the symptoms of her mysterious illness.

"They put a tube down me and looked around but didn't see anything. And I had all these blood tests, but nothing ever showed up. And then Dick disappeared."

"When was that?"

"About two and a half weeks ago. Well, I wasn't about to stay in that house alone with all the spooks, and Fiona and Nigel were kind enough to let me stay here. And you know the rest."

"Not quite," Mark said. "How did Dick disappear? Were you in the house at the time?"

Doris explained that she and Vicky had gone shopping in Los Angeles and hadn't gotten home until late. She'd looked everywhere, she said, including the barn, but hadn't found him.

"His car was still there, but he wasn't in it. That's when I called Fiona."

"Can you remember what day that was?"

"I'll say. I'm not likely to forget a thing like that. It was June 10, and you two ought to know that because I called to report him missing and got the usual song and dance about having to wait forty-eight hours. I could show you the shopping receipts if you need proof that I wasn't here."

"It would help," Mark said, "if we knew for sure what day Dick was killed. He was too decomposed for the county coroner to be able to pinpoint it that close."

Mum made a face, but Doris was on a roll. "And I wish you'd explain to me how I could possibly avoid hearing someone slam Dick's head in the dumbwaiter and then haul him up from the basement to the second floor and throw him down the stairs if I was in the house. But you only have my word on that, don't you?"

Tyrone poured himself a glass of iced tea and helped himself to a canapé. "She's got a point, boss," he said.

"You could talk to Vicky," Doris said. "That's Victoria Maxwell Jones, attorney at law, but you probably won't believe a word she says because she's my daughter. Are you done with me now? Because I need to visit the little girls' room. I promise not to escape out the bathroom window."

"Thank you, Mrs. Campbell," Mark said. "I have no more questions at this time."

As soon as Doris was out of the room, Mark wiped his forehead with the back of his hand. "Whew! She's a pistol, isn't she?"

"You'd be testy too, if you'd gone through what she has," Mum said. "She's almost back to normal. Do have some iced tea, Leftenant."

"No, thanks, ma'am. When did you call your daughter to come and stay?"

"About a week later. I don't remember the exact date. Doris was getting impatient because she hadn't heard anything from the police."

"And they arrived when?"

"The fifteenth," Hal said.

"And you went back to the MacTavish house that same day?"

"Yes."

"Was that the day you found the passports?"

"No," I said. "That's the day we found the blood in the dumbwaiter and called you."

"And the day Toni found the arsenic," Hal added.

"That's also the day we called it a crime scene," Mark said, "but that didn't stop you from going back inside, did it?"

"No. Sorry about that."

Mark gave me a severe look. "You were lucky I didn't arrest you for that."

Meekly, I said, "Thank you. At least I found a body and the passports and driver's licenses. And now *you* know that Sonia stole them and slammed the door to the secret staircase on me."

Tyrone looked surprised. "Did you tell her that, boss?"

"No," I said. "His brother did."

Mark gave a disgusted sigh. "Bernie and his big mouth." He popped a canapé in his mouth.

"I don't look at it that way," I objected. "Bernie was trying to warn me that Sonia had another motive for killing me besides me stealing Bernie from her, which I didn't do, by the way. She was afraid I'd accuse her of killing Dick. She had every reason to think I'd die in that staircase and she'd be safe."

Mark put his head in his hands. "Oh my God. Fiona, I believe I'll have some of that iced tea now."

"Of course, Leftenant." She poured a glass and handed it to him.

"Well, we're on the same page about that," Nigel said. "She was the first one we suspected."

"Especially when we found out her husband drives a neon-green Volkswagen," I said.

"Let's not talk about neon-green Volkswagens," Mark said. "What happened to Quentin St. George after we let him go?"

I handed him the obituary on Quentin St. George. "He took his boat out, said he was going to sail it to Catalina, but he never got there."

"And I suppose no body was ever found," Mark said sourly.

"No, and no boat either."

"Of course not," Tyrone said.

Mark took a long pull at his glass and wiped his mouth with the back of his hand. "Too bad it isn't something stronger."

"We have beer and Scotch," Hal said.

"Thanks, but I'm on duty. So let's talk about the passports. Doctor?"

I picked up my cell phone and brought up my pictures. "The earliest one was John McNabb, who Doris actually knew. As far as Doris knew, John McNabb wasn't married at the time, but he did have a wife later, when he disappeared and was found to have died in a cabin fire up in Big Bear."

"We know about that," Mark said. "We have the records from San Bernardino County. So McNabb is out of the picture. What next?"

"It wasn't him," I said.

"What do you mean, it wasn't him?"

"Someone else died in that fire, because John McNabb reappeared as ..." I changed to the picture of the next passport. "Samuel Tobias Cartwright. The police just assumed it was him because he owned the cabin. His wife said she didn't even know about the cabin. Her name was Frances, by the way, and she disappeared right after he did."

"How do you know all this, Toni?" Tyrone asked.

"Google," I said economically, "and the public library." I handed them printouts of the two obituaries of Frances Diane McNabb and the material on Bradley McNabb and his construction company. "Is this the guy you know as McNabb?"

"That's him," Tyrone said. "I'd know that sourpuss mug anywhere."

"A face only a mother could love," Hal commented.

"Gladys told us that she actually knew Frances McNabb and that she'd moved up to Northern California, remarried, and had a son whose name she thought was Brad," Mum put in. "She said that Frances died a few years ago."

"So if McNabb's parents' names are John and Frances, he could be a suspect?" Mark said.

"Correct," I said.

Mark made another note. "Okay. Moving on. What about this next guy, Cartwright?"

I handed him the printouts on Samuel Tobias Cartwright. "He married wealthy widow Susan Mary Worthington Welles in 1980. She was the widow of wealthy industrialist Winston Welles, and Sonia's mother.

"Susan Mary Worthington Cartwright died mysteriously six months later, and Samuel Cartwright disappeared three months after that. They suspected suicide, because he had been depressed over the death of his wife, but a body was never found."

"That figures," Tyrone said.

"That gives Sonia a motive for killing Dick, if she thinks that he killed her mother. And you know, if you don't mind my saying so, you could cut Sonia some slack," I observed.

"I do mind," Mark said flatly. "It's none of your business."

"Think about it," I pursued. "She would have been only sixteen in January 1981. Winston Welles was the only father she'd ever known, but he hadn't seen fit to adopt her. We know that because her name was still Caligari when she married Bernie. Then when her mother died, she was left with a stepfather she didn't know very well and didn't much like. Maybe he didn't pay much attention to her, or maybe he did, and that might have been worse. Maybe he paid *too* much attention to her, if you get my drift."

"Sexual abuse?" Hal wondered.

"Maybe. It would sure explain why she ran away from home, wouldn't it?"

"It sure would," Hal said. "No wonder she's so messed up."

"It's also a hell of a motive for murder," Mark said.

I handed Mark another printout. "Here's an article about the drowning death of a three-year-old boy named Samuel Tobias Cartwright in 1951. If you check the passport and driver's license, you'll see that the birthdates match."

"Identity theft," Mark said. "I suppose you've got one of those for Quentin St. George too?"

"Right here," I said. "And here's one for Richard Alexander Campbell." I handed them both over. "And Gloria Buchanan St. George died mysteriously only five months after the wedding. Her son suspected foul play and went to the police, which you already know about."

"Right," Mark said, "and the autopsy didn't show anything."

"But now they've both been exhumed, and we know that both of them were poisoned with arsenic."

"Oh, yeah, I almost forgot," Tyrone said. "Toni asked me to get Doris's Metamucil tested. It had enough arsenic in it to kill a horse."

Doris came back in just in time to hear this last remark. "So that's what happened. I was wondering where it got to."

"But you didn't know that I started using it too," Mum said.

Doris gasped. "Oh, Fiona! I'm so sorry!"

Mum put an arm around her. "Not your fault, lovey."

"So we both got treated for arsenic poisoning," Doris said. "Whodathunkit?"

Mark closed his notebook with a decisive bang. "So now we have two possible suspects: McNabb and Sonia."

"Don't forget Derek Buchanan," I said. "He had the same motive as Brad McNabb and Sonia. And don't forget Frances McNabb either."

Mark gave me that sharp look again. "I thought you said she died. You gave me her obituary."

"I gave you two obituaries," I said. "Obviously one of them isn't true. Maybe neither one is true. Maybe they were both planted."

"You're suggesting that Frances McNabb is still alive? What gives you that idea?"

"Wait till you hear this," Hal muttered sotto voce.

"I followed the money," I said and told Mark and Tyrone my theory. "What if the McNabbs came up with the idea that John could keep on marrying wealthy widows and kill them for their life insurance?"

"You mean, what if Frances came up with that idea so that John wouldn't kill her?" Hal said.

"Yes, hence the Scheherazade angle," Nigel said. "Quite ingenious, actually, don't you know."

"So how did they go about finding these well-insured widows?" asked Tyrone.

"She would have to get a job in an insurance company," I said. "Or companies. We don't know who insured Susan and Gloria, but we do know who insured Doris."

"Are you suggesting we go around interrogating the clerical personnel in the hundreds, nay, thousands of insurance companies in the Long Beach and Greater Los Angeles area?" Mark asked theatrically. "And who's to say they'd tell the truth, even if they knew?"

"What I'm suggesting is that you start with Bob Maxwell's company, Advantage. If you find that they insured Gloria St. George and Susan Cartwright, I can give you a likely suspect."

"Who?"

"Gladys Pierce."

"You're kidding."

"No, I'm not. She's worked there forty years, which would be 1974, the year they both disappeared. She could have easily picked out likely widows for John to marry and kill. They could have made a killing. No pun intended."

Tyrone smiled broadly. "I believe I can solve this particular problem. You see, not all of those boxes in the speakeasy contained money."

"You mean they contained insurance policies?" I asked.

"That's right. They were all insured by Advantage."

"So we can add Gladys Pierce to the suspect list," Mark said, opening up his notebook again and making a note. "But what was her motive?"

"She's Frances McNabb," I reminded him.

"But why, then, would she kill Dick?" Nigel asked. "He was the golden egg-laying goose, so to speak."

Mum threw up her hands. "Oh, you men! You don't know anything. Do you really think poor Frances would just sit by forever and keep hooking her husband up with other women? Don't you think they agreed that at some point they would just stop and take the money they had accumulated and spend their golden years in the South of France, or something? But what if he wouldn't stop? What if he just got greedy and kept on doing it? They were both in their sixties. If it were me, I'd be furious!"

"She's right," I said. "I can see it. If he didn't stop, she might just kill him with the intention of taking all the money for herself and living on the Riviera without him. As a wealthy widow, she could easily find another man, if she wanted to."

"Okay, okay!" Mark said, holding up his hands. "I give you Frances McNabb, whoever she is, as a possible suspect."

"Not to mention," I added, "you could get DNA from Gladys and McNabb and see if there's a match."

"Well," Mark said, rising to his feet, "I guess we got all we can get from you folks. You know, I wouldn't be surprised if we could release the crime scene in a couple of days. We'll let you know, Mrs. Campbell, when you can move back in."

They gathered up their materials and prepared to leave. I followed them out to their cruiser.

"Are you going to stake out the house?" I asked.

Mark turned. "What for? We got all the money out of it already."

"But the suspects don't know that," I said. "Do they?"

"I don't know how they would," Mark said.

"I don't know about that," Tyrone said. "McNabb might. He was there yesterday."

Mark opened the car door and placed his notebook and papers on the seat. "Not when we found the money."

They both got into the car, and Mark started the engine. I held on to the door so he couldn't close it. "If you stake out the house, you might see who comes back to get the money," I suggested.

"We'll take it under advisement," Mark said and pulled the door closed. I went back inside the screened patio, letting the screen door slam behind me.

"Did you hear that?" I demanded of Nigel. "Take it under advisement, my ass."

"I heard it," Nigel said. "What are you suggesting?"

"Seriously?" Hal asked. "Have you *met* Toni? She wants to stake out the house herself."

"Antoinette, you'll do no such thing," Mum said severely. "I won't have it."

"What if I go with her?" Nigel suggested.

Mum shoved her chair back and stood up, hands on hips. "Nigel Henry Gray, you're seventy years old! Have you taken leave of your senses? You're not going *anywhere* if I have anything to say about it."

"What if I go with them?" Hal asked.

Mum tossed her head angrily. "Oh, so you can *all* get killed?"

Doris stood up and put her arm around Mum. "Fiona, you're overreacting. If they all go, they can protect Toni. They'll have cell phones. At least one of them will be able to call 911 if necessary. You need to have *some* confidence in your family."

Nigel stood up and took my mother in his arms. She buried her face in his shirtfront. "Fiona, my dearest love, please do give over. I do know how to run a stakeout. We're not going to take anyone down. We'll merely take pictures, call our police counterparts, and then disappear. We'll be fine."

Mum raised her head and looked Nigel in the eye. "If anything happens to any of you, I'll kill you all myself." She disengaged herself and wiped her eyes. "You'll need a hot meal before you go. Doris, will you help me in the kitchen?"

Because it was June, it didn't get dark until after nine o'clock. Because there was no place to hide the car at the MacTavish house that we could be sure it wouldn't be seen, Mum agreed to drive us up to the house and leave us there while she went back down to the bottom of the lane to watch and alert us if anyone turned into the lane.

Doris insisted on going along so that Mum wouldn't be alone. So it was rather crowded in the back seat as we drove up the lane and along the driveway up to the house.

We met nobody in the lane or the driveway, but when we drove around the house, we saw a McNabb Construction truck already parked there.

"Shit," Hal said. "McNabb beat us to it."

"Well," I said, "it *is* his house. Maybe he's not here after the money. How do we know?"

"The fact remains," Nigel said, "that he's entered a crime scene, for whatever reason. We need to let Mark know he's here."

"Does that mean we don't have to leave you here?" Mum asked hopefully.

"No," Nigel said. "We need to document that he's here. We need to photograph him in the act of disturbing a crime scene."

"Very well," Mum said with a sigh. "If you insist." She pulled up behind the truck, and we got out of the car. She turned her car around and went back down the driveway.

"Well," I said as I watched her taillights disappear, "at least we don't have to worry about them meeting McNabb on the way out."

"They could still meet a neon-green Volkswagen," Hal said.

"Well, it can't be Sonia," I said. "She's in jail."

"Too bad we don't know what Derek Buchanan drives," Hal said.

"Or Frances McNabb," I said.

Nigel said, "Enough chat. Let's get on with it. Now, we need someone to catch him coming out the kitchen door, someone to catch him coming out the front door, and someone to catch him coming out the outside cellar door. Phones on vibrate, please."

Hal took the barn, I took the front steps, and Nigel took the cellar door.

I was pretty sure my assignment at the front door was because we had very little reason to suppose that McNabb would come out that way when his truck was around back.

I had no reason to think that he'd come out the cellar door either.

This, I figured, was going to be a very boring stakeout. McNabb would come out the kitchen door, get in his truck, and drive away. Hal would get a picture, we'd call Mum to come get us, and that would be that.

What could McNabb be doing in there? I wondered. Sure, it was his house, but as far as he knew, Doris was going to move back in once the crime scene was released. Was he, perhaps, going to repair the cellar stairs? Fix the broken cellar door? Replaster the door to the speakeasy? Close up the stairs leading from the speakeasy to the cellar? Because once he went into the speakeasy, he'd know the money was gone. If he went into the cellar, he'd know that all the boxes and the coffin were gone. He'd know he was too late.

Maybe he was cleaning up the mess we'd left on the landing of the secret staircase and in the cellar.

Maybe he was going to burn the house down and collect the insurance.

My cell phone vibrated. I looked at the display.

Vicky.

I retreated farther into the brush at the edge of the property, turned my back so that my voice wouldn't be heard from the house, and answered in a whisper.

"Vicky?"

"Hi, Toni. Why are you whispering?"

"We're staking out the MacTavish house. McNabb is here."

"Who's we?"

"Me and Hal and Nigel."

"Why?"

"Because the cops didn't want to."

"Oh. Well, I thought you'd want to know. Sonia is out on bail. Greg says her trial is set for July 3."

A frisson of fear raised the hairs on the back of my neck. "How the hell did she manage that?"

"No idea."

"Mum is going to plotz."

"Greg says you have nothing to worry about."

"Easy for him to say. He's not the one in her crosshairs."

"Be careful!"

"Thanks, Vicky."

"You're welcome."

We disconnected.

I texted both Hal and Nigel.

vicky says sonia out on bail

Well. *That* was exciting. What next?

Something crawled along my arm. Reflexively, I slapped it. Then I realized what I'd done. *Some sleuth you are, Toni,* I thought. I held my breath and waited to see if the sound had alerted anyone. I didn't hear anything but the chirping of tree frogs, so I gradually relaxed.

Was Bradley McNabb ever going to come out of the house and release us from this?

I couldn't stand this any longer. What the hell was he doing in there?

I left my post and tiptoed up the front stairs. I flattened myself against the wall at the side of the door and listened. I heard nothing.

Cautiously, I reached out and depressed the latch. I waited, heard nothing, and gingerly pushed on the door. It appeared to be unlocked, but would it squeak if I pushed it open and give me away? I didn't remember it squeaking when we came here with Doris, so I took the chance that it wouldn't do so this time either.

I pushed the door open, darted inside, and closed the door as noiselessly as I could. I concealed myself in a dark corner and listened. Silence.

I tiptoed down the hall past the darkened living room, hid behind the wall, and listened before tiptoeing down the hall past the library, also dark. The kitchen was dark too. Luckily, my night vision was already operational since I'd been in the dark for the past half hour.

I stopped and flattened myself against the hallway wall and waited. I still didn't hear anything. *Christ, this is scary,* I thought. No lights. No noise. Could McNabb be hiding somewhere, waiting for me to find him? Would he spring at me out of a dark room, like our cat, Spook, always does?

Suddenly, I heard the sound of a band saw cutting through wood. It was coming from the end of the hallway, where the doors to the cellar stairs and the stairs to the second floor were located.

Well, what do you know? I thought. *He* is *repairing the cellar stairs. Looks like he's going to be there for a while.*

I began to tiptoe back toward the front door when my cell phone vibrated again. I looked at the display. A text from Mum to me, Hal, and Nigel.

Green VW coming yr way

Shit. Now what?
I texted back.

Mcnabb fixing cellar stairs

The band saw stopped. I was now in danger of being trapped between Sonia and McNabb. Without hesitation, I went in the only direction I could: up.

I turned and quietly opened the door to the stairs and ran on tiptoe up to the second floor, where I went into the bedroom that I assumed had been old MacTavish's. I certainly couldn't call it Dick's uncle's bedroom any more since Dick wasn't really Dick and his uncle was fictitious.

The laird's lug was still open. I heard a woman's voice call out, "Where are you?"

I was pretty sure she wasn't asking me that, so I kept quiet.

She called out again.

The band saw started up again. I couldn't see her, but I heard her walk down the hall and open the cellar door, and then there was light.

I drew back from the laird's lug so that she wouldn't see me.

The band saw stopped.

"How's it going?" the woman asked.

"Damn slow," McNabb growled. "I've gotta get this done. That damn Campbell woman is moving back in here in two days."

"I see you got the money out of here. Where'd you put it?"

"I didn't. The police took it."

"The coffin too?"

"I don't know about the coffin. I wouldn't be surprised."

"You idiot!" the woman screamed. "You had one job. You blew it. What are we supposed to do now?"

"Goddamnit, Mom, I was busy! I've got a business to run too, you know."
Mom?

"Don't you swear at me, young man."

Could that possibly be Frances McNabb?

The dust up here was playing hell with my nose. I pressed a finger to the side of it to close the nostril, but it was no use.

I tried to sneeze quietly, but it wasn't quietly enough.

The woman said, "What's that?"

"What's what?"

"Somebody sneezed. Didn't you hear it?"

"No, I didn't."

"Well, I'm gonna check it out. It better not be that pesky daughter of Fiona's that keeps getting in my way. You'll have to take care of her just like the others."

"Whatever," McNabb said. The band saw started up again.

I heard the door to the stairway open.

Shit!

I was trapped.

No, I wasn't! I scrambled for the fireplace, flipped the switch on and off again, and the wall swung out. I stepped inside, and the door swung shut behind me.

Did Frances know about the switch? I wasn't about to take the chance.

I ran down the stairs, opened the door to the speakeasy, ran across the room to the other door, opened that, and tiptoed down the stairs to the cellar.

I peered around the corner, trying to see if the wall was open or closed.

It was open. Damn! Hal's pry bar was still holding it open. Apparently, McNabb hadn't seen it, or didn't care. Was there any chance I could remove it without McNabb hearing me, close the wall, and escape through the cellar doors?

The band saw stopped. I held my breath. Then I heard the woman's voice. "There's nobody up there."

"The hell you say," McNabb growled. "Did you look on all the floors?"

"Well, no, just the—"

"Goddamnit! You've gotta look on all the floors. Whoever it was coulda just climbed up another flight!"

"Don't you swear at me, young man."

"Sorry, Mom. Wait. I'll come up there, and we'll look again."

Now was my chance. McNabb would climb out of the cellar on his ladder, because certainly he would have gotten into the cellar that way.

To my dismay, I heard McNabb heading in the direction of the wall.

Shit!

There was only one thing to do.

Well, maybe two. I could run over and grab the pry bar and knock McNabb over the head with it, but there wasn't time.

So I turned and ran back up the stairs to the speakeasy. But how was I going to open the door at the top? The switch was on the outside.

I ran behind the bar and tried to conceal myself by squeezing into a space between the sink and the refrigerator under the bar. My phone vibrated, but I sure as hell wasn't going to answer it now.

It worked.

McNabb came pounding up the stairs and ran across the speakeasy without even looking in my direction. He went out the door and up the secret staircase.

Apparently, Frances had flipped the switch on and off, because I heard McNabb's footsteps pound across the bedroom above and then up the stairs. Or was it down the stairs? Were he and Frances headed for the fourth floor or the first?

McNabb had said Frances needed to look on all the floors, so probably the fourth. Now was my chance.

I left my hidey-hole and went back down the stairs and out into the cellar, where I grabbed Hal's pry bar and tried to pick it up.

No dice. The pry bar was wedged so tightly between the two halves of the wall that I couldn't budge it. It was as if the wall, in trying to close, had wedged the pry bar in like this. What would happen if I pushed the brick that opened the wall?

I pushed the brick. The wall moved a fraction, but it was enough. I picked up the pry bar. Then I heard McNabb and Frances coming back.

There was only one thing to do.

I ran to the cellar doors and pushed up on them.

But no dice. The police had thoughtfully locked them.

But wasn't one of them broken? It was the one on the right, I recalled. I moved over to the right and pushed up. The broken edge of the door moved—enough for me to get an arm out. Nigel should be out here. I waved my arm and called out. "Nigel! It's Toni! I'm here!"

Nobody answered.

What the hell? Where was Nigel?

My phone vibrated again. Again, I was in no position to answer it.

I couldn't get the rest of me through the opening, no matter how hard I pushed, but I sure as hell was not going to stay here like a sitting duck for McNabb and his mother to catch me. So far, they didn't even know who I was. They hadn't seen me.

I extricated myself from the jagged, splintery edges of the door with difficulty, tearing my tank top and scratching my arm badly enough to draw blood. Nothing I could do about that. I ran back up the stairs to the speakeasy and back to my hidey-hole.

I waited. Nothing happened. I pulled out my cell phone and looked at the display. Two missed calls. Hal. I texted him.

Trapped in speakeasy hiding from mcnabb and mom.

Another text came in, from Nigel this time.

Not sonia gladys

I texted back.

Gladys is frances mcnabb

Had anyone called 911? Or Mark or Tyrone? They knew McNabb was here. Shouldn't someone be here by now? I texted both Mark and Tyrone.

Trapped in speakeasy hiding from mcnabb and his mom

If Hal and Nigel had shared any of this with Mum and Doris, Mum would be frantic by now.

It wouldn't be long now. No doubt I was in for a scolding from both Hal and my mother, not to mention Mark, for being stupid enough to go into the house in the first place.

I waited.

CHAPTER 20

Like one that on a lonesome road
Doth walk in fear and dread,
And having once turned round walks on,
And turns no more his head;
Because he knows a frightful fiend
Doth close behind him tread.

—Samuel Taylor Coleridge

There was one difference, however.

This time, I was armed. I had the pry bar. With it, I could, if McNabb discovered me, do him a mischief, as Mum would say.

As if McNabb had read my mind, he came down the stairs into the speakeasy, stopped, and looked around. I held my breath. He flipped on the light switch, totally destroying my night vision, came around behind the bar, and walked its length. He obviously didn't see me. At one point, he nearly stepped on me. When he got to the end, he turned around and walked back. As he walked by me for the second time, I stuck the pry bar between his legs. He crashed to the floor, hitting his head with a metallic clang on some kind of tank, and lay still.

I stepped over him and went back downstairs to the cellar. The wall was still open. I walked over to the opening and looked at McNabb's handiwork. He'd made quite a bit of progress, but the new stairs were nowhere near finished.

I also noticed a ladder lying on the floor. All I needed to do was use the ladder to climb out of the cellar and walk right out the front door.

I walked through the opening in the wall, which promptly closed behind me, trapping Bradley McNabb in the speakeasy. The secret staircase was closed at the top, unless, of course, his mom opened it for him. The cellar doors were locked, and if I couldn't get through them, McNabb sure couldn't.

I set up the ladder and climbed out of the cellar into the hallway. When I got there, I saw a tall, thin elderly woman with wild gray hair and even wilder eyes run at me, hands out with the intention of shoving me into empty space.

I dropped to my knees.

She fell over me, somersaulting, screaming, and landing with a sickening thud on the stone floor of the cellar.

I averted my eyes. Instead of feeling triumphant, I felt a little sick.

"Toni!"

I looked up to see Mark and Tyrone coming toward me with guns drawn. Hal and Nigel were right behind them.

When Mark and Tyrone saw me, they lowered their guns instantly. "Where's McNabb?" Mark demanded.

"In the speakeasy," I said. "He tripped and hit his head. He may still be unconscious."

"What about Frances McNabb?"

"She's in the cellar. She's unconscious too."

The cellar door was still open, and all four of them clustered around it to look down at the motionless form of Frances McNabb. Mark climbed down the ladder, went over to the body, and felt for a pulse.

He looked up at us. "She's dead. What the hell did you do to her, Toni?"

"Nothing," I said. "She came at me like she was going to push me, I dropped down like this"—I demonstrated—"and she fell over me."

Mark climbed back up the ladder. He gave me a sharp look. "And I don't suppose you had anything to do with McNabb tripping and hitting his head either."

"I tripped him with this pry bar," I said, brandishing it, "and he hit his head on a tank."

Mark said, "Well, we'll need at least one body wagon. Come on, Tyrone. Let's see if we need two."

Tyrone said, "Yassuh, boss."

When they had gone, Hal wrapped his arms around me and held me tight, my face pressed into his shirtfront. "Damn it, Toni, don't you ever do anything like that again." He didn't sound especially mad, though, and when he let go of me and I could raise my head to look at him, there were tears in his eyes.

"Sorry," I said.

"You're bleeding," Nigel observed.

"What did that son of a bitch do to you?" Hal demanded.

"He didn't do this. I did it trying to squeeze through that broken cellar door. All I could do was get my arm out and wave. Nigel, where were you? I was trying to get your attention."

Nigel shrugged. "The cellar doors were locked. Nobody was getting out that way, so I went over to the front door and looked for you, and you weren't there, so I took up your post. I texted Hal that you weren't here and that you probably went inside the house."

"Oh."

"Sorry I wasn't there for you, old girl."

"It's okay. No harm, no foul."

"Where are Mum and Doris?"

"Right outside. Mark told them it wasn't safe inside."

"Oh, terrific," I said. "It wasn't safe, so you two came charging in here anyway. Mum must be *beyond* frantic."

I ran down the hallway to the front door and went outside. Someone had turned on the front door lights. The police van with the cage in the back sat in the driveway, its lights still flashing. Mum's Chevy sat right next to it. Doris leaned on the front bumper, arms folded, while Mum paced.

Doris saw me first. "Fiona!"

"Mum!" I called and ran toward her.

"Antoinette!" She ran toward me, arms outstretched, and I ran into them. She hugged me tight. She was crying.

"Oh, kitten, you're safe. What on earth is going on in there? And what is Gladys's car doing here?"

"Where?" I couldn't see it from where I stood.

Mum pointed. "Just around the corner."

I walked a few steps in that direction. There was the neon-green Volkswagen.

"Gladys is Frances McNabb," I told her.

Mum looked at me with something like awe. "That's what you tried to tell us, kitten. How did you know?"

"I didn't. As far as I knew, it could have been Sonia, or maybe even Derek Buchanan. I thought it *was* Sonia, at first. Apparently, Gladys drives a neon-green Volkswagen too."

A black van with Los Angeles County Coroner on it pulled into the driveway, and two men got out. They pulled a gurney out of the back and took it into the house.

Doris said, "Who's dead?"

"Frances McNabb," I said.

"How?" Mum asked.

"She fell into the cellar," I said, without further detail. I could tell her everything later.

And then I heard sirens.

"What on earth," Mum began, but she was drowned out by the sirens as the ambulance pulled into the driveway with its lights flashing. Two men got out, took a gurney out of the back, and took it into the house.

"That's for Brad McNabb," I said. "Apparently he's not dead."

"Kitten," Mum said, "just what went on in there?"

Hal and Nigel came out of the house and down the front steps just in time to hear Mum's question. "That's what we'd like to know," Hal said.

"Apparently your daughter is Wonder Woman," Nigel said. "She vanquished one foe and seriously injured the other."

I smiled. "I cannot tell a lie. I did it with my little pry bar."

Hal said, "Is that the same one I ..."

"Held the wall open with? The very same."

"Can we go home now?" Mum asked. "I'm fair knackered."

"We can," Nigel said, "but Toni has to go to the police station and give a statement."

"And I'm going with her," Hal stated.

"Me too," Nigel said, "but we can drop the girls off at home first."

We did that and then went straight to the police station, where the same female sergeant was on desk duty that had been on when Sonia was brought in for attacking me in the restaurant.

She put one fist on a hip and leaned on the counter. "Okay, which one are you this time?"

"I'm Toni," I said. "I'm here to give a statement."

She looked at Hal. "And who are you?"

"Her husband," he said and gave his name.

Nigel said, "I'm her stepfather, Nigel Gray."

"Who told you to come in?"

"Lt. Mark Kincaid."

"The Richard Campbell case?"

"Yes."

She looked through a pile of folders on the desk and selected one, which she placed in the exact center of the blotter. "Lt. Kincaid isn't back yet, but he's expected any minute now. Would you please wait in the waiting room? I'll show you where it is."

"We know where it is," Hal said. "We've been here before, you know."

The waiting room was quite full when we got there; some of the people were a little scary. Suddenly I was very glad Hal and Nigel were with me.

Tyrone came in a few minutes later and sat down next to Hal. "The boss is here, but he's busy with paperwork. In the meantime, I can put you in a conference room where you might be more comfortable."

He led us to a room that looked exactly like the one where I'd given my statement about Sonia.

"How is Brad McNabb?" I asked as soon as we were seated.

"He's alive but unconscious. They're taking him to Memorial."

"I heard Sonia made bail," I said.

Tyrone chuckled. "Not for long. Didn't Mark tell you? She's been charged with attempted murder."

"For locking me in the staircase with Dick?"

"Well, to be fair about it, she didn't know Dick was there. But yes, you could have died in there, if you were left there long enough."

Hal asked, "Will we be able to stay while Toni gives her statement?"

"If it's okay with the boss."

Hal asked the same question when Mark breezed in just a few minutes later. "I'd rather you didn't," he said. "Your wife is a material witness, and she needs to be able to speak freely, for the record."

"Toni and I have no secrets from each other," Hal protested.

I put my hand on his. "I'll be okay," I told him.

He and Nigel left. Mark closed the door. "Doctor, do you want legal representation?"

"What for?" I asked. "I haven't done anything."

"Well, let's review. We have a dead woman on the cellar floor, and a man with a serious head injury in the speakeasy, and the only other person there was you. You could conceivably be charged with murder and attempted murder, or manslaughter at the very least."

Christ on a crutch. No wonder Mark hadn't wanted Hal and Nigel to stay.

"Maybe I'd better," I heard myself say.

"Do you have anybody in mind?"

"Greg Jones."

"Do you want to call him, or shall I?"

I held up my cell phone. "I can call him."

"Go ahead. I'll be right outside."

I guessed that since I'd opted for a lawyer, Mark couldn't be a party to any conversation I might have with him.

I had Vicky in my contact list, so I called her. Despite the late hour, she answered right away. "Toni?"

"I need to talk to Greg," I said.

"Sure, but why? And I note that we aren't whispering anymore."

"No, I'm at the police station to give a statement about what happened at the MacTavish house tonight, and Mark Kincaid told me I should have a lawyer because I might be charged with murder or attempted murder or manslaughter."

"Holy shit. You will tell me all about it later, right? Here's Greg."

"Toni? What's up?"

I told Greg the same thing I'd told Vicky.

"What the hell happened at the MacTavish house?"

I gave Greg the *Reader's Digest* condensed version of my evening activities. "And as a result, there's one dead and one serious head injury."

"But weren't they trying to kill you?"

"That's what I thought at the time."

"And now you don't?"

"Oh, no, I still think so."

"It sounds like self-defense to me," Greg said.

"Will you come? Please?"

"Of course. I'll be right there."

Greg was there within ten minutes, during which I badly wanted to talk to Mark, but he didn't come back into the room, so I couldn't. He hadn't Mirandized me, but he may as well have.

I paced the room, mentally reviewing what I'd be saying in my statement, trying to find any detail that would tend to incriminate me. I still hadn't found one by the time Greg walked in.

"Toni, are you all right? What happened to your arm?"

"I was trying to escape through a broken cellar door. I got my arm through, but when I pulled it back, I got scratched."

"That's looking a little inflamed. You need some triple antibiotic cream on that. And a tetanus shot too."

"Thank you, Doctor," I said with a mock bow. "I have some at home, and I'm up to date on my tetanus."

Greg pulled out a chair and gestured at it. "Toni, sit down and tell me all about it. Leave nothing out."

I did so. Aside from an occasional question for clarification, Greg let me talk, while he made notes on a laptop. When I was done, he closed it.

"Toni, are you sure you've told me everything?"

"Yes."

"Well," Greg said, pushing his chair back, "I didn't hear anything you can't put in your statement to the police."

"Thanks," I said.

"You're welcome. And take care of that arm!"

He went out, and Mark Kincaid came back in. This time he had a tape recorder. He sat down opposite me, informed me that I would be recorded, and started asking me questions.

I told him exactly what I'd told Greg. When I was finished, he turned off the recorder. "Off the record, Doctor, what possessed you to go running into that house? What were you even doing there in the first place?"

"I asked you if you were going to stake out the house, and you blew me off."

"You do realize that you once again disturbed an active crime scene?"

"Sorry," I said. "Are you going to arrest me?"

"No," Mark said. "That would be counterproductive."

"There's just one thing that bothers me."

"Just one?"

"Why would anybody smash someone's head in a dumbwaiter? Why go to all that trouble?"

Mark got up, came around the table, and sat down next to me. "We don't usually do this, but this time I'll make an exception. The CSIs were able to figure out from the footprints in the blood in the speakeasy that two people were fighting in front of the dumbwaiter. The way they reconstructed the scene, the killer hit Dick over the head and pushed him into the open dumbwaiter door and hit the button. The car plunged down from the third floor and darn near took Dick's head off. The car went on down, crushing Dick's head between the wall of the shaft and the side of the car. Meanwhile, Dick bled into the shaft, and the blood pooled on the bottom of the shaft, and when the car landed in it, it splashed everywhere, and that's how it got on that wall panel."

"So nobody had to move the body up to the second floor and throw it down the stairs," I said.

"Nope. All the killer had to do was move the body to the landing and then plaster over the door to the speakeasy."

"So that means one person could have done it without help."

"Not exactly," Mark said. "Dick was a pretty big guy. I suppose a woman could have moved him, but she'd have to be pretty strong. Besides that, both sets of footprints were size twelve."

"Well, that would eliminate Sonia and Frances," I said. "Their feet are no bigger than mine, and I'm size eight."

"That pretty much eliminates everybody but Brad McNabb."

"Unless it was Derek Buchanan," I said.

"We have absolutely no basis for thinking Derek Buchanan is involved," Mark said. "There's not a scintilla of evidence pointing to him."

"I suppose they were fighting over the money," I said.

"More than likely," Mark said. "Now let's get you back to your family. You've got to be exhausted."

"One more thing," I said. "What's the matter with Sgt. Baker?"

Mark looked surprised. "What do you mean?"

I told him about my interview.

Mark sighed. "Sgt. Baker badly wants to become a homicide detective. He can't seem to pass the exam."

"Ah," I said. "So that's it."

"He tends to take it out on other people that he perceives as smarter than he is. Someone like you, a smart, successful doctor, would really piss him off."

Hal and Nigel greeted us at the door of the waiting room. All the other people who were there when we arrived were gone.

"What the hell took so long?" Hal asked. "It's been two and a half hours."

"I'll tell you at home," I said.

"We'd best get some sleep," Nigel said. "We have a big day tomorrow."

"We do?" I asked.

"Doris called and said the Realtor has released her house and she can move in right away."

"Really?" Mark asked. "She isn't moving back to the MacTavish house?"

"She wants nothing more to do with the place," Nigel said. "Except that she needs to move her furniture out of it."

"But it's still a crime scene," I said.

"Maybe not for much longer," Mark said. "I sent a crew of CSIs over there tonight after the ambulance and the morgue wagon left. They should be done by now. It's quite possible that she can move her things out tomorrow. I'll let you know in the morning."

Nigel glanced at his watch. "Blimey, it's morning already."

"Well then," Hal said, "let's make like the good shepherd and get the flock out of here."

CHAPTER 21

The Moving Finger writes, and having writ,
Moves on: nor all your Piety nor Wit
Shall lure it back to cancel half a Line,
Nor all your tears wash out a word of it.

—Edward FitzGerald

I didn't wake up until after ten the next morning. Before I came out from the apartment after my morning ablutions, I put on a clean tank top and capris, Hal having declared yesterday's outfit unsalvageable.

I felt three hundred years old. I had muscles aching in places where I didn't even know I had places. But I'd put triple antibiotic ointment on my arm before I went to bed; it looked like hell, but it felt much better.

To my surprise, a police cruiser sat in the driveway. I heard voices coming from the screened patio. Apparently, everyone else was up already.

I went into the kitchen and got myself a cup of coffee and then went out to the screened patio. Mark and Tyrone were both there. Mum had gone out and gotten doughnuts from the Long Beach equivalent of Jim Bob's back in Twin. I sat down, grabbed one, took a bite, and moaned with pleasure.

"Good morning, Doctor," Mark said. "How do you feel?"

"Better now," I said.

"Well, I for one am glad you came," Mum said. "Doris and I have been dying to know what happened last night, but by the time this intrepid trio came home last night, all they wanted to do was go straight to bed."

"Okay," I said. "We decided to stakeout all the entrances. Hal took the kitchen door, I took the front door, and Nigel took the cellar doors."

"What for, dear?"

"We were waiting for McNabb to come out, so we could photograph him and disappear."

"That was all you were going to do?" Doris asked.

"That was it," Nigel said.

"But it was boring," I said. "The most exciting thing that happened was that Vicky called and told me that Sonia was out on bail."

Mum put a hand to her mouth. "Oh, dear. I'm glad I didn't know that last night. I wouldn't have slept a wink."

"So when you texted and said there was a green Volkswagen coming, naturally I thought it was Sonia," I said.

"Well, as it turns out," Tyrone said, "Sonia is back in jail awaiting trial for attempted murder."

"For shutting me up in the secret staircase," I said.

"Oh, thank God," Mum said.

"What was McNabb doing there?" Doris asked.

"Repairing the cellar stairs."

"Why do you suppose he was trying to kill you?"

"His mother was the one who wanted to kill me."

"What for?"

"Well, as I heard her telling her son, because I was 'that pesky daughter of Fiona's who kept interfering.'"

"Interfering in what?" Mark asked.

"In her scheme to accumulate all that insurance money," I explained. "She's a modern-day Lyda Southard."

"Who?"

I told him the story of Idaho's Lady Bluebeard. "She and her husband, John McNabb, faked their deaths to collect each other's life insurance. Then she got a job in Doris's husband's insurance company so that she could introduce him to wealthy widows collecting their husbands' life insurance, and he would marry them and then poison them and collect their life insurance in addition to inheriting the insurance they'd already collected. She did that three times, with Susan Worthington Welles, Gloria Buchanan, and Doris."

"So who killed John McNabb?"

"She did," I explained. "Or rather, she got her son to do it for her."

Mark's brow furrowed. "Why would she do that?"

"Mum can explain that better than I can," I said.

"I think Doris was supposed to be the last one," Mum explained. "Gladys, or Frances, or whatever you want to call her, wanted to go somewhere out of the country with all the money and live happily ever after with her husband. Dick, or John, or whatever you want to call him, didn't want to stop. So she killed him."

"Maybe you have to be a woman to understand that," I said.

"Enough with the feminist claptrap," Mark snapped. "I'm not a complete male chauvinist pig. I get it."

"Why do you think she got her son to kill Dick instead of doing it herself?"

"Well, actually, I don't know that she didn't hit Dick over the head herself, but she'd have needed help with all the rest of it. I mean, you saw her. She's a little old lady."

"She's no older than Fiona and me," Doris said tartly.

"So how were you supposed to have interfered?" Tyrone asked.

"Well, first, I found the body. Then I convinced the doctors to test Doris for arsenic, and then I found the passports and driver's licenses. So Doris didn't die, and there was no insurance to be had. Then Mum and Nigel showed up in the office asking uncomfortable questions, and Gladys was there. And now we know that she was really Frances McNabb."

"How did you figure out the scheme in the first place?" Mark asked.

"I was trying to think of a way that both John and Frances McNabb could each collect on the other's insurance, and the only way I could think of was for both of them to fake their deaths. Then they could assume other identities and keep on scamming people for insurance money."

"It was a pretty diabolical scheme," Hal commented. "It bothers me just a little that my own wife could conceive of such a thing."

"I do have a diabolical mind," I said. "That's why I'm so good at solving murders. One has to be able to think like a murderer to catch one. Plus, I'm a pathologist, so I can figure out the medical details."

Hal shivered. "Remind me not to get you mad at me."

"Do we know the identity of the body in the freezer yet?" Nigel asked.

"Oh, yes," Mark said, digging in a pocket. "I've got it written down right here." He pulled out a slip of paper. "Linda Lee MacTavish Martin."

"Oh, I know who that is," I said. "Isn't she, or wasn't she, I should say, the daughter of Dougal MacTavish Junior? The original Dougal MacTavish's granddaughter?"

"Yes."

"How'd you figure that out?" I asked.

"Dental records. We found a dentist who she went to as a child."

"So what was she doing here?" I asked.

"The coroner's report said that she'd been dead at least five years."

"What happened five years ago?"

"That was when Brad McNabb bought the house for a song at a county auction."

"Maybe she tried to buy the house from him and he wouldn't sell."

"Or maybe she bid against him at auction," Mark said. "We'll never know now. She probably thought she should have inherited the house."

"Maybe she threatened him, and he killed her," I said.

"I guess we'll never know," Mark said. "We certainly can't ask her."

"Speaking of McNabb, how is he doing?" Nigel inquired.

"Still unconscious, as far as I know," Tyrone said. "I heard that they might have to drill a hole in his head."

"What are his chances?"

Tyrone shrugged. "Fifty-fifty is what I heard."

"So if he lives, what happens then?" Hal asked.

"He'll be charged and tried for murder, attempted murder, and accessory to attempted murder."

"Does that mean we have to stay?" I asked.

"Well, you are a material witness, but we won't actually need you until the trial."

"When will that be?"

"We won't know that until after the arraignment. How much longer can you stay?"

"I have to be back to work on the seventh," I said, "so we'll be flying out on the sixth."

"I doubt that it'll be that soon. Can you come back?"

I looked at Hal. He shrugged. "I don't know," I said.

"Can she do a deposition or something?" Hal asked.

"It's possible," Mark said. "We'll see what we can do. In the meantime, I believe we can release the crime scene later today."

"Jolly good," Nigel said. "I'll hire the moving van."

The next morning, we met the moving van at the MacTavish house.

Doris, seemingly having forgotten that she'd sworn never to go back inside this house again, was the first one up the stairs to unlock the front door.

The movers stood next to their truck looking up at the house in dismay. The big-bellied driver took off his baseball cap and scratched his bald head.

"I hope there's an easier way in than this," he said. "No way can we get a dolly up those stairs."

"We'd need a conveyor belt," said his younger and skinnier companion.

Doris pushed the front door open. "Then I assume you have one with you. Why would you not?"

The younger guy threw up his hands. "Okay, lady, whatever you say."

"Ray," the older man said. "Be polite."

"The name is Mrs. Campbell," Doris said severely. "And the furniture came in through this door, so you can sure as heck get it out this way."

The movers looked at each other, shrugged, and followed Doris into the house. The rest of us followed them. "Where do you want us to start?" the older man asked. "By the way, my name is George, and this is my son, Ray."

"How do you do," Doris said. "We'll start upstairs. Come with me."

The movers exchanged another look of dismay when confronted with the narrow staircase that led to the second floor. Doris looked back at them in annoyance. "Come on," she said impatiently. "What are you waiting for? Christmas?"

"How many rooms does this place have, anyway?" George asked.

"Only one up here you need to worry about," Doris replied. "The master bedroom, here on the right. The bed and the dresser are mine. The clothes in the wardrobe are mine, but the wardrobe isn't. And there are some personal items in the bathroom, which I'll take with me."

Hal held up some grocery sacks. "We'll help with that."

"What about downstairs?" asked Ray.

"In the library, there's my couch and Bobby's recliner," Doris said. "Also, the coffee table, end tables, and lamps. Everything else stays here."

"What about the rolltop desk in the kitchen?" I asked.

"That stays here too," Doris said. "But the appliances are mine. We just bought those."

"That doesn't sound too bad." Ray said. "We can handle that, can't we, Dad?"

"I suppose," George said, in a tone that suggested he wasn't so sure. "Ray, you may as well go get the dolly. We'll start with the bed."

Ray cast a dubious look at the king-size bed as he went out of the room. I sympathized with him and was glad it wasn't Hal and me who had to squeeze that mattress through those doors and down that narrow staircase. But someone had managed to get it upstairs that way, so it wouldn't be impossible to get it down again.

Mum and I grabbed a few grocery bags and went into the bathroom to retrieve Doris's personal effects. "What shall we do with Dick's things?" I asked.

"We might as well take them too," Mum said. "The city won't want them, and Doris might."

"Maybe, but I doubt it," I said. "Let's put them in a separate sack so we can just toss them when we get home if she doesn't want them."

By the time we'd sorted out the bathroom paraphernalia, the movers had removed the mattress and box springs. The hardwood floor under the bed had been home to a family of dust kitties that had been happily reproducing since God knew when, which made me wonder if anyone had vacuumed before moving the bed into the room in the first place.

Not my problem, I thought, but as we left the room, something gleamed in the light from the window. "What's that?" I asked Mum.

"What's what, dear? I don't see anything."

I put down my bags and stepped closer to the object. "It's a cell phone," I said.

"It must be Dick's," Mum said, "because Doris has hers." She stooped to pick it up, but I stopped her. "Don't touch it, Mum; it may be evidence."

Mum straightened up. "Sorry, kitten. I should have known better."

I took out my cell phone and called Mark. "We found a cell phone on the floor in Dick and Doris's bedroom."

"You didn't touch it, did you?"

"No, we just left it there."

"Good. I can't figure out how the CSIs missed something that obvious."

"Maybe because it was under the king-size bed in about an inch of dust."

"I'll send a CSI over to pick it up. Don't let anybody touch it."

"Okay."

When Mum and I left the room, I shut the door behind us.

George and Ray made short work of loading Doris's furniture and the new kitchen appliances and were preparing to shut the doors of the van and take off when I stopped them.

"You forgot Doris's boxes," I told them. "In the barn behind the Mercedes."

Grumpily, they hauled their dollies back out and stomped off to the barn, with us following them.

"I say," Nigel said, "what about that Mercedes? Doesn't it belong to Doris now?"

For an answer, Doris pulled a key ring out of her purse, got into the Mercedes, which miraculously started on the first try, and drove it out into the driveway, out of the way of the movers, and then got out. "When the movers leave, I'll drive it over to my house. I need to be there when the movers get there to tell them where everything goes."

By the time I got back around to the front of the house, a police van had arrived with a pair of CSIs in it. I showed them to the master bedroom and left them to it.

When the movers left, Doris took the Mercedes, and we followed her to her old house on Olive Avenue. Vicky and Greg were there waiting.

By nightfall, Doris was all moved in, with her furniture back in place. Dick's Mercedes was safely in the garage.

Greg reminded me of Sonia's upcoming trial for assault on July 3 and said he'd pick up Hal and me at nine o'clock in the morning.

Unlike the arraignment, the trial was an exercise in boredom. Sonia appeared in street clothes and behaved herself with such decorum that I wondered if she'd been sedated.

During my testimony, she sat with her head bowed and never looked up, not even when the damning pictures of my purple face were shown. She was sentenced to a year's probation and court-ordered psychiatric treatment and counseling.

The next day, Hal and I gave depositions, in the hopes that we wouldn't be required to come back for the trial of Bradley McNabb.

With all that going on, my upcoming fiftieth birthday had completely slipped my mind. So it was with a sense of shock that I awoke on the morning of July 4 to see black banners and over-the-hill-themed decorations everywhere.

Mum and Hal had prepared a sumptuous breakfast of scrambled eggs with cheese, an entire pound of bacon, and fresh cinnamon rolls drowning in frosting, just the way I like them. When I went out on the screened patio to eat it, I noticed that the backyard was decorated too.

Clearly, a major birthday bash was in the making. Hal and Nigel set up the bar in the shade of the open patio, but the food and birthday cake were set up inside the screened patio to keep flies out.

The birthday cake was a sheet cake frosted in black with white tombstones and a gallows.

People started arriving around noon. Doris came with Vicky and Greg. Larry and Louise Murphy came too, and Hal and I finally got to meet them.

Patti came with her partner, Syd, whom I hadn't seen in twenty years. Syd hadn't changed much, aside from having put on a few pounds. Her blonde hair was as long and luxurious as ever.

Tyrone and Mark came with their wives.

When they moved on, Mark took Hal and me aside. "Just thought you'd like to know—that cell phone wasn't Dick's. It was Gladys's."

"How the hell did it get under Dick and Doris's bed?" Hal asked.

"I'll bet I know," I said. "I'll bet that the day he was killed, he and Gladys started the day with a little afternoon delight. Doris wasn't home, so why not?"

"You're right," Mark said. "They were husband and wife, after all."

"Hey, look who else is here!" Hal exclaimed.

I turned to see Hal's parents, Ida and Max, approaching. My heart sank.

But Ida Shapiro hugged me and handed me a small wrapped package. "Toni, dear, my son has told me everything about what you've been doing, and I'm so proud that you're my daughter-in-law. I have to admit that I was sorry to lose Shawna, because she was such a nice Jewish girl, but that was wrong. I don't feel that way anymore. My son is lucky to have you."

I couldn't help it. My eyes filled with tears. I put my arms around my mother-in-law and hugged her back. "So you're not going to call me 'that shiksa' anymore?"

Ida drew back and looked me in the eye. "Did Hal tell you that?"

"I heard you," I said.

She put a hand over her eyes. "Oy gevalt," she murmured.

"I told you that, my dear," Max Shapiro said, slinging a burly arm around her shoulders, "but you didn't believe me."

"I'm so ashamed," Ida said, "and I apologize."

"You're forgiven," I said.

"So open it already," Ida said, indicating the package.

"I will," I said, "but you've already given me the best present anyone could give me."

"What's that?" Ida asked, looking quizzical.

"Love," I said. "Nothing beats that."

"Well said, my girl," Max agreed.

I opened the package. Inside was a silver bracelet with a Star of David on it. I immediately slipped it on. "Thank you, Ida. This is perfect."

"Very pretty," Mum said. "It matches her necklace."

Hal had given me a Star of David pendant on our first anniversary. It was silver with diamonds and sapphires, and I never took it off.

Nigel came up and put an arm around Mum while he too admired my bracelet. "Toni, old thing," he said. "Congratulations on wrapping up this whole schemozzle so neatly. Next time, let's have it not be such a deadly homecoming, eh what?"

ACKNOWLEDGMENTS

There actually is a Country Club Drive in Long Beach, but the MacTavish house is a figment of my imagination.

There is also a St. Mary's Hospital; I did my internship and part of my residency there.

Mum and Nigel's house on Lemon Avenue is based on the house my mother and I lived in while I was in junior high and high school. I attended Charles Evans Hughes Junior High and Long Beach Polytechnic High, and I actually *was* a Polyette.

But Tyrone Jeffers is a figment of my imagination, as are all my characters, because this is a work of fiction. Any resemblance to any person, living or dead, is coincidental. That being said, I may borrow a trait, a physical feature, a turn of speech from someone I know and combine them to make up a whole new person.

Thanks to my BFF, Rhonda, for reading my drafts and pointing out all my egregious errors, letting me bounce ideas off her, ad nauseam, and coming up with ideas of her own that she lets me use.

Not to mention all the folks at iUniverse who helped me get it into print for my expectant and impatient reading public.

Printed in the United States
By Bookmasters